THE
WANDERER
Scorned

Book 1 in The Wanderer Series

By NATASHA WOODCRAFT

WW&S PUBLISHING

Published by WW&S Publishing 2022.
ISBN **978-1-7396055-1-3**

A catalogue record for this book is available from the
British Library.

AUTHOR'S NOTE

Dear Reader,

This is a work of fiction. It is based on a story from the Bible, but you do not need to be a Christian to read it. I hope many will enjoy it, whatever their beliefs. The questions asked by Kayin are ones we all struggle with.

For those who are Christians, it is worth noting that this work is the result of my imagination and is not intended to replace or add to the Bible. I approached this story with trepidation, aware that some of the content may raise eyebrows. If you have difficulty with anything in the text, please refer to the appendix where I discuss the reasoning behind my decisions.

This story is the first in a series. I have used British spelling and punctuation conventions throughout. Included at the start are maps and a cast of characters for ease of reference. The Appendix and some suggested study questions are at the back for those interested in reflecting further. The songs are on YouTube if you want to know what they sound like.

My thanks must go foremost to my Father, Saviour and Comforter, who gave me the idea for this novel and held my hand every step of the way. He allowed Himself to be disparaged on Kayin's lips and gave me the assurance I needed to continue.

Thank you to my wonderful Beta readers: Richard Fairbairn, Sophia Anyanwu, Amanda Bedzrah and Maressa Mortimer; to Deirdre Lockhart for your timely and excellent advice; and to my editor, Hannah Morrell, without whom this novel would undoubtedly be poorer. To all at ACW who have supported my journey – you know who you are – I appreciate each one of you. Lastly, thanks to my husband, Ben, and my children, who have graciously allowed me countless hours away from them for the sake of this manuscript.

N.W.

MAP OF THE EAST

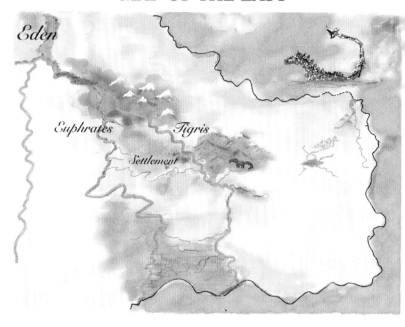

DETAILED MAP

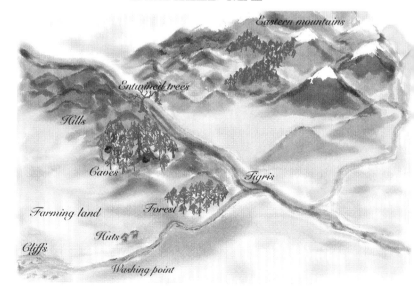

CAST OF CHARACTERS

In order of appearance

Abba means Dad/Father. It applies most often to Adam, but also to Kayin in the prologue.
Ima means Mum/Mother. It applies most often to Chavah, but also to Kayin's wife in the prologue.
Elohim means God and **Yahweh** means LORD. They refer to the same being, **Yahweh Elohim** (see Appendix for more).

Chanoch	*Eldest son of Kayin (Also city name)*
Lamech	*5th generation descendant of Kayin*
Adah	*1st wife of Lamech*
Tzillah	*2nd wife of Lamech*
The Wanderer	*Byname of Kayin*
Adam	*1st man (Also known as Abba)*
Chavah	*1st woman (Also known as Ima)*
Kayin	*Eldest child of Adam & Chavah*
Havel	*2nd child of Adam (Twin to Awan)*
Awan	*3rd child of Adam (Twin to Havel)*
Chayyim	*4th child of Adam & Chavah*
Avigayil	*5th child of Adam & Chavah*
Shimon	*6th child of Adam (Twin to Channah)*
Channah	*7th child of Adam (Twin to Shimon)*

PROLOGUE

Unpleasant laughter erupted from the throng of bodies that filled the expansive hall. Chanoch was beginning to feel uncomfortable. The heat was stifling, smoke was drying his throat and the mingled smells of meat and sweat created a sickening in his stomach. Chanoch loosened the neckline of his tunic and coughed, just as his host – a large, burly man with a thick dark beard, tinged with hints of red – rose from his seat and lifted his voice.

'Adah and Tzillah, hear my words; you wives of Lamech, listen to what I say!'

The orator – Lamech himself – grabbed the waist of a woman standing near him and pulled her against his side. He spoke suggestively into her ear which made her squirm. She was a fine-looking woman. Her skin, the colour of iron-rich clay, shone in the firelight while jet-black hair, plaited into several braids, fell the length of her back. Chanoch knew her as Adah, Lamech's first wife.

His eyes darted to another woman near him, who was serving wine from a large, clay pitcher. Her hair was free and wild, bronze curls cascading around her neck, and she wore a low-cut tunic nipped in at the waist. At Lamech's summons, Tzillah placed the pitcher down on a trestle table and threw her hands up in a gesture of exasperation.

'Lamech, you old fiend! Leave Adah alone,' she exclaimed. She made her way across the room, dodging the bodies slumped in various positions around it and stepping over one or two who were reclined on the floor. Raucous tittering greeted her as she did so, with several men grabbing at her ankles and almost pulling her down. Unfazed, she kicked them off or swatted them over the head, providing further entertainment for the men.

Ascending the raised platform on which Lamech stood, Tzillah reached her husband. Planting a firm kiss on his lips she allowed his spare arm to grasp her. Lamech released his first wife and encircled Tzillah in his arms before pulling her roughly in for another embrace. The room erupted in a drunken cheer at their display. However, Chanoch noticed Adah standing behind them, staring at the floor in embarrassment.

'That's better!' Lamech proclaimed loudly. 'Now I have the attention of both my beautiful wives, and the rest of you despicable lot, I have an announcement to make.'

He stepped into the centre of the room, ensuring all eyes were trained on him, then lifted one arm in an oratory posture and spoke with a clarity that echoed through the hallways:

> Adah and Tzillah,
>> Hear my words,
> You wives of Lamech,
>> Listen to what I say!
> Today – this very day – I killed a man merely
>> for wounding me,
>> And also his boy for striking me.
> If Kayin is avenged sevenfold,

2

> Then may Lamech be avenged seventy-
> sevenfold!

There was a moment of shocked silence. Chanoch stared aghast at Lamech. He knew his host had slipped into underhand measures in order to gain his current position in the city, but he never expected Lamech to brazenly admit to murder. Chanoch's eyes scanned the room, waiting to see how the people would react. Several of the revellers were shifting uncomfortably or muttering under their breath, but some had begun to smile, even chuckle. The murmur was escalating into acceptance. Suddenly, a prominent member of the city elders stood and raised his cup.

'To our fearless brother Lamech!' he cheered. Then, as a mob follows its master, the majority decided Lamech's announcement was hilarious and erupted into hoots, laughter and catcalls.

'May he live forever and ever be avenged!' another declared above the noise.

Pleased with the response, Lamech rewarded his audience. 'Refill the wine!' he shouted, to further cheers. His wives quickly dispersed to retrieve more from the storehouse. Lamech sauntered down the steps, into the crowd, to relay more details of his triumph.

Amidst the revelry, Chanoch slipped out unnoticed. The cooler night air tickled his skin as soon as he left the main hall, giving considerable relief. Tiptoeing down some steps, he entered the dim corridor that led through the centre of Lamech's complex, trying to keep the slap of his leather sandals to a minimum. He then traversed several courtyards before reaching the guards watching at the gate.

Chanoch didn't need to say a word, his instruction was intuitively understood. A guard exited and returned a moment later with a saddled creature. Mounting it,

Chanoch rode out of the gateway, stealing into the darkness of the night. He quietly navigated the city, passing numerous dwellings belonging to his kinsfolk which rose on either side of passageways cluttered with pots, pitchers and animal fodder.

As Chanoch arrived at his own dwelling near the city gate, he hastily called an attendant, requesting a second animal. When it was brought, he hooked a rope around its face, grasping the other end in his free hand, then scratched the animal's stubbly forelock. It snorted, unhappy to have been roused from its slumber, but Chanoch pushed on. Once outside the city gate, he pressed his mount into a faster pace, forcing the second creature to keep up, and rode on until he reached the foot of a hillside. Then, the two cloven-hooved animals picked their way up a narrow path until the mouth of a cave appeared. Chanoch dismounted, secured the beasts together and entered the cave.

Inside, the remains of a simple meal sat alongside the dying embers of a fire. The embers gave just enough glow to reveal a man and a woman lying huddled together under linen blankets and sheepskin. The man slept on his side; his head tucked into a folded arm. The other arm was draped over his wife. Chanoch knelt next to the couple and gently placed his hand on the shoulder of the man below him.

'Abba,' he whispered, 'wake up.' There was a groan as he persisted in shaking his father's shoulder. 'Abba, please wake.'

Drowsily, the man turned over and squinted, trying to make out the features in the dark.

'Chanoch?' he said at length, 'What are you doing here?'

'Abba, I'm sorry to wake you, but you need to come with me.'

'In the middle of the night? Why?'

As the elderly man's arm lifted from her body, his wife began to stir. She groaned and rubbed the sleep from her eyes.

'Chanoch!' his mother said pleasantly, on recognising her son. 'What a lovely surprise.' She sat up and drew him into an embrace. Chanoch was not a young man himself and his back, doubly stiffened from his ride, clicked as he leaned into her.

'Listen to you; you are getting old,' she chuckled, affectionately. 'Sounds like you need to eat more fish.'

Chanoch laughed. Trust his mother to always be thinking about such things. She was right, though. He was nearing his seven-hundredth winter, and although time had been good to him, there was no denying he was not as sprightly as in the youth of his first few centuries.

Seeing no cause to delay the explanation of his unexpected quest, Chanoch told his parents about the events that night in Lamech's house, urging them to return there with him.

'Should I know this Lamech?' his father asked.

'Lamech is the son of Methushael. He has become one of the most wealthy and influential people in the city,' Chanoch replied.

'Hmm. I have no desire to visit that house, son. Methushael's people have wandered a long way from the truth. No good can come of me going there.'

'Abba, please reconsider. I believe they need to hear your story. Perhaps if they do, they shall turn from this evil.' Chanoch did not want his journey to have been in vain.

'And what makes you think they shall listen to me?'

'You are the founder of our people! You may not be an elder of the city, but your word still holds sway.'

The older man sighed. Chanoch knew his father had not ventured into the city for many moons, yet hoped he could see the wisdom in going now. He looked at his mother. She nodded and offered a gentle smile of encouragement.

'Alright, I shall come,' his father relented. 'Do you have a mount?'

'I have two,' Chanoch replied. 'You may both come.'

Outside the cave, they mounted the creatures. Chanoch's mother was slight of build so swung up behind her son and wrapped her arms around his waist. They carefully descended the hill and, once on the plain, rode fast back to the city.

Arriving at the house of Lamech, the sounds of intoxicated merriment could now be heard from the outermost courtyard. The party was certainly not dying down yet. They entered through the gatehouse and surrendered their mounts then Chanoch led his parents through several large archways on their way to the great hall. Stopping before the main entrance, the three huddled together for a moment, speaking quiet words into the night. Then they drew apart and walked through the passageway until they reached the steps leading to the hall.

A wolf-like creature lay there. It jumped up and growled at the newcomers. The older man recoiled in fright, but Chanoch held out his hand to the animal and called its name. As soon as it recognised him, it wagged its tail and, after a brief welcome, went back to dozing on the step.

As they entered the hall, his mother's eyes flew to one corner and she gasped. Six people were sat there, playing musical instruments. Some reeds, with holes along the length, were being blown. Others – carved wooden crescents, with strings suspended from a crossbar – were being plucked, producing a melody in harmony with that being blown. For a moment her face lit up before she caught the words being sung by the musicians. They were sensuous and lewd. In response to the music, others were dancing around the floor, barely covered by their clothing; clasping cups of wine from which they sipped as they continued their display.

'Those are the people of Yuval. He is a gifted musician, yet he has ceased to use that gift for good things of late. His mother is Adah,' Chanoch said, indicating Lamech's first wife. 'She is an honest woman, but the evil of her husband seeps into her children.'

Chanoch watched as his parents scanned the rest of the room. On the opposite side to the musicians the fire was still lit inside a stone circle. Suspended above it was a tall spit made of wood and pointed with hardened bronze. Hanging from one end was the upside-down head of a boar, its tongue lolling out. Its body was being carved and those around were eating its cooked flesh.

Just then, Tzillah caught sight of the newcomers and stopped in the centre of the room.

'Well! If it isn't The Wanderer, come to grace us with his presence at last! Lamech, witness who has entered our humble halls!'

Lamech was lounging on an impressive chair that stood on the same raised stage where he had delivered his earlier speech. A young woman – not one of his wives – was reclined on his lap, feeding him grapes. At Tzillah's shout, he rose abruptly from his chair, throwing off the girl, and stood proud and tall in the presence of his ancestors. He began to utter words of perplexed welcome.

Chanoch's mother held back with her son, while his father walked calmly across the room towards their host. As the older man ascended the steps, his height began to dwarf that of the person in front of him. For although Lamech was of impressive physical stature, his ancestor stood a whole head taller. Despite his age,

Chanoch's father had a muscular form from many years of toil and constant movement – he was a man not accustomed to rest. Strength and authority exuded from him. As he approached his grandson-many-times-removed, Lamech's garbled greeting silenced.

Now the one they called The Wanderer turned and faced the people. The room quietened as, one by one, the revellers took in the scene before them and ceased their activities. Deflated, Lamech retreated into the shadows.

'People of Chanoch!' The Wanderer began. 'My son, the most senior elder of this city, has called me here tonight so that I may tell you a story. I suggest you take a comfortable seat.'

CHAPTER 1

It all started with the banishment.

As soon as the truth was known about their disobedience, my parents were driven out of the Garden. It had been planted for them by the LORD God, Yahweh Elohim – a garden pleasing to the eye and filled with every kind of food. Yet, for them, it had not been enough. And so, Elohim drove them from His presence, from the place where He had walked with them.

For a time afterwards, they dwelt just east of the Garden and could still see the flaming sword if they went too close: the blade held by the cherubim that turned every which way to prevent access to the Tree of Life. The sword was a constant reminder that the way was barred; that immortality and glory were just out of reach.

Season after season passed. My parents wandered, rarely settling in one place, but moving between areas of trees that they could harvest. They gradually moved south, following the River of Life that flowed from the land of Eden, passing through arid areas before turning east again into a fertile area studded with olive trees. Then they continued south until they came across the mountains that border my childhood home. These magnificent highlands, covered with mighty oaks, were cold in the winter so they huddled together in caves, creating fires to keep warm. Once the weather improved, they wound their way down through the mountains.

Here, streams had formed as springs combined with the melting tips of the highest peaks. Had they followed these streams, they would have discovered them running to join the gushing Euphrates that branched off from the River of Life.

When winter approached once more, they moved southeast into the valley below the mountains. There the air was less bitter, and forests of pine, pistachio and terebinth grew on the nearby hills. When they realised my mother was with child, they finally settled in those fertile plains, and my father began to tend the ground.

In accordance with the curse, my mother gave birth to me in excessive pain. Such pain as humanity had never known before. When telling the story in later years, my father recalled the night in horror: seeing his wife in distress, helpless to do anything, knowing nothing about the workings of a woman's body or how he could relieve her of the child. However, his face always changed at one point in the retelling. He would recollect how, after having intense pains for an entire cycle of the sun, towards dawn my exhausted mother cried out for mercy. Now expectant of death, Elohim's name sprang to her lips, and she screamed for Yahweh to fulfil His promise: to spare her so that she could fill the earth.

Moments later, a man appeared at the mouth of the cave. My father could just glimpse a ray of sunlight as the covering over the cave entrance was lifted. The newcomer said little but gathered water and cloth. Then quietly, calmly, he guided my mother through, and the child out. After he cut the cord and wrapped the babe, the man simply left. In this way, I was born, and my parents finally obeyed the blessing to multiply.

I questioned my father about that man, in later years. 'Did you see him again?' I asked.

'We did not, son,' my Abba replied.

'Why not? Why didn't he stay?'

Abba sighed and gazed into the distance. 'He could not. He cannot. It is all part of the banishment; this must be our fate.'

Seeing my bereft face at that moment, he put a hand on my shoulder and squeezed it. 'It is not all bad. That day was the first time we called on Yahweh after He cast us out. He provided for us then and gave us you.'

'So, the man won't come back?'

'No, son. I don't believe so.'

My mother named me Kayin, meaning *acquired*. For she said, 'I have acquired a man with the help of Yahweh.' For my parents, the years of my childhood were sweeter than those that had come before. My mother doted on me, her firstborn, seeming to forget what she had been through to bring me into the world. We were always busy with many tasks, but everything felt like a game to me. I rarely disobeyed, having no cause to, as I had my parents' attention most of the time. I didn't realise that true happiness rarely graced their faces during that time, for I knew no different.

We settled in a cave, not a quarter day's walk from the smaller river, the Khabur, which lay between the two great ones and joined them together. There were steep drops down to faster waters at points along the river, yet in other areas it was flat and regularly flooded, nurturing the ground with the water of life and providing good soil for the small crops my father began to plant. It was hard labour moving water around when the river wasn't flooding. The mist that used to cover the ground in the mornings had not appeared since the banishment, and it rarely rained.

Fortunately, the valley was populated with trees suitable for food and grapevines grew near the river's edge. As a child, I enjoyed climbing the trees to pick olives, figs and dates, and watching my father tend the vines. I was fascinated by the river, and helping my mother collect water did not feel like a chore. I saw it as an opportunity to build up my strength so I could one day be as tall and strong as my father.

From the higher ground that our cave nestled into, we could see the winding Tigris far off to the east, but we never went that way, fearing the massive mountains on the eastern side that held animals of great size and strength. Occasionally, we would catch glimpses of the giant lizards that my father called *tanninim* as they meandered from the mountains to water at the Tigris. But they never crossed the river or came near our land. We saw no predators in those early years of my life.

One day my father ran back to our cave with excitement on his face. 'I have found a flock of animals. A smaller variety than the ones I named *cattle* in the Garden,' he said to my mother. 'They have multiplied beyond that ridge to the north. I believe we could tame them; keep them for milk, clothing, perhaps meat?'

My mother grimaced slightly but did not disagree. Before the banishment, only plants had been permitted for food. After the first death (when Yahweh slew a creature to provide clothing for their nakedness) my parents had occasionally eaten animals when plant life was scarce. Graceful creatures, such as the many-horned and slender-horned deer, frequented the woods near our home, but we had not yet come across anything we could tame. Out of respect for the lifeblood of the creatures and our responsibility to care for them, any hunting trips were rare. Skins acquired from the hunt were always carefully preserved for bedding or clothing and bladders were fashioned into water carriers.

I was eight years old at this time and ready for an adventure, so I begged my father to take me on the trip north. He agreed. As we set out, we took water-skins, slung over our shoulders, along with some long branches we had sharpened at one end, in case of trouble.

My father and I had been walking for half a day, enjoying the rare respite from work, when we found a fallen tree in the middle of the plain. Its roots were unearthed – some even pointing up to the sky – and its branches were scattered over the ground. My father gave me a lift and I climbed onto its trunk, skittering along its length until I reached the end where the branches began and some of the leaves were still green. I climbed through those great branches, devising a den and imagining adventures.

During this time, my father sat on the ground and stared at the tree. At first I thought he was resting from the walk, but he looked sad after a while as if something about the fallen tree was significant.

'What of it, Abba? Come join me in the game,' I implored him. He didn't answer directly, for his mind was in another place. Eventually, though, he seemed to recall I was there, and he replied.

'The great tree that was pleasant to the sight of Elohim falls. It is another sign of our sin, Kayin,' he said, shaking his head. 'This tree would not have fallen if we had not taken the fruit of another like it. Because of us, this earth is destined to decay and destruction.'

'But Abba, look!' I said, pointing to the ground beneath the roots where I had found a colony of beetles. 'There is new life here!'

He came round to where I was sitting and observed it. My father smiled then, crouching beside me and letting a beetle run onto his palm. 'You are right, Son of Adam. Perhaps the earth shall show the grace of Elohim and bring forth new life, even where we have destroyed it.'

The next day we found the flock of small cattle that we called *sheep*. They were still grazing where my father had seen them: eight ewes and a ram. It was the wrong time of year for lambs, which was another grace, for we would have struggled to move them with young in tow. We walked around the sheep, trying to encourage them into place with our sticks.

It didn't work. Many years later, my brother Havel would laugh at our recounting of this tale. How we had tried for the whole afternoon to call the flock to order, not knowing how to control them as they scattered in all directions at every approach.

As night fell, we found a glade where moss and ferns covered the ground in musty patches and a stream trickled fresh water down from the northern mountains. I refilled our water skins and dipped my head in the refreshing flow. Then I splashed some at my father, who laughed and chased me around the glade, splashing me in turn. As we fell onto the soft moss in a fit of humour, a noise from the thicket startled us. My father grabbed me around the waist and drew me behind a rock, putting a finger to his lips.

We crouched there, waiting to see what would emerge. A small creature half my size crept out, making a slight clicking noise. Another followed it. They looked around, scanning the water's edge for predators. Their scaled bodies were perched on two legs, with claws at their feet like a bird. A light scruff of feathers jutted from their necks, though the rest of their skin was smooth like a lizard. They had pointed teeth that looked suited to eating smaller animals, though they would surely take a man's arm if provoked.

As they scanned the area, their eyes swept over us but did not register our presence. We didn't move a muscle, scared that if we did they would spot us immediately. They proceeded to drink at the stream, then crossed it, disappearing into the undergrowth on the other side.

We exhaled together. 'Let's make our bed on that raised area in case other visitors come for a drink in the night,' my father said. We climbed onto a ledge that jutted out over the stream and found more soft moss where we could lie. 'There were no creatures like that in the Garden,' Abba murmured as I crawled into his outstretched arms. Oblivious to his fear, I felt deep contentment as he wrapped his cloak around us both. In mere moments I was sound asleep, exhausted from the day of unsuccessful sheep-herding and sure of safety in Abba's arms.

My father woke me as the sunlight was beginning to filter through the trees. He held a finger to his lips once more as he pointed towards the stream. This time, out of the thicket, the sheep were emerging. We counted them as they drew up to the water's edge for a drink. All of them were there, and they were unsuspecting of our presence. We watched the sheep for some time, taking in the way they interacted with each other: how they all followed the actions of one if startled.

Abba cautiously picked up his water skin and stick and gestured for me to do the same. He walked around the back of the sipping sheep, his bare feet making no noise on the undergrowth. He raised his palm, motioning for me to stay where I was on the other side of the flock.

The ram raised its head and spotted my father. He became uneasy, his legs jittering as he considered whether to go forward through the stream or backward through his ewes. Then his brown face switched to wide-eyed panic as he turned and barged through the ewes. They began to scatter, but my presence on their flank surprised them and rather than dispersing to the sides, they rushed through the thicket, two at a time. My father jumped over an opening and got ahead of them. He stayed behind the ram, stopping the ewes from moving to the sides once they were through the thicket. Copying his movement on the outer flank, I held my stick horizontally, and we began to gain some control of the small flock.

The sheep calmed as they spied their familiar patch of lush grass ahead. We drove them onto it, then relaxed, letting them graze as a sign we meant them no harm. We stood watch there well into the morning, keeping the flock within a small area. All that time, I beamed at my father over the top of the creatures, and he grinned back. My legs were beginning to ache, but the excitement of what we might have achieved prevented me from weakening.

We didn't talk to each other for the rest of that day, afraid of raising our voices and alarming the sheep. Instead, we moved along leisurely and silently, walking a little way at a time, then allowing the sheep to graze when we came upon good pasture. That afternoon, we led them to a watering hole we had spotted on the way, and they drank appreciatively as they stood in the hot sun.

I studied them as they drank. They were brown-faced with lighter-coloured coats on their backs which were smooth around their faces and neck but curled slightly across the rump. Some of them had tangles and matts under their bellies which were thick with waste and dead plants. Their tiny hooves allowed them to balance on the rocky surface around the watering hole with ease. The ram's horns curved down around his long flat ears and almost jutted under his chin. Now that he had settled, his eyes looked kind and not unintelligent.

It was late into the evening when we once again approached the fallen tree. It felt like a long time since we had been there. A boy had scampered over that fallen trunk just two days ago, but now, I quite suddenly felt like a man. It was a suitable place to make camp for the night as there was some cover in the other trees around.

'Do you think you could keep a watch during the night?' my father whispered as he neared me.

'Yes, Abba,' croaked my voice, the sound of it startling me as I heard it for the first time that day. Although I wasn't sure what I should keep watch for.

'Good. I'll take the first shift; then I'll wake you for the second,' he replied with a smile, patting my shoulder as he walked back to the other side of the flock.

It took me longer to get to sleep that night. Although just as exhausted, my head felt busy with thoughts of the days to come. I was so pleased that my Abba would trust me with these creatures during the night that I didn't want to close my eyes. I watched my father silently standing guard. He always remained conscious of the sheep, whilst scanning the surroundings for movement. The striking night light shone brightly on the landscape, highlighting the water hole in the distance and the tops of the mountains far away. Billions of smaller lights also flooded the sky.

It struck me in a new way what my mother, Ima, had told me about Elohim:

He fashioned the skies with His words,
He ordered everything into its place;
That He might be shown glorious,
And we might have life to the full.

Ima had always looked sad when she had recounted this saying, recalling only the life that had been lost. But I felt hopeful in that moment. Hopeful of something beyond the banishment that weighed so heavily upon my parents.

CHAPTER 2

We had an excellent harvest that year, for the spring had not been so hot that the sun scorched the land. My favourite produce was the grapes, which came after the grains. They were sweet and tender, and my young taste buds couldn't get enough of them. My father had begun to train the vines that were already here when we arrived, pruning and supporting them, so they produced more fruit.

He had gained his knowledge of farming during his time in the land called Eden (which meant *delight*). As we worked to harvest each variety of food, Abba told me stories of how Elohim instructed him in the Garden of Eden.

'He walked with me, Kayin, talking to me and teaching me, as I'm doing with you. It took Him many years to explain to me how to sow, harvest and prepare the different grains, grasses, reeds and fruits. Yet His patience was never-ending. He delighted to fill my mind with wisdom and spend time with me.' He was smiling as he spoke, but there was always a hint of sadness in his eyes, an ever-present grief.

'When Elohim drove us out of the Garden, He told me to continue working the ground from which I was taken, yet I did not wish to. I could not imagine doing it on my own, without Yahweh by my side. So instead, we wandered and scavenged, not settling down until you were born.'

I gleaned from Abba's stories that there had been no true toil in Eden, for the ground had not yet been cursed. Growing food to sustain life had been a pleasurable experience. But the delight of Eden had departed when they did. Now the weeds grew as quickly as the crops. It was a daily chore working to remove them. Occasionally my father would stop work with a puzzled expression.

'That is a new plant, son. I have not seen it before,' he would say. I knew not to touch those new plants. They were the result of the curse, and nothing good could come of trying to eat them. There seemed to be more of those plants appearing every year.

My mother helped us in the fields at harvest time, taking some of the crops back with her part-way through the day, ready to sort for drying, soaking or storing. She had also taken to getting up early to milk the sheep. Having milk was exciting in those days, and I gladly jumped up to help her if I heard her rise at dawn.

Together, we discovered a new method of preserving the milk. Turning it in a skin over and over made it thicken, separate and eventually, harden. Then we could eat it on bread and it lasted for longer. The first time we made butter, Ima picked me up and swung me around, tickling my neck with kisses. 'You are so gifted, Kayin,' she said. 'I am so proud to call you my son.'

Sometimes the sheep would wander off and my mother and I would go out to search for them. I enjoyed those days with her, exploring the terrain further afield from our home and climbing the higher ground. Together, we would collect herbs on the hills and search the forests for mushrooms, while keeping an eye out for lost sheep.

When springtime came, it brought us lambs. Five had already been born naturally before I experienced my first lambing. Ima and I were sitting outside the cave grinding fresh flax seeds for oil when Abba ran into view.

'Kayin, there is a ewe in trouble. I need your small hands,' he panted. I followed him out to one of the further fields, where I saw the ewe collapsed on the ground, bleating pathetically. 'I think there are two lambs; the first is stuck,' Abba said, pointing to a tiny foot that I could see enclosed in a sac at the ewe's rear.

'What can I do?' I asked.

'Use your small hands to pull it out. I don't think I can do it.'

The dripping sac was the most disgusting thing I'd ever seen. I pulled a face and stared back at my father as if he'd gone mad.

'Kayin, she will die if you don't help!'

I wanted to run the other way, but I couldn't. I was a man now and shouldn't show my weakness to Abba. So, I screwed up my eyes and moved forward, blindly feeling around for the body of the lamb inside the ewe. After some time, I found what I thought was the other leg. Tucking the stray leg back so that both legs were straight, I pulled.

The lamb tumbled out onto the ground. Still enclosed in its sac, it was even more disgusting than before. The ewe grunted, and a second lamb slipped easily out. She rose, used her teeth to remove the sac, and cleaned the lambs before nudging them toward her milk.

My father clapped me on the back and sang my praise, but I felt my stomach churn, like the milk we turned in the skin. Suddenly retching, I deposited its contents on the ground right in front of my father. Embarrassment flooded my body. I quickly rose and ran to the river, throwing myself into the water to wash all remains of sheep, and humiliation, from my skin.

Several more years passed much the same as that one. As I grew, I became fascinated with the land and increasingly less keen on the sheep. I soaked up everything my father told me about farming and performed my own experiments. I discovered new ways of spacing the crops to increase the yield and tried growing new varieties. I didn't just use the seeds Abba had brought out of Eden, but also took seeds from the more vigorous crops that grew on the plains and replanted those.

Using strong digging sticks and pointed stones, I dug channels from the river directly to the crops so that it was easier to keep them watered. While doing this, I discovered that there was water under the ground if I dug down far enough. So, I dug a well to provide us with permanent water storage and ensure we always had a supply near the crops when the river wasn't flooding. I also made a strong twine by twisting together several types of grass from the riverbed. This new twine was tough enough to lift a water carrier from the well and Abba began using it to tie up the grapevines. I loved finding ways of improving life for my parents. It gave me great satisfaction to see the pride on their faces with each new thing I discovered.

By this time, I'd seen fourteen summers, and we were still sleeping in our cave in the hills, which was away from the river's edge. A small stream near our cave satisfied our thirst, but every day we had to walk some distance into the plains to water the crops, then climb back up to the cave at night. The sheep had no trouble climbing – their nimble hooves were adept at it

– but their night-time shelter in the woods outside the cave was dangerous. New variations of the animal kinds had emerged in the hills: predators with a thirst for blood, whose visits were growing increasingly frequent. Accordingly, my senses grew attuned to threats and I slept with one ear always alert to the bleating of sheep.

One night, I suddenly woke, thinking I'd heard a sound. However, there was silence outside the cave; the sheep slept undisturbed. Perhaps I had just imagined it. I turned over and tried to get back to sleep.

After a short time, I heard the sound again, barely discernible: a hiss accompanied by the low rustle of slithering. I knew that noise. It had haunted my dreams since childhood when my mother had told me the story of the Deceiver in the Garden. Her words now came back to me:

> I had been innocent then, Kayin, believing all creatures to be Elohim's and there for our benefit. When one spoke to me, I hadn't thought it strange. Indeed, I thought it to be a messenger from Elohim himself. The words he spoke were coated in honey: they seemed wise. I barely realised that they were questioning the Maker, undermining Him. On the hiss of his tongue I heard the things I wanted to hear: that I could gain more wisdom; that only good would come from taking the fruit.
>
> I was transfixed by the eyes of the serpent, which drew me in and promised something better than what Elohim had pledged to us. I had no notion what better might be, for to us life was, and had always been, perfect. But the serpent convinced me there was more: that life was incomplete without the forbidden fruit. Then I began to feel a hunger, a longing for

something that I didn't believe Yahweh could provide. I believed the lie that Yahweh Elohim was not supremely good.

I heard that hiss now – the same whispering deception. I tried to discern where in the cave it came from. I listened for the words. There were none, only a gentle sliding of scales on rock and the hiss of a tongue between teeth. And yet, I thought I could still hear those words: *Did Elohim really say...?*

Suddenly, the creature threw itself onto my shoulders, curling around my neck and beginning a chokehold. I jumped from the ground. That deceitful tongue was in my ear now; whispering and lying as it sought to devour with words. As its mouth opened, revealing its fangs, I thought, *This is the end. The creature will win, will destroy my life, take away the blessing once and for all.*

Then a shaft of light entered the cave. Looking up, I saw a gap in the rocks that I hadn't noticed before. It illuminated the serpent, revealing its head next to my own. Quickly, with a power I didn't know I had, I grasped its neck, pulling it away from mine. Its chokehold loosened. I threw it to the floor, and in one swift movement, my heel came crashing down on its head. Next, in the shaft of light, I saw a large stone. Grabbing it, I brought it down fast onto the creature's skull, crushing it repeatedly until it lay lifeless and limp on the ground.

The shaft of moonlight moved on, and darkness once again enveloped the cave.

I needed to move away from that place. My parents agreed when I told them about the serpent. They explained that Elohim had spoken a curse against the snake in the Garden; how it meant there would always be enmity between it and humankind. They seemed pleased and somewhat awed that I had crushed the serpent's head, as if it had significance. I wondered if there were other curses they had neglected to tell me about.

CHAPTER 3

We built a new dwelling nearer the crops and away from the danger of creatures in the night. My father showed me how the clay around the river was strong and able to stand up in banks. So I set about collecting this clay and packing it together with barley straw to build walls. After the summer harvest, I gathered several dried bushels of wheat stalk and tied them with twine to make thatch for a roof.

In addition to building and farming, I spent much of the following seasons searching for and sharpening stones. I was sure there must be other materials on the earth that would be more useful for tools. My father maintained that Elohim had created all we needed to flourish in the land – we just hadn't found it all yet.

One day in my seventeenth year, my parents called me into the hut. Nervously, they told me that my mother was with child. I'm not sure why they were nervous. Though I knew little about the ways of men and women, I thought it strange that I had been on my own for so long when they had been commanded to fill the earth.

Over several full moons, my mother's stomach grew until it looked like she couldn't possibly hold more weight on her slight frame. Abba and I increased our share of the work so she could rest as her back became painful.

It was another excellent year for lambs, so that spring we often spent nights out in the fields. In the last few years, our flock had grown substantially in size, yet we rarely slaughtered the sheep. If we did, my father said a prayer beforehand and offered Elohim the first portion of meat on the fire as thanks for His provision. I don't recall Abba speaking in prayer apart from at those times.

Towards the end of Ima's pregnancy, I asked my father if we could slaughter a sheep so my mother could use the full sheepskin to lie on, for the few sheepskins we possessed had grown thin. Abba agreed, so we prepared the animal, being careful to drain its lifeblood first, as Abba had seen Yahweh do when preparing the first skin-covering.

My mother, finding it difficult to rise from her pallet, talked me through the process of roasting the meat on a wooden spit over the fire. She told me what herbs to push into the flesh for the best flavour. The organs of the animal we kept back to stew with dried barley, water and herbs, using a cooking pot made from clay. I had found this extra use for clay, recently improving the design by waterproofing it with resin from the terebinth tree.

Whilst appreciating the meat, we hung the sheepskin on wooden posts to dry for seven cycles of the sun. After this, I scraped the underside with a flat stone to make it smooth and preserved it by rubbing it with the boiled brains of the animal, as my father had taught me. Finally, I took the skin to the river and cleaned it several times, then left it to dry again. It was a long process, but worth it to see my Ima get some relief from her discomfort.

The labour began only a few days after I'd given her the finished sheepskin. It was earlier than expected. She said I had taken more cycles of the moon to be ready. After an afternoon pacing about, she moved indoors. I listened to her wails and panting all evening as I sat outside the hut. Although I didn't especially know how to talk to Him, I remembered my birth story and I begged Yahweh to help my mother through her pain.

The labour seemed to last forever, but it couldn't have been as lengthy as mine, for the sun had only just set when I heard Ima's cries stop. Moments later, my father appeared with a babe in his arms.

'We thought she was finished but the pains have renewed. There is another coming,' he said anxiously. 'Will you hold your brother?'

I stood quickly and held out my arms. Abba placed the tiny, swaddled bundle into them, and I had my first glimpse at the boy who would change our lives forever. He looked like my father; he had the same skin the colour of dry earth, with a thin nose and wisps of dark brown hair covering his head. Loose curls already danced around his ears. I was instantly besotted. I smiled up at my father, whispering, 'He's amazing!'

Abba grinned at me then disappeared back inside the hut.

Once again, I heard Ima's cries of pain as she laboured to deliver the second child. Not wanting to stay in earshot this time, I wandered out towards the fields, brother in arms. Desiring a distraction, I talked as I roamed, describing the land we lived in, the river that was central to our lives and the fish that we had begun to spear and eat.

'Ima cooks a wonderful fish on the fire,' I told the sleeping babe. 'Ah, what is fire, you ask? Well, mastering the fire is the secret to becoming a man. I first managed to create a spark when I was sharpening a new type of stone I had found. The spark burnt my fingers. Despite that, I immediately tried to recreate it, having been fascinated with flames since my earliest days as a boy, when I would stare into the blaze Abba created at night.'

I proceeded to recall all the ways I had practiced getting the spark to light dried grass and become a flame. 'Once I had mastered the art, I showed Abba my new skill. He was both impressed and very severe, warning me to be careful with the flames and not to misuse them.'

Then I talked about the way Ima used the fire for cooking my favourite foods. 'Her bread is the best. She grinds wheat from the field and combines it with water to make a dough, then stretches it thinly and cooks it on a flat stone over the flame. It bubbles at first until she turns it, and it puffs up into a circle. It is delicious eaten warm. Abba and I can't get enough of it.'

I meandered about, constantly talking, until I heard my father shout for me. I saw in the moonlight that his arms held another bundle. As I approached he said, 'Meet your sister – a girl, like your mother.'

'How is Ima?'

'Exhausted, but well,' he replied. 'She would love to see you.'

I lifted the skin at the entrance to our home and crept in, still clutching my baby brother. Abba followed behind with the other bundle. My mother looked up and smiled, then reached her arms to me. I knelt, carefully tucked my brother into one of her arms, then buried my face in her shoulders. A sob escaped me, then another, as I released the fear I'd been holding and hiding.

'All is well, my precious boy. We have two more beautiful children in our family now.'

'It explains why your belly was so massive,' I managed to say.

'Indeed,' she chuckled. After holding me a few more moments, she sighed. 'I must feed the babies. I don't know how you kept this one quiet all the time I laboured with your sister.' She smiled at me again, brushing the hair from my face and tucking it behind my ear. Then she wiped a tear from my cheek.

'What will you call them?' I asked.

'Your brother is Havel – for he swiftly drew breath – and his sister will be Awan.'

I looked at my sister for the first time. Her eyes were wide and deep brown, framed by thick, black eyelashes. She had smooth umber skin and a head full of tight black curls. A snub of a nose widened toward a pout of lips. She didn't look anything like her twin, but she was perfect.

As the babies grew, so did my responsibilities. I was now overtaking my father in height and strength. I spent most of my time out in the fields and the hard work had honed my body, so every shape was well defined. My strength proved useful in every way, from digging the soil to carrying fallen logs from the forest. I was also becoming more proficient with the crops, so Abba began leaving most of the management to me while he dealt with the menial tasks and the sheep – who I still found slightly repulsive.

Little Awan proved to be lovely inside and out. She was content to be anywhere, with anyone, as happy placed on the ground as carried, satisfied with just a few sticks to chew on as soon as she could sit up. However, it was Havel that made the light shine in my mother's eyes.

After that first night, Havel was a tetchy, rather demanding child. He cried constantly for milk and refused to be put down. Yet nothing he did could anger my mother. As he grew bigger, he seemed permanently attached to Ima's hip while Awan crawled around. Ima performed her tasks one-handed, laughing at Havel if he put his fingers into the grain and threw it in the air or poked at her nose. I had never seen her so full of delight.

On the twins' first birthday, we were sitting together outside the hut. In a rare moment, Havel was not in my mother's arms but was crawling on the ground with Awan. They had invented a new game, climbing over the top of each other and then giggling furiously when one of them tumbled. I shifted my weight to my hands and knees and crawled towards them. Havel looked at me wide-eyed, but Awan chortled and came crawling forward. I swept my arm under her belly and tickled her until she rolled over on to her back, legs in the air and holding her toes.

Havel decided to join in. When he crawled forward, I tickled him in the same way. However, he resisted rolling over and continued towards me, grabbing hold of my arm. I swung him up and around onto my shoulder, where he grasped my ear and started chewing it. I laughed aloud as he'd found my single ticklish spot. Then, he fell into my arms and I blew on his stomach, reducing him to fits of giggles. When I looked up, Ima was watching us, her face radiant.

Then Abba began to sing, his low voice rumbling through the valley:

Give to Elohim all praise,
He is our source; by His breath, we were made.
Formed from the dust to subdue the land,
Taken from my side, she was placed at my hand.

Then blessed to procreate, producing more
Offspring to fill the earth and adore
Yahweh, for in His name is might,
All power and goodness are His right.

We fell; alas we listened
To the lying tongue that glistened,
In the light of the fading day.
Only darkness evermore would reign.

Or so we thought.

Yet Yahweh has blessed us again,
For we followed His command, when
We multiplied! And blessed we have been
With three to bring glory to Elohim.

Yahweh – my rock – forgive our iniquity;
Set us free, provide sanctuary.
Cleanse us, make us new once more.
May we fulfil all you have designed us for.

We sat silently afterwards for many moments. Even the babies were still. Then a gentle wind whipped around us and caressed our hearts.

CHAPTER 4

The day my father sang that song was the first day I remember us celebrating Shabbat. Apparently, Elohim had blessed the seventh day in the Garden. We were supposed to rest from work and keep the day holy by using it to praise our Creator. But my parents had not been practising Shabbat since the banishment. The song changed this.

The decade following my father's song was more joyful than my childhood – and became far noisier. Before the twins were three years old, Ima was with child again. My second brother was born one cold night during the season for figs and was named Chayyim, meaning *Life*. Two summers following that, the blessing continued with the birth of my second sister. She was named Avigayil – *My father's joy* – for nothing could contain his delight in his fifth child or Elohim's continued favour.

Around this time, Ima began singing songs on Shabbat, and sometimes at mealtimes. When I asked her where she had learnt them, she said they were songs from the Garden. Encouraged by my mother, Abba started to pray more regularly, until it became normal to speak thankfulness at every meal, rather than just before eating meat. There was little variation in his words, and Ima usually held his hand and smiled at him as he spoke.

Four barley harvests after Avigayil's birth, another set of twins were born. The names my mother chose reflected my father's song once again. The boy's name, Shimon, meant *He hears,* and the girl's name, Channah, meant *Grace*.

By this point, my body had fully matured, and I stood a whole head taller than my father. My shoulders and chest were also broader than his. I wore my hair – chestnut with hints of red – around shoulder length. My beard thickly covered my chin, though I kept it tightly cropped with the careful use of a sharp stone.

Of the children, Havel looked most like my father, although his hair was darker, and Avigayil favoured my mother. Awan was similar in appearance to Shimon, who shared her skin tone and curly black hair. By contrast, Shimon's twin, Channah, had skin like sandstone and hair even lighter than mine. Chayyim was somewhere in between the two. His beige locks were as straight as a reed and never stayed in one place, flopping about with every bound of his little legs.

I enjoyed playing with the young ones on rest days. We invented games of chase and hide and seek. My parents began to tell us stories of their travels over the land, of the many creatures they had seen and sights they had beheld. They regaled us with anecdotes about running with wild cats or climbing trees for food, only to find themselves amongst the monkeys. These were creatures we didn't see often on our plain and my younger siblings loved to hear about them.

My mother started asking Yahweh for provisions and praying over the children when they grazed knees or fell from trees. I continued to see glimpses of worry in Abba's face from time to time, but nothing that gave me cause for concern.

One Shabbat day, we were just sitting down to eat when Chayyim began crying hysterically. My mother ran to scoop him up.

'What is wrong, my love?' she inquired as she brushed Chayyim's mop of hair from his head and kissed him.

'Havel bit me!' Chayyim cried. He held up an arm with bright pink teeth marks on it.

'Havel!' said my father, coming over. Havel was standing behind Awan, with a scowl on his face.

'He stole my space! I wanted to be next to Awan!' Havel declared.

'Havel, you must not bite. Chayyim is hurt!' Ima replied.

'Awan is *mine*. He deserved it!'

My parents looked at each other, shocked and unsure how to respond. Havel was still headstrong and liked to get his way, often taking advantage of his younger siblings. I was sitting on the other side of Awan and decided to intervene.

'Havel,' I called. 'Come to me.'

Havel walked round until he stood before me, arms crossed and face defiant.

'I am sitting next to Awan too. Would you like to bite me?' I asked.

Havel's eyes opened wide. 'No! You are too big!' he exclaimed.

'So, it is alright to bite Chayyim because he is small?' I asked. 'What if I was to bite you. Would that be acceptable?'

Havel screwed up his face and looked at his feet. 'He shouldn't have taken my place,' he muttered.

'Your place on the ground, Havel? Whom does the ground belong to? Is it you?' I asked.

Havel looked at me from under furrowed brows and pursed his lips. 'It belongs to Elohim,' he replied. Then Havel gave a dramatic sigh and rolled his eyes. He shuffled over to stand in front of Ima, who was sitting down, holding Chayyim.

'Have you something to say, Havel?' Ima asked.

'Sorry, Chayyim,' Havel said as quietly as possible.

'Havel,' said my father. 'What must we do when we have been wrong?'

Havel took a deep breath. 'Will you forgive me?' he slowly asked Chayyim. Chayyim reached out his arms, and Havel leant into them, reluctantly accepting his little brother's embrace. Abba patted me on the shoulder, then took his place next to me so we could begin our meal.

By the time the older twins had seen eleven summers, Chayyim was growing in confidence while Havel had settled down somewhat. Havel discovered a love for the sheep and consequently spent most of his days in the pastures with my father. By contrast, Awan usually preferred to stay by the hut with Ima, helping with her younger siblings.

As my father spent more time with Havel and the multiplying flock, the responsibility of growing food for the family increasingly fell to me. One day I was working in the field furthest from our home. There was rocky ground leading to a slight cliff edge to the south. The river ran below it, in fast torrents, so I could hear it from the field but could not see it. A new type of weed had come up, and I was labouring hard to remove it before it destroyed our seedlings. No matter how much I pulled up, it just seemed to reappear.

This weed had dark pointed thorns and grew like a vine, weaving itself around the shoots and strangling them. With a small, pointed stick, I was digging at their roots one-by-one, trying to avoid the precious seedling, then gently unwinding the binding weed from the rest of the plant with my bare hands. I had been at it all morning and had barely made an impression on the field. My hands were sore and bloody from contact with the thorns.

The hot sun beat down on my back, scorching and blistering my skin. I began to envy Father and Havel, who never suffered such discomfort and could stay in a shaded glade as they watched the sheep. I grew angry. Before I realised what I was doing, I cursed the day my mother had listened to that lying serpent, and my father had listened to my mother. That day had brought thorns and thistles on the earth and made my work hard.

Knowing of my difficulty with this weed, Abba had promised to come and help, but he had not appeared yet. Bitterness crept in that he had chosen the sheep over me and left me to do all the hard labour. As the sun peaked, I saw a lone figure approaching. As he drew near, I realised it was only Havel.

'Kayin, we have lost a sheep. Have you seen it?' he asked, worry etched on his youthful face. I had no cause to be angry with Havel, but my temper was stretched thin.

'No, I have not. Perhaps the stupid thing fell off a cliff,' I snapped. Havel looked taken aback for a moment, then thoughtful.

'Perhaps you are right,' he pondered, and began walking off.

'Havel! Ask Abba to come and help me,' I shouted at his retreating form as I turned back to focus on the ground and the large patch of weeds I still had to tackle.

I was out there until the sun had retreated and the day had finally cooled. My father never came. I made a small fire away from my crop to burn the weeds then began to walk towards home, taking a detour to the river at a point where I could wade into calm waters.

I felt such relief as the gentle current swept around my legs that I submerged fully into the river and lay there for some time, floating as the cool water ministered to my burnt back and swollen hands. My long hair swirled around my face and my eyes absorbed the orange, pink and yellow hues of the sunset – interspersed with blue sky and wisps of white cloud – as the ripples of the river dislodged the stresses of the day.

Sometime later, I reluctantly pulled myself out of the water and rubbed my hair with a strip of linen I had removed from my waist before entering. Ima had made it from the flax that I'd grown intentionally for all the cloth we required. I began wandering back towards our hut, feeling much better. However, as I approached home, it became clear that all was not well. My youngest siblings were huddled by the fire, looking bewildered, with Awan hovering behind them. Her face held fear and grief.

'Kayin!' My mother shouted out, 'Finally!' Then she looked past me as if she expected to see someone else. 'Where is Havel?' she asked.

'How should I know?' I replied.

'Your father said he went to the far field to ask you to help find the sheep. No one has seen him since; neither he nor the sheep returned. We thought he must still be with you, looking for it.'

'I have been washing in the river. Where is Abba?'

'Your father had gone in the other direction and returned just a short while ago. Since then, we have been anxious for you both.'

'Havel came to the field at the high point of the sun but stayed only a moment. I was busy with the crops – which Abba said he would help me with,' I said, sending a pointed look towards my approaching father.

'You sent your brother off to search on his own?' he asked incredulously. 'He is eleven years old!'

'He is nearly twelve And I didn't send him off; he just left! How was I to know he wouldn't return to you?' I had never spoken with a raised voice to my parents, but their accusations – blaming me after I had laboured all day in the field, shedding my blood and skin for the sake of their crops – were entirely unjust.

'Oh, my boy! My precious boy!' wailed my mother, throwing herself into my father's arms. He stared at me, disappointment weighing on his face. I walked past him to the fire, grabbed a piece of bread from the stack next to it – for I was famished – then a thick, burning stick. Turning around, I stalked back towards the fields.

'I will search for him until he is found.' I threw the words behind me. I did not look back, but I heard my father retrieve a burning stick and follow me. We did not talk to each other as we walked the distance towards the farthest field where Havel had last been seen. I ate the bread silently, gaining no pleasure from its taste.

The moon shone brightly in the sky, giving us a smattering of light. My father went off to the right where the forest began at the foot of the hill country. I searched in the rocky places to the left, near the river.

My heart was heavy, and anger clouded my thoughts so that nothing seemed clear. What had I said to Havel? Every part of me protested my innocence and my parents' unfairness. Yet still, a voice crept in, warning me that I had indeed sent Havel off with a harsh word. What if that was the last thing he ever heard? What if he had been attacked by a serpent or fallen off a cliff? I fell to my knees and groaned aloud, crying to Yahweh.

'Yahweh, my Elohim, do not let my anger be the undoing of this family and of this blessing! Forgive me!' My face fell into the soil, my wet hair collecting the orange dust.

It came to me then: A cliff! *Perhaps the stupid thing fell off a cliff.* That is what I had said. I jumped up and began to climb the nearby rocks. Pain shot up my arms where my already raw hands touched the sharp stone. As I reached the cliff's edge, I held my burning branch over the side, desperately hoping to see my brother safe.

'Havel!' I shouted, 'Havel, are you down there?'

The sound of rushing water filled my ears. If he replied, I wouldn't be able to hear it. I looked around for a safe place to climb down, but it was hard to see in the dark. I scanned the area again, looking for anything that might suggest Havel was there. Then I saw it: a glimpse of white against the rocks, moving slightly.

It was the sheep! I turned this way and that, then saw another branch lying near me on the ground. I used my torch to light it, then threw the old one down the cliff edge toward what looked like a dry shrub below. Miraculously, it caught alight, and began to light up the rock face. The sheep was startled but could not move away from the fire. I saw that it was tangled in some of those same thorns that had grown up around my crops. And there, by its side, was my brother, clinging to the wool of the sheep, terror in his eyes.

'Havel! I am coming. Stay there!' The light from the burning bush lit the rock-face enough that I could see several ledges large enough to climb down. Before descending, I shouted for my father, hoping my voice would carry to him on the wind. Then I turned and began my descent. With my face to the rocks, I moved slowly down the cliff edge, trying to find a route between where the shrub burned and my brother lay.

My bleeding hands did not want to grip the jagged edges, but I persevered. Partway down, some vines were growing, and I was able to grasp them for support. They proved strong enough to hold most of my weight. I leaned back and stepped down the last flight of rock.

I practically ran to Havel then, as fast as I could over the steep rocks. He was balanced on a narrow ledge, not stuck in the thorns himself, but clearly unsure how to move without losing the sheep. I reached him and threw my arms around him.

'I was trying to reach her, then I slipped. I shouted for you, but—'

'I couldn't hear you over the river,' I finished for him. He looked at me with those wide, fearful eyes and I drew him closer. A tear fell down my cheek and dripped onto his. 'Havel, I'm so sorry for speaking harshly to you. Forgive me.'

He looked up at me again, the fear melting away. 'I forgive you. I love you, Kayin.'

We grasped each other for a moment longer before I realised the fire was lessening. We needed to be quick.

'Come, we must get you back up the ledge.'

'But the sheep!' he insisted. I looked at the poor beast, tangled in the thorns. It would be far safer to leave it here to become food for a predator, but my brother's face implored me to help it. It was hopeless to resist.

'Alright,' I relented. I began untangling the thorns from the creature's legs, gently unwinding them as I had done with my crops. My blisters screamed and new blood flowed. Havel calmly stroked the sheep's flank and whispered to it skilfully to keep it still. The ember light was fading fast when I eventually freed it.

'Come on, it's alright,' Havel spoke to the sheep, gripping its fleece. We crept back along the ledge, then I grabbed hold of the vine I'd used to climb down and tied it round Havel's waist.

'Climb with this around you. It will support you if you fall.' Looking up, I could just about see my father's face peering over the cliff's edge. He was trying to say something, but it was impossible to hear. He had also renewed his torch with a second branch. His free arm motioned for us to move to the side as he flung the branch down toward another scorched shrub growing a little further off. Within moments we had more light to see our way up the cliff.

Abba climbed down a short way to a ledge, then held his arms out for Havel, grasping him as he climbed near, then pushing him on above his head so he could reach the top of the cliff. With Havel safely returned to Abba, I turned my attention to the sheep. How would I get it up? There was no climbing the cliff with it in my arms.

My father held out a hand for me. I shook my head then shouted over the noise of the rushing river, 'Take Havel and get him home. I will figure out the sheep.' He nodded at me then pulled himself up from the ledge to the top of the cliffs.

My eyes scanned the surroundings once more. From this angle, and with the fire's illumination, I could see across the river. On the other side, a wider ledge snaked its way up a cliff that was far less steep. Although the river flowed fast here and was certainly deep enough to have drowned my brother if he had fallen in, I was much taller and more robust than he was, and confident I could cross it.

Sighing, I resigned myself to what I had to do. Kneeling and ducking my head under the sheep's belly, I grasped its pairs of legs with my two hands and stood up again. Laid across my broad shoulders, the sheep struggled for a moment, then fell still.

I looked back at my father, now clutching Havel at the top of the cliff, and wearily smiled. I hoped all would be forgiven between us now that I had rescued my brother and was trading a quick climb for a challenging crossing, for the sake of this stupid animal.

I waded into the river for the second time that night. This time, the water surrounding my legs offered no relief. Rather, the current pushed at me incessantly. It would have been hard enough to balance on my own, let alone with a sheep on my back and no hands to steady myself.

I pushed through as the torrents grew deeper until waves were up to my chest and spitting foam into my face. Halfway across, I stopped to catch my breath. My chest heaved with the effort of standing upright, and blood dripped from my hands into the water. For the second time that night, I appealed to Elohim as I felt my strength ebb. I expected any moment to be hurtled downstream by the current and thrown into the rocks that I knew were close-by. With the spray in my eyes my vision was useless, so I closed them and concentrated on the ground beneath my feet. Step by step I moved forward, praying that the water would not grow deeper.

It didn't. Before I realised it was there, my foot struck a boulder, and I re-opened my eyes to find myself staring at the rock-face on the other side of the river, now mere strides away. Exerting my last strength, I stepped up the bank. The water receded first to my middle, then my thighs, and finally, only covered my feet.

I fell to my knees on the pebbled surface and laid the sheep down, still gripping one leg to stop it taking flight. I heaved and panted as my chest fell towards the earth and my forehead met the ground.

I must have fallen asleep right there with my feet in the water, for when I next opened my eyes, the sun was just rising in the east. I basked momentarily in the sound of birds singing a morning chorus. Then I realised my hands were empty.

Panicking, I looked around – the sheep was gone! Seeing the ledge I had spied last night, I sprinted up it as fast as my shaky legs could go on the uneven surface. There, at the top, was a meadow of lush grass and in the centre was Havel's sheep, contentedly munching as if nothing had happened the previous night.

I laughed then – a deep throaty laugh, releasing all the mixed feelings. 'Come on, you,' I said to the sheep as I grabbed a stick and approached it. 'Let's get you back to your master.' I herded it the long way home, making my way downriver until I found a calm and shallow crossing place back to the other side.

CHAPTER 5

My mother didn't stay angry at me for long. One look at my bloodied hands that morning and her tender nature kicked in. She bathed them, poured olive oil over them and wrapped them in new linen cloths, then kissed them profusely. So, I blessed the hands that had caused me so much pain but enabled her to forgive me for losing her favourite son. I didn't see my father. He had already left for the pastures when I got home.

I rested my hands that day and did not go back to the grain fields. After a short sleep, I went for a walk to clear my head. As I passed the point in the river where we washed our clothing, I heard a voice singing. It was Awan.

Yahweh is my light and my salvation,
My heart shall not fear,
Though the waters roar and darkness creeps in,
Yet, I will be confident.
For He will bless those who love Him,
And protect those who draw near.
Bless the toil of my hands, my Elohim,
Clothe me in your love,
As I clothe those who are dear to me.

I had never heard Awan sing alone. Her words seemed too mature for her eleven summers; perhaps that calm demeanour hid a more complex soul. I drew nearer to where she was crouched over the water, scrubbing at some dirty rags. I realised they were the linens Ima had cleaned my hands with, stained with my blood.

'You sing well,' I said, lowering my tall frame to sit beside her. She looked up at me and smiled, her eyes glistening as if they held back tears. 'What was it about?'

She hesitated then answered in a quiet voice.

'I sometimes get fed up with doing all the chores for Ima. She relies on me so much while the babies keep her busy. I have taken to singing, to remind myself of Elohim's goodness. It stops me being ungrateful.'

'I am grateful for you cleaning my blood off that cloth,' I smiled. 'It is good that Ima has you to help her now. I used to do many of the things you do.'

'You did?'

'Yes, in the early days, before I knew my way around the fields, I would stay with Ima during the day while Abba was out working. I would help her at the river, as you do now, and with collecting food. I loved climbing trees to pick fruit and nuts! To keep myself entertained, I'd play all sorts of tricks on Ima in the forest.' I chuckled as I remembered the time I'd hidden in a thicket and made animal noises, fooling her into thinking I was a predator. 'We had fewer crops then; we relied more on what we could scavenge from the land. The crops have only multiplied recently, as our family has.'

'You mean as you have tended them, rather than Abba?' she asked, grinning. Awan was perceptive. I couldn't deny the truth of what she said, and I was pleased she had noticed.

'It is true, Abba never found pleasure in the ground as I do. For me, it brings many rewards. For him, just reminders of the past. He prefers to be with Havel and the sheep now.'

'I think they told you more about the Garden than they have told us. I should think it would make Abba happy talking about his time with Yahweh Elohim, but it seems to make him sad.'

I sighed. It was true that although my parents were now keeping Shabbat and appeared closer to Yahweh than they had been before, they rarely spoke of what they had lost. And whilst we worshipped the Creator with our words and deeds, I still didn't know much about Him. Besides calling to Him in distress, I didn't know how to relate to Him or get Him to talk to me. Even so, I wanted to help Awan.

'Has Ima told you the part about the talking snake?' I asked her.

'Oh yes! I once saw a grass snake in the field and she pulled me away from it, giving me a stern warning about listening to creatures that talk, even though it hadn't said anything. I have always feared the serpent since then.'

'I do too. Did you know it attacked me once when we used to sleep in a cave at night?'

'No! Did it really? What did you do?'

'I crushed it.' I grinned as Awan gasped. 'Is that the fear you were singing of? Fear of the serpent?' I enquired.

'Oh,' she paused. 'No, that is not it.' She seemed reluctant to continue.

I took her hand – still wet and cool from the washing – and placed it between my own. 'It's okay, you can tell me.'

Awan raised her lashes to gaze at my face as if assessing my sincerity. Once again, I thought such perception did not belong in one so young. 'I am afraid of the darkness and the rushing water.'

'Though the waters roar and darkness creeps in,' I quoted back to her.

'Yes. That's why I do not come out to the fields; why I always stay with Ima. I am afraid of being caught out in the dark, away from the fire. I wanted to help you and Abba look for Havel. As his twin I thought I would know where he was – we seem connected in that way. I tried to find the courage to follow you, but I couldn't walk out into the dark.' She shivered and crossed her arms over her chest.

'I don't think Abba would have let you come anyway,' I smiled. 'He's rather protective over you younger ones. He wasn't like that with me, but I suppose the creatures are more dangerous now.' I paused. 'What about the water?'

'I have never learnt to swim. I come here, where the water is calm, to clean the linens, but I do not like it upstream. I fear the day Ima asks me to collect the rushes for baskets: the water is much deeper over there.' She hesitated then refocused on me. 'How did you do it? How did you cross the rushing river with the sheep?'

'I don't really know. I suppose I just knew I had to.'

'You are so brave.'

I smiled at her. Perhaps I should have mentioned how scared I had been and how I had cried out to Yahweh Elohim for help, but it was nice to feel appreciated.

I jumped to my feet and held out a hand. 'Come on.'

She looked up, questioningly.

'I'm going to teach you to swim,' I grinned. Awan shook her head furiously, fear creeping back into her eyes. 'Come on,' I encouraged, 'you will be safe with me. And as you said, the waters are calm here.' I unfastened the pouches I kept tied to my waist and discarded them on the bank, then removed my outer tunic, leaving my undergarment in place.

'I can't believe Abba & Ima haven't taught you yet. They taught me when I was much younger than you.' Wading into the water, I stretched out my hand further and caught hers.

Awan nervously took a few steps into the water. Her confidence grew as she clasped my hand tightly and kept wading in deeper. When she was thigh deep, she suddenly squealed, 'There's something in the water!'

'It's just fish, don't worry. Perhaps we can catch some for supper. After I've taught you to swim,' I replied, mischievously. Keeping her eyes on mine, she took a few more steps until she was waist deep. Her breath caught as the colder current swept around her. 'I'm afraid it's not as warm in the deep,' I added.

Our lesson began. Firstly, I showed her how to move her arms in a circular motion. Then I showed her how to kick her legs and held her as she tried it. Once she had mastered these two movements, and I was confident her slight figure would stay afloat, I turned her around so she was facing the water and could try the two movements together. She wasn't naturally coordinated, and we regularly burst into fits of laughter when her arms and legs refused to work together. But, by the time the sun had begun to lower in the sky, she had mastered the basic strokes.

'You're tired,' I said, 'Let's stop. We can try some more tomorrow.' I helped her walk back halfway towards the bank then affectionately ruffled her damp hair. Her tight curls flicked water back into my face, and she giggled. 'Now you can help me catch some fish. Stay where you are; it's a good spot.'

I waded up the rest of the bank to retrieve a sharp stone from the pouch in my pile of clothes. I used this to cut a stiff willow reed from the water's edge and sharpen it to a point, then carefully passed her the reed.

'Hold it high, and stand completely still, watching the water.' I waded in and stood behind her. 'When the water settles, we'll be able to see, but we must be quiet,' I whispered. Once the mud had resettled, we could indeed see the fish swimming around our legs. 'Those with the dark, pointed fins are the tastiest. When one comes near you, plunge the reed into it as quickly as you can.'

On her first attempt, she completely missed. Concealing my amusement to spare her pride, I continued to instruct her. 'Now we have to start again because we've spooked them.' I bent down and grabbed a handful of muck from the riverbed. Squirming in amongst it, on the palm of my hand, were some tiny worms. 'When the water settles, I'll throw the worms in. They will draw the fish back.'

Four attempts later, Awan speared a fish. She squealed with an equal measure of delight and horror as I wrapped my hands around it and lifted it out of the water. I turned and slapped its head against a rock behind me, then tossed the dead fish onto the bank. 'Now go again; that won't feed our whole family,' I grinned.

'Ah! I'm exhausted. My arms cannot hold this reed high any longer!' she moaned, revealing that she was, after all, still a child. I noticed she had also started shivering. I relented and took the reed from her.

'Go, sit on the bank then. Use my clothes to wrap yourself up,' I instructed. She did so. 'Has Ima taught you to scale fish?' She nodded, picked up the fish and my sharp stone, and began to remove the scales, screwing her face up and muttering that this was the worst bit, as the scales flicked off around her.

After a few more attempts I had caught two more fish. I scaled the last one while Awan worked on the second. Once finished, we rinsed our fish and hands in the river and began to make our way home.

'Ima can gut the fish,' Awan said as we walked, sticking her tongue out. 'I've had enough of them for one day. I don't think I'll want to eat it now.'

'You'll change your mind later, after we've smoked it over the fire,' I laughed.

The next day I went to the nearby fields, checking over the vineyard and watering the younger plants. It would soon reach the hottest time of the year and I needed to make sure the roots were strong enough to withstand the heat. By the afternoon my hands were hurting and I'd had enough, so I sought out Awan for our second swimming lesson.

She was near our hut, playing with the children. Havel was with her. The older twins had formed caves with their bodies which the youngest ones toddled and ducked underneath, while six-year-old Avigayil and eight-year-old Chayyim tried to catch them. Whenever Channah or Shimon were under the cave, they were safe. Anytime they ran out, they were fair game for their older siblings. The little ones were not confident moving at speed and kept wobbling and falling over as they tried to run, much to everyone's amusement. I stood and watched the game for some moments before I felt Ima walk up behind me and snake her arm through mine.

'I used to put my arms around your shoulders, but now I cannot reach,' she chuckled. I looked down at her fondly. Then she continued more sombrely, 'I am sorry you had no brothers or sisters to play with when you were growing up. I see now that wasn't for the best.'

'It's fine, Ima. I enjoyed spending my days with you. I was content,' I said, placing a kiss on her forehead.

'At the time, things were still raw from the banishment. It felt hard enough to provide for three of us, let alone more children. It took all our time searching out enough food to sustain us.'

'I don't remember that; it always seemed to me like we had plenty.'

'Well, we did once you learnt to climb trees,' she laughed. 'Then the pistachio nuts and dates came swiftly in, usually landing on my head from above, as you threw them down!'

'Ha! I think it is time you took Chayyim to the forest. I have a taste for some more pistachios.'

'Perhaps you could take him? He reminds me of you. He never sits still now; he is always up to something. The other day I caught him catching ants and putting them down Avigayil's back. She didn't stop itching all afternoon!'

I guffawed. 'I would definitely have done that if I'd had a sister!'

'I also wish we chose a different name for him. Chayyim sounds far too much like Kayin. I am forever calling him the wrong thing, particularly when he's causing mischief,' she grinned.

'It is good to see Havel playing nicely with the others,' I commented.

'Yes. I think he just has a busy mind. Helping with the sheep has benefitted him enormously, for it wears him out! It's also done him good to be away from Awan. He's loosened his grip on his sister. Awan told me you are teaching her to swim?'

'Yes.'

'She is very fond of you.'

'And I of her. She has a good heart.'

'Kayin,' she looked up at me, suddenly serious. 'I am sorry I turned on you the other night when Havel was missing. I was so scared.'

'It's alright, Ima. I understand.' I put my arm around her elegant shoulders and pulled her into an embrace. 'I know how much you love Havel.'

'I love you all,' she replied, with a tremor in her voice.

CHAPTER 6

We didn't manage to swim that day. I stayed by the hut and helped Ima churn some of the milk Havel had brought in that morning, revelling in spending some time with her again. I had rarely done this since the other children had been born and I had found myself in the fields every day. Conversation with Ima came effortlessly. I desired to ask her what Abba thought of me – whether he was pleased with me for rescuing Havel and his sheep, or still angry – but I didn't find the courage for it.

I enjoyed watching the children play around the hut as we worked on the milk. Havel was in charge, but he was gentler than before, and the younger ones crowded around him, seeking his attention and instruction. Occasionally I caught Awan's eye and she smiled at me. She was devoted to her twin brother and enjoying his presence when he would usually, these days, be with the sheep.

The following morning, I went back to the far field to see what damage the thorns had done in my absence. My hands were still painful, but scabbed over, and I thought I could work with them wrapped in their linens. Awan had said she would come and find me when she could get away from her chores, so I was looking forward to a reprieve after a few hours of work.

By midday I was sweating from the exertion of digging and unbinding the thorns. My hands had begun to sting, and a few wounds had reopened and bled through the linens. Fortunately, I had brought my tunic with me which protected my back from burning again.

I was just stopping for a water break when I saw two figures approaching. It was Havel and my father. Havel was in front and was jauntily walking towards me as if it wasn't the hottest part of the day and the sun was nothing to him.

'We have come to help,' Havel said, cheerfully, sweeping his arm towards Father. 'I reminded Abba that we promised to help you the day the sheep ran away, and he agreed to come with me today instead.' He looked around, 'These are the same thorns the sheep got caught in.'

'Yes, they seem to be taking over this patch of ground. I think I will need to move these crops to a better place next year. The problem is, the further I plant from the water, the harder it is to keep the ground moist.'

I looked past him to my father. Abba did not look as if he was happy to be here. I wondered what Havel had said to convince him to come. There was no pleasure at seeing me, no happy greeting like I usually received. My stomach tightened into knots at the thought he might still be angry. I was desperate for an apology like I'd received from Ima. I knew I wasn't completely innocent, but I'd done what I could to fix it, and Havel was safe now.

We had been so close when I was young, yet recently I had barely spent any time with my father. I thought he'd withdrawn from the fields because he preferred the sheep, but perhaps I'd been wrong? Perhaps all the time he'd been spending with Havel had changed his preference. That my mother favoured Havel had been clear since his birth; I hadn't realised until now that my father might also value his second son more than his first.

The last thing I wanted was to make things worse. Although my heart yearned to cry to him and ask him to forgive me, I feared his rejection more than anything else. So, I buried my feelings and kept my thoughts hidden as I showed Abba & Havel the method I was using to remove the thorny weeds. I tried to be grateful that they were here, grateful for the effort my little brother was making.

I retrieved two more tools from my pouch for them and they got stuck in. As the time wore on, Havel happily chatted away about all manner of things, from the sheep (each one had a name and a history) to Shimon's wakeful nights as he was cutting a back tooth.

My father said scarcely a word the whole afternoon; he just quietly got on with the work. At one point, a thorn cut his hand badly, and he stood up, cursed at it and began to stomp towards home. Havel and I watched him in shock. After a few steps, he paused, turned back and slowly resumed the task. I exchanged raised eyebrows with my brother. This wasn't a pleasant job, but we had never seen our father react that way.

Havel began a fit of the giggles, cutting the tension. 'Perhaps you now understand why Kayin was angry with me the other day, Abba! He was doing this very task when I asked him about the sheep.' He continued to chuckle to himself as he attacked the next thorn. I glanced at my father, but he maintained his scowl and did not look back at me, only stared at the spot he was digging. I could see Havel was doing his best to heal the rift between us, but it didn't appear to be working.

Fortunately, shortly after that, Awan appeared on the horizon. She was a welcome sight; I had certainly had enough of the thorns that day: the ones growing out of the ground and the ones coming from my father.

'I'm ready to call it a day,' I said, standing up. 'Havel, would you like to join us at the river?'

'Thank you, but are you sure you don't mind me leaving these?' He motioned towards the thorns. 'I can try to get a few more out.'

I looked at his hands. They were cut and bloodied, but he hadn't once complained. 'No, leave them and join us in the river. The water will soothe your hands,' I smiled, reaching out to help him up. Once he was on his feet, I extended a hand to my father.

'I'll stay and do a few more,' he grunted. He looked up briefly, and I tried to understand the look in his eyes. Was it anger? Frustration? Or was there a glint of remorse?

'Thank you,' I replied quietly, then clapped Havel on the back. 'Can you swim yet, little brother, or did our parents forget to teach you as well?' I laughed. Behind me, I thought I heard Abba stifle a sob.

I often missed family meals as my trek back from the fields meant I arrived too late. So the times I tended to see Havel and Awan together were on Shabbat. On those days, Ima always prepared the day's food ahead of time so that we could spend longer enjoying each other's company. Even so, I was often so exhausted from six days of labour that I slept most of the day on my own in the hut, only joining the family later in the afternoon.

Because of this, I realised I had missed much of the interaction between Awan and Havel in recent years. They had a different sort of connection to the rest of us, I supposed from sharing a womb. Havel was obviously the more dominant character, and Awan submitted to him as she did to everyone. Yet, she seemed more at ease in his company than apart from it. Her eyes trailed him constantly; even when she glanced and smiled at me, she seemed aware of her twin's presence. He treated her differently too, as if she was one of his limbs rather than a separate person.

Now they were together in the river, all the nervousness Awan had shown towards the water disappeared. She laughed and splashed at Havel. When they practised their swimming motions, I noticed their movements were synchronised without them realising.

My tall, strong frame meant I could hold one twin upon each arm, so I stood in the centre of them as they practised until I was confident that they were ready to try the water without my aid.

'Havel, you go first,' I said, but Awan interjected and asked that they try it together. 'If you sink, it shall be harder to catch you both!' I warned with a laugh. She relented, as always, and Havel took the first turn.

He was a natural swimmer, and twin or not, I couldn't deny he was more coordinated than Awan had been. Within moments he was confidently swimming into deeper water and laughing as the gentle current took him and he had to fight his way back to us. I offered him plenty of encouragement to do so by himself, before swimming out and retrieving him when the force of the current got too strong.

Awan did just as well on her turn. A terrified look briefly crossed her features the moment she realised she couldn't reach the riverbed, but Havel and I offered her so much praise and reassurance that she quickly gained confidence and found her way in the water. When I swam to retrieve her, she was glowing with pride at her achievement. I'd never seen her look so happy.

'Thank you, Kayin,' she said softly as I helped her back to shore. Havel stood in the shallows, laughing and slapping the surface of the water. As I approached him, a water-fight inevitably began. Awan looked exhilarated – her fear of water waning and finally enjoying the feel of it. I was glad my sister would now be able to enjoy the relief I always felt when I bathed at the end of a long, hot day.

After we'd had our fill of river and laughter, we made our way back to the hut. Meeting our father on the way, Havel ran to him and embraced him enthusiastically around the waist. He proceeded to chatter about everything that had happened in the water. Abba looked at him and managed a small smile, but it was not enough to smooth the worry lines that were drawn over his face.

When Chayyim was a baby, I had built a smaller hut next to the first one. Much of the grain and fruit we still carried to our old cave during harvest as it was too hot on the plain for long-term storage. We'd rolled a stone in front of the entrance to deter animal intruders. But in this second hut we kept enough supplies of food and materials to prevent having to travel to the cave often.

When I had grown so tall that I took up too much space in the main hut, I'd moved into the storage hut alone and built myself a pallet bed of wood, straw and sheepskin. Having some privacy as an adult was welcome. And, as I often came in late, my return didn't now disturb the sleeping little ones.

That night I struggled to get to sleep. I'd enjoyed my afternoon with Havel and Awan but my rift with Abba was disturbing me. After tossing and turning for some time, I rose from my bed, thinking I'd go for a walk to clear my thoughts. I paused at the skin that covered the entrance when I heard voices outside. It was my parents.

'You cannot continue to be angry, Adam.'

'I am trying, Chavah, but I cannot shake it. It eats at me. I am reminded of it everywhere I go, especially when I am in the fields with Kayin.'

'You must not bear this; you must let it go.'

'How can I? What if Havel had not been found? What if he had died?'

'But he did not; he came home safely. Elohim is protecting us, my love. Despite everything, He still wishes to bless us. See how He is blessing Kayin! All the ground Kayin works bears good crops.'

'Not so. The far field is now covered in thorns. No matter how hard Kayin works, he will never overcome those.'

'Then you should help him! The sheep do not need as much care as you give them.'

'I cannot bear to be in those fields with Kayin, don't ask it of me, Chavah!'

'You cannot leave Kayin to do everything, Adam. You are living a life of avoidance.'

'He can manage. In time Chayyim will help him.'

'Oh, my love! Why can't you be free? Can you not speak with Yahweh, as Havel has?'

'Havel is only a boy! Soon he will grow up, and then he will feel the same way as I do.'

'I will pray that does not come to pass.'

'What right do you have to do that, Chavah? What right have you to approach the Eternal One? You are guilty too!'

'How dare you? Do not place the blame on me as you did in the Garden! I cannot live like that again, as we did for all those years before the children were born. I thought we were past it.'

I had heard enough. I moved back to my bed and pulled a skin over my head to block out the rest of their conversation. I lay there with Abba's words running through my head like the river's current. He would not let it go. He was still angry at me for putting Havel's life in danger! I thought we were meant to forgive; why couldn't he forgive?

When the voices ceased, and I guessed they had gone to bed, I got up and walked, desperate to wear my body out to the point where it had no choice but to collapse in sleep. I paced furiously away from our camp, out towards the hills. If anyone had wanted to catch up with me, they wouldn't have been able to do so. Yet, of course, no one did want to follow me. Had I become an outsider in my own family? I was the firstborn. I had served Abba for years before the others came along. I had never disobeyed him. Yet now he was so angry he didn't even want to be near me.

His words reverberated in my head: *I cannot bear to be with Kayin.* Everything I did was for him. I longed for him to be proud of me, to love me. I had spoken one harsh word. Was his love for me so weak that this one mistake would make him despise me? Havel had a childhood of naughtiness behind him but had never been rejected.

What if Abba was right and Havel grew up to feel the same way as him? My brother loved me now – he said he had forgiven me – but what if later he hated me for causing him to fall off that cliff? What if he was haunted by the hours of fear, stuck between a sheep and a rock face?

As strong strides were interrupted by broken sobs, I fell to my knees. I sat in the dust, head leaning on my forearms. I thought about the second part of the conversation. I could not comprehend why Abba had also called my mother guilty. Did he think the curse on the ground, a consequence of her sin, was worsening because of me?

I thought Elohim was good and true, but I couldn't make sense of such a curse. Perhaps Elohim was angry with me now, as He had been with my parents. My shoulders racked with weeping as the pain sank deeply into my soul. It twisted inside me and made my gut retch.

Then a light flickered over my face as the moon crept out from behind a cloud. As it did so, the sweet, small voice of Awan came back to me. *Yahweh is my light and salvation…Clothe me in your love,* she had sung. I wanted that: that confidence in Yahweh. I wanted the light, the love.

Yet, though I searched for it, I could not find it. The pain of rejection was too great. How could I believe what she did about Elohim? He'd banished my parents from paradise for eating one piece of fruit. If He could not overlook one mistake then, why would He do so now?

My mother had defended me and seemed to believe we were being blessed. I had thought so too as all the babies had been born. Yet, if Elohim was merciful, why hadn't He forgiven my parents back in Eden? Why curse them at all? And the ground *was* getting worse every year; my father was right about that. Was he right about me? Was it my fault? What had I done to cause it?

As the confusion continued to grow inside me, so did the urge to walk, to clear my head. I stood up and headed further into the hills, passing the entrance to the tall forest. Soon, I was enveloped by the trees, and all around me was deep darkness. I had to slow my pace to avoid tripping over anything in the dark, but I had walked these paths since I was a boy and I knew them instinctively – every tree, every turn.

Soon I came to the rocks we scaled to get to our storage cave: our old home. Instinctively, I climbed the steep rocky path using hands and knees, even though I could see little. Rolling the stone from the entrance to the cave, I went inside. I had not been here in the dark since the night the snake attacked me. I sat down near the entrance and tried to empty my mind.

It was then I heard the near silent sliding of a serpent's body stroking the earth. It was probably just tricks inside my head from associations embedded in my memory. Even so, I stared into the darkness of the cave, watching for movement.

I felt it rather than saw it – a tongue flickering over my foot. Then the body of the serpent began to weave its way between my legs as if caressing them, its entire length massaging my skin. I stayed completely still, trying to steady my breathing. When it had passed through my legs, it turned and began to weave its way back again. I waited. Waited for the attack, for the bite that might end my life.

It didn't come. Instead of condemning me, the serpent went back the way it had come, returning into the darkness. I exhaled, letting all the tension drain out of my body.

I dozed in that cave until the dawn began to shine through the tops of the trees. Then I summoned the courage to move my rigid limbs. I had to go back to my family and face them. I had nowhere else to go.

CHAPTER 7

After that night, I didn't know how to interact with my father. Whenever he made eye contact with me, I looked hastily away, feeling the colour rising in my cheeks. We barely talked on Shabbat, and I noticed his enthusiasm for those days waning. They became drained, bled of the life that had previously characterised them.

Over the next few years, our relationship grew more strained. Looking back now, I am not certain that he treated me very differently. But at the time, I felt every awkward moment like a punch to the stomach; each pause magnifying the impression that he no longer cared for me. With so much work to do, it became increasingly easy to avoid Abba, so that is what I did. I spent more time in the fields, getting up at first light and often returning well after the evening meal. I took to swimming in the river every day after work, honing my muscles by pushing them to new limits when they were already tired from a full day's labour.

As Chayyim grew, he proved to be even more like me, demonstrating a natural aptitude for farming crops. I began to gently wake him at dawn. He would come with me and work in the fields until the high point of the sun, at which time he would go home to Ima while I'd continue working on my own.

Chayyim followed my every move, learning quickly and occasionally even finding new ways to improve the crops. He was an ideal student, and I began to enjoy his company after several years of solitude. He didn't constantly chatter like Havel, and he wasn't sullen like Abba; he just got on with the task at hand in quiet contentment.

He also had my mischievous streak, as my mother had rightly noted. He would sometimes set traps for me in the ground and howl with laughter when I stood on something or fell into a hole. I didn't mind his tricks. They broke up the monotony of my days and helped keep me aware of my surroundings.

Once a week (the number of days marked between the Shabbat rests) we would go together into the forest and gather what we could there. At some points of the year it might be nuts and garlic; at others, berries or mushrooms. As he was still light and agile, I sent Chayyim right to the top of the trees for the best nuts. He copied my behaviour from years earlier and threw them down onto my head as I'd done to Ima.

By the time he was thirteen, Chayyim could work a full day and I began to give him more responsibility in the fields. He was a naturally hard worker and was good with vegetables, enjoying tending each plant individually and figuring out how it would best grow. His figure was still scrawny, but with each passing season, he grew more capable of completing demanding tasks. He also grew more precious in my eyes. Of all my siblings, he became the closest. Chayyim and I understood each other, whereas Havel – much as I loved him – didn't always seem to inhabit the same world as me.

I also taught Chayyim to make and use weapons. It had become increasingly necessary to defend ourselves from predators – especially in the forest. So we fashioned slings from long twine and slips of leather, and spears from branches. We spent hours contentedly sharpening our stones and fixing them to the ends. I wasn't sure how effective they'd be against a scaled tannin, but these new spears could undoubtedly kill a large-tusked boar if it charged.

One day, when Chayyim had passed fifteen winters, we were in the forest later than usual and dusk was approaching. It had been a difficult harvest and a hard winter, so food was scarce. Havel was now so attached to his flock he never liked to give one of them up, so feeling the familiar responsibility to feed my family, I had brought Chayyim to the forest to see what creatures we might find. We had been stalking a deer for some time, but the elusive animal kept losing us.

The forest was never completely silent, but a hush had fallen on it as the sun slowly lowered in the sky and the daytime birds settled. The quiet made me uneasy. As the nocturnal animals would start to come out it was unwise to be in the forest.

'I think we better head home, Chayyim,' I said, for the fourth time, and I began to gather our things.

'Kayin, we've been hunting her all day. Let's not give up now, please!' he responded, pushing his hair out of his eyes. He implored me so fervently that I agreed to hunt for a bit longer, although I knew our chances were slim. The eyes and ears of the deer worked much better than ours at this time of day.

As the sun began to set in earnest and it became too dark to see more than a short way in front of us, I insisted that it was time to leave.

Chayyim began to protest again, then he suddenly froze. I turned my head to follow his stare. There, several strides from us in a thicket, was a wolf. Its brownish-grey fur was barely distinguishable from its surroundings, but the black point of its ears contrasted with the white surrounding its face. Its eyes sparkled in the waning light and its bared teeth snarled.

'What do I do?' Chayyim whispered.

Havel had told me of this new form of canine that had begun to hunt the woods in groups, even coming for the sheep some nights, but I had not seen one up close before. I moved slowly towards where my brother stood, trying not to do anything that would startle the wolf. 'It will not be alone. We must get out of here now.' I entwined my fingers with his. 'Run!' I whispered in his ear.

We took off. Chayyim was a fast sprinter and sped in front of me. In one hand I held my spear; in the other, I held Chayyim's hand. I dared not loosen my grip on either. Yet, it was harder to move through the bush in tandem. With no spare arm to move them out of the way, branches whipped into my face. I kept glancing behind me. Occasionally I caught glimpses of the wolf; it was keeping up with us. Then I saw what I had dreaded: more wolves were joining the chase.

Their fur shone in the brief glimpses of moonlight that filtered through the trees, yet it was their teeth that still stood out – always displayed, always seeming to get closer and closer to us.

Stealth would do nothing for us now that there was a pack behind us. Recognising the line of the trees just ahead, I realised that we were nearing the western edge of the forest.

'Shout for help!' I cried to Chayyim. I began to make as much noise as possible, hoping against hope that someone might be nearby, as we were not far from where the sheep often grazed.

Just then, Chayyim's foot snagged a protruding root and he tumbled, face first, to the ground. Hitting his head hard on a rock, he was knocked unconscious. I couldn't stop in time and tripped over the top of him. I felt a pain in my head, but I managed to roll and stand back up. A wolf was strides away. Seizing the moment, it pounced, its claws outstretched, those glistening teeth headed straight towards my brother's neck.

I screeched as I threw myself towards it, spear first. Its tip impaled the creature's chest. It fell limp. The sudden weight on my spear set me off balance. I dropped it to the ground as I fell forward onto my hands and knees, over the body of the dead wolf.

I righted myself and lifted my eyes, only to see another wolf. He was taking a more cautious approach, growling at me and encircling Chayyim's slackened form.

I briefly surveyed my surroundings. Above Chayyim was the tree whose roots he had tripped over. Stretching out from its trunk was a low hanging limb. I launched myself forward again, jumping to grasp hold of the lower branch. Swinging my feet forwards, I kicked them into the side of the wolf that was circling my brother. It fell sideways. I dropped and lunged forward to clench the dazed wolf's throat. I squeezed it as tightly as I could. The creature yelped and rolled its eyes. Then its legs curled under, and it managed to sink a claw into one of my forearms. Instinctively, I loosened my grip on its neck and the creature retreated hastily back into the bush.

Two more wolves prowled in my peripheral vision. I scooped Chayyim into my arms and ran towards the clearing, desperately hoping the wolves would give up the chase once out in the open. I felt one of their noses at my heel. I could see the sheep ahead of me. I flew towards them. Better a wolf take one of our sheep than take my brother.

Just as I escaped the trees, the wolf that had been on my heels caught my ankle and sunk its teeth into my flesh. I fell, with Chayyim tumbling in front of me, and threw my body around my brother. I felt my ankle bone crack and screamed in agony. Another wolf jumped onto my back and sunk its claws into my shoulders then dragged them down my spine. Crying out, I reached my arms behind me and grasped hold of its feet, toppling it from my back.

The other wolf still hung onto my foot. I grasped around for a stone and, finding one, aimed a throw at its head. The range was too close to do great damage, but the shock at least loosened its hold on my foot. I gathered Chayyim back to my chest and tried to stand, but my foot gave way. I knew there was no way I could run again.

I noticed a fire burning off to the right of the panicked, scattering sheep. Before I could register what that meant, from nowhere another stone hit the wolf sharply on its head. This one took effect, sinking into the creature's skull and ending its life. The wolf that had attacked my back then howled as a further stone struck its rump. It turned and fled into the forest.

'Kayin! Kayin!' I heard my name. As I fell onto my side and looked up, I just registered Havel's face – filled with concern – and, in his hand, the sling that must have slain the wolf. Then I fell into senselessness.

CHAPTER 8

When I opened my eyes again, it was Awan's face that greeted me. She had just seen her nineteenth birthday, and her appearance had changed dramatically in the last few years. Her face had matured and she had grown a woman's body, like my mother's. She had also developed confidence. Now she often sang with others in times of worship, during which she seemed to bloom like a flower.

Looking around, I realised we were in my hut. Awan was kneeling next to my pallet.

'You're awake,' she smiled. 'You had us worried there.'

Everything in the room was blurred. I tried to sit up but got a sharp pain in my head. I clapped my hand to it, then shooting pains ran down my back and up from my feet.

'Shh, stay down. You are injured,' Awan soothed.

'Where is Chayyim?'

'He is here too, in your hut, but he's still sleeping.'

'How long?'

'It is the morning after the wolves' attack. You must have hit your head; you have a gash here,' she motioned to the top of her head.

'Chayyim hit his head hard on a rock, he went immediately limp, I had to carry him—' Images of the previous night flooded my mind, but as if a dream: hazy and out of order. My head pulsated, and the room began to spin. I let my head rest back on the sheepskin.

Awan dipped a cloth in water and gently wiped my face. The cool liquid gave relief to my skin, which felt burnt from being whipped by the branches in the forest.

'You are both covered in injuries, but you definitely look worse than Chayyim. The wolves attacked you badly; they have severely maimed your ankle.' She flushed. 'I had to wash your back while you slept, to remove the dirt from your wounds. Havel helped me to roll you over and remove your covering.'

'Is Havel well? Wasn't it he who saved us?'

'Oh, he's unscathed and enjoying all the attention!' She laughed, then continued as I raised my brows, 'The twins are so excited about their brother who defeated the wolves. We were all out by the fire last night; we saw the whole thing. Ima and I had brought food out to Abba and Havel. They had decided to stay with the sheep through the night as Havel had heard the wolves howling close-by.

'We had gathered round their fire and were eating together when we heard your shout coming from the woods. It was hard to see as the sun was setting, but Havel and Abba lit torches and ran towards the noise. As soon as he saw you appear out of the forest, Havel ran forward without a hint of fear. He swung his sling with such skill – those wolves didn't stand a chance. Shimon was enraptured by it. He won't leave Havel alone now; he was up at dawn asking for lessons with the sling.'

I tried to smile with her, but something about the story didn't sit right with me, and my head ached.

'I think I need more sleep,' I murmured, 'please rouse me when Chayyim wakes.'

'Of course,' she replied, stroking my head again. I heard her move to the other side of the room as I let my body succumb to the exhaustion.

When I next heard that gentle voice whispering my name, my eyes flickered open. This time the room and its few objects looked clearer, but the dimness indicated it was already evening.

'Chayyim is awake. You asked me to rouse you,' Awan said. 'Let me help you,' she added, as I tried to sit up. My brother was already sitting up on his pallet. He had gained a large, red lump on his forehead, along with a few scratches across his cheeks and arms, but he looked a lot better than I felt. He held and sipped a bowl of broth.

'I am so relieved to see you alive,' I tried to laugh. It hurt.

'Yes, Havel saved us.' Chayyim grinned as if there had been no terror in the events. 'The twins have been in here telling me all about it.'

Again, a flicker of something in my heart prevented joy. Had no-one acknowledged my efforts to save Chayyim? 'How long has he been awake?' I asked Awan.

'Not long, but the twins saw me go out for broth, so ran straight in here and tried to jump all over him, just to make sure he was ok.' Awan gently chuckled. 'I let them leave before I woke you, in case the noise was too much for your head.'

She was always sensitive to the needs of others. I realised I would have liked to see the twins too and wanted them to be excited by my waking up. But she was right. My head was still pounding.

I sat up, pushing through the intense pain that shot up my leg as I did so. It made my head swim and it was some moments before I could reopen my eyes to examine my foot. From what I could see through the gloom of the room and mangled mess of my ripped flesh, it looked like the connection between my foot and ankle was damaged. My foot was at an awkward angle and my ankle was twice its normal size. Would it ever bear weight again?

Awan left the room briefly and Chayyim's mischievous face looked at me with a question in his eyes but said nothing. Awan returned moments later with some broth for me. She was followed by Ima, who ran in and embraced both her sons in turn as if we had been asleep for a year, holding and kissing our faces. Tears wet her cheek, and her eyes were red.

'Don't you dare do that to me again, you cruel children,' she said, trying to mask her earnestness with jest.

'I am hardly a child, Ima,' I chuckled, planting a kiss on her forehead.

'Yes, Kayin, which is why you should know better than to be hunting in the woods at night.' She sounded severe this time.

'It was my fault,' piped up Chayyim, 'I kept goading him to stay, even though he warned me we should head home.'

'It is not your fault; you are just a boy. He should have been more responsible!'

'We would not have been hunting at all if Havel had given us a sheep to kill!' I protested. 'His selfishness got us into this mess.'

'Don't blame the brother that saved your life for your foolish actions,' Ima retorted.

'If it wasn't for Kayin I'd definitely be dead!' Chayyim defended. 'Besides, Ima, I am not *just a boy*. Look at these muscles!' He flexed his arms, gently batting Ima with one.

My mother did not look amused, and she didn't take her eyes from my face. I realised this was no mild scolding. She was angry, even though she was trying to hide it. Nevertheless, she waited a moment, as if choosing to soften, and addressed me. 'Forgive me. I was so scared for you both.'

'Of course, Ima,' I said, but I wasn't convinced she meant it. Could it be that I had broken more than my foot with this latest act of folly – my mother's trust?

The scratches on my back were relatively shallow and seemed like they would heal quickly. Only the deeper cuts on my shoulders, where the claws had first sunk in, prevented me from making any quick movements. Awan did her best to keep the wounds clean, bathing them daily in water boiled with herbs and changing my linens, but she expected I would have scars in some places.

My foot showed a slight improvement in the first week. The skin began to heal, the swelling reduced, and the colour turned first to blue, then purple, before beginning to fade. Yet my foot still sat at an unnatural angle, and none of us knew how to fix that. I certainly couldn't put any weight on it. My recovery looked like it would be slow and painful.

Immobilised, I had never spent so much time at the hut. At first, it was pleasant to be surrounded by my family. Havel and Awan took turns spending time with Chayyim and me. Havel was full of stories, as usual, and the young twins would come in twice a day with Ima when she brought us food. They would sit on Chayyim's pallet, relating everything that was going on outside.

As it became clear I would be having a more extended recovery period than Chayyim, Avigayil insisted on making me a seat outside so that I could watch the goings-on while I recovered. She was a feistier kind of girl, more like my mother than Awan. And she had a gift for weaving reeds. When I'd tried to protest how long she would spend on the project, she'd rolled her eyes at me and dismissed my concern, 'You can't stay stuck inside this hut with only animal skins to keep you company.'

'I am used to being on my own,' I'd said. 'It's fine.'

'Tush,' was all she'd replied as she walked out of my hut, waving an arm.

Four days later, she finished the seat and came to fetch me. 'Now, big brother, do as I say and put yourself down outside on the seat that I have made you.'

She insisted on helping me hobble to it, even though I was twice her size. I was astonished as I beheld the seat. She had woven a vertical section between two branches and suspended the whole seat off the ground by weaving a base around three more crossing branches, firmly fastened. I would be able to sit back and rest without having to lie down all the time or getting a numb backside on the hard floor. The seat was lined with linen, and there was even a stool for me to rest my foot on.

'Avigayil, I don't know what to say…' I began.

'Then say nothing,' she retorted. She instructed me to sit down and proceeded to tuck me in with blankets. I laughed at her.

'Watch it; she will be force-feeding you her disgusting broth next,' Chayyim smirked from his position near me. Avigayil was a talented weaver, but she had not inherited my mother's ability to cook. Being so close in age, she and Chayyim were constantly goading each other.

'Where is my chair, sister?' Chayyim continued. 'I am injured too, you know.'

She stuck her tongue out at him and walked off. Chayyim was no longer injured. Within days, he had been back on his feet and was now keen to continue working in the fields. So, I began to give him instructions each morning, and he would go out to work all day. Often Abba, and sometimes Havel, would accompany him.

'Though I am sure even three of us will not manage to achieve near the amount of work you can do in a day,' Chayyim had joked. It was probably true.

Upon waking one morning, nearly two weeks after the attack of the wolves, my foot felt suddenly worse – throbbing and hot. Ima uncovered my wound and gasped. It had changed colour overnight. There was a green tinge around the broken skin. She checked my back; the deepest cuts in my shoulders were also weeping. She went out and spoke in hushed tones with Abba and Havel, out of my earshot. I heard Havel walk away.

Sometime later, he went back to speaking with my parents. They talked for a while, my parents seeming to disagree about something. Eventually, it seemed that Ima had her way, for she led the procession back into my hut.

'Havel has consulted with Elohim,' she said. *How did my brother do that*? I wondered. 'He revealed a tall tree in the mountain forests that contains the ointment you need for your wounds. Havel has offered to take the journey to retrieve some.'

I looked at their three faces. My mother looked worried but firm, Havel was smiling confidently, Abba looked sullen.

'I do not wish to put Havel in any danger,' I answered, trying to appease my father. Abba opened his mouth as if to say something but was cut off.

'Nonsense,' Havel answered. 'Yahweh will show me the way and protect me. I will gladly go for you, my brother.'

'Abba should go with you,' I suggested.

'No, someone needs to stay with the sheep, and Chayyim is needed in the fields. I suspect I will be gone for a quarter moon, and your foot may get worse before it gets better. You will need the women to look after you. Ima, Yahweh told me that you should continue to bathe the wounds every day with water that has been boiled and cooled,' he added.

'Perhaps you should take Awan?' my mother said. 'She will be good company for you, and that girl is stronger than she looks. Avigayil can help me with Kayin.'

Havel looked at me in indecision. We shared a small moment of understanding – only he and I knew of Awan's fear of being out in the dark.

'I will ask her,' he finally said.

As they turned to leave, I called to my father, needing to understand something. 'Abba?'

He stopped in the doorway while my mother and Havel left.

'Yes, son.'

'Why don't you want Havel to go?'

My father slowly knelt next to my pallet. Now unused to his proximity, I trembled.

'It is not the northern mountains Havel is journeying to, but the eastern ones,' he replied.

I gasped. 'Where the tanninim dwell?'

'Yes.'

'But the creatures there—'

'Indeed. I fear for his life.' We were silent for a moment, before he spoke again, more wistfully. 'Did I ever tell you about the behemoth?'

'No.'

'The behemoth are the most gigantic of the tanninim. One day, Elohim brought one to me. I heard it before I saw it, a great crashing noise that shook the earth. Then I saw a neck reaching as high as the cedars of the Garden, and a tail so long I could not see the end of it! Its skin was smooth and hairless and a tiny head perched on top of that immense neck.

He continued, 'There are behemoth in the east, Kayin. Havel and I have seen them from the hill of herbs. Yet, it is not them that I fear, for they are peaceable, with teeth like a deer. It is something else... You remember the creature we saw the day we found the sheep?'

'The one that clicked?'

'Yes. I have seen another like that, but far larger. Not as gigantic as the behemoth, yet more deadly. It is that tannin I fear.'

Images of enormous predators invaded my mind as I considered his words, and I realised the danger Havel was walking into. I also understood that, for my father, the conversation outside had been like choosing between the lives of his two sons. And I knew which he valued more highly.

'I suppose we must trust in Elohim?' My words were framed as a question, needing the reassurance of my father's faith.

Abba fiddled with a stray thread on his tunic.

'I suppose,' he muttered.

Havel and Awan set off together that afternoon. Awan evidently hated the thought of being separated from Havel more than she hated the idea of being in the wild at night. Our home immediately felt strange without them. Everyone seemed to be on edge. Even

Chayyim could not cheer us up at dinner that night with his attempts at light-hearted banter.

As for myself, I was grateful to Havel, but I did not understand how he could be so confident and jovial in the face of such danger. Or how he could drag my sister into it.

CHAPTER 9

Fear for Awan permeated my mind. I spent a restless night with my foot throbbing and my dreams populated with danger.

At first, I was in the field digging at weeds, then the thorns began to grow around my arm, sinking into my flesh and pulling me down into the earth. I fought against them, but I was powerless to resist as they grew larger and wrapped around my ankle and shoulders, cutting them open.

Then the earth opened beneath me and pulled me into it. I travelled through fire – feeling it singeing my broken flesh – then I was thrown into a forest. Wolves surrounded me and took up pursuit. As one came near and bit at my heels, it transformed into a tannin with feathers around its neck. The strange, clicking noise it made resounded angrily in my head. Chayyim had been running in front of me at first, but suddenly, he looked like Awan. We ran together. I was grasping her hand, but our fingers kept slipping apart.

Then she was attacked – not just by the tannin, but wolves also surrounded her. The former grew until it towered above the earth. Awan let go of my hand as she fell and hit her head on a rock. I tried to reach her but, again, thorns grasped hold of me, pulling me back into the earth. Helplessly I watched as a wolf sunk its teeth into her neck. Then the magnified tannin took her body in its jaws and flung her further into the forest, dashing her slackened form against a tree. Chunks of her flesh were left hanging in its huge jaws.

I woke in a cold sweat. Sitting up, I tipped water into my hand and splashed my face. On the other side of the hut, Chayyim slept soundly. My flesh prickled. My body felt like it was still roped in thorns. The heat was intense. I longed to get up and find my sister, but my head ached so profoundly that I could do nothing but lay it back down on my bed. My eyes stung in their sockets, forcing my lids closed. I tried to fight sleep, desperate not to return to those nightmares. Yet, almost immediately, sleep claimed me again.

I was transported to a cliff face above a wide, gushing river, far more extensive and violent than the Khabur. As I watched, a sheep tipped itself over the edge of the cliff. Then Havel ran past me and threw himself after it, taking no care with his life. Darting to the edge, I watched as he fell into the rushing currents. He caught his sheep and held onto it. They began to sink. I tried desperately to reach him, throwing my arms towards the rapids impotently. A serpent grasped hold of me and the more I reached, the further it pulled me away. 'Perhaps the stupid thing fell off a cliff,' the serpent hissed in my ear, as it coiled around my neck, strangling. Helplessly, I watched until the river carried Havel downstream and split his body violently against the rocks.

The serpent finally retreated. I ran down to the riverside and dragged my brother's broken body from the water. He lay in my arms, lifeless and pale, covered in blood. Suddenly, my father was standing before me. His voice began cursing me, blaming me for killing his favourite son and his beautiful daughter.

He was shouting at me, 'Why did you kill them, Kayin? It should have been you!'

I covered my ears. I rocked back and forth, trying to block out the sound of his voice. Then, just as I could bear his condemnation no longer, the nightmare drove me into a desert. I wandered countless miles, having nowhere to go – parched and alone.

Several times during this night of horrors, I woke. Each time sleep reclaimed me, taking me back, forcing me to relive the deaths of my siblings over and over again.

I experienced those delusions constantly while Havel and Awan were gone. Each day I feared more for their safety. I knew that the further they got from home, the more dangerous it became. Each night I dreaded succumbing to nightmares that grew in length, detail and peculiarity – as the pain in my foot also increased. Night after night, I relived the deaths of my loved ones. Night after night, I faced my father's condemnation and blame. Morning after morning, I tried to readjust to reality, even as the heat and pain in my body grew more intense.

The first day was a day of rest, so all of us that remained gathered. I sat on my wicker chair while the others sat, as usual, on the ground or on bushels of straw. Abba had brought the sheep near the hut and herded them into a stone circle we had constructed some years previously, so they would not be out of sight while he rested.

We tried to act as if we weren't missing them, but nothing was the same without Havel and Awan. We tried to sing songs of thankfulness to Elohim, but the songs sounded shallow without Awan's sweet voice to enrich them. Abba said the usual blessings over the food, but the words seemed rehearsed and empty without Havel's lively and sincere input.

On the second day, the men went back to the fields. I was, of course, confined to my chair with little to occupy me. I spent some time carving bone and sharpening tools, but it wasn't long before I ran out of things to do. I tried to help with some of the chores, but most I couldn't manage without standing.

I began to grind some grain between stones but twisting my back towards the ground while keeping my foot up was very uncomfortable. Soon, my tender shoulders ached from the exertion and I had to stop. Having been active my whole life, I hated feeling utterly useless.

Sensing my frustration, on the third day Avigayil brought me things to do. She even tried to show me how to weave, but my large hands couldn't manage the intricate entwining of reeds in and out of small spaces. When my failure ceased to be amusing, Avigayil got bored of tending to me and got on with her tasks alone.

By this time, Ima seemed to be regretting her decision to let Havel and Awan go. She was often at the river doing the cleaning that Awan usually took care of. When she was nearby, she was lost in thought and didn't pay the younger twins any attention. Consequently, they sought attention like feral creatures: getting up to mischief and getting in everyone's way.

By the fourth day, I was suffering from extreme boredom, coupled with a lack of sleep and now agonising pain. My once easy demeanour had transformed into a temper shorter than ever before. I snapped at the twins when they were running around. When Shimon knocked over a bowl that held my soup, I shouted at him, berating his clumsiness. Reacting to my tirade, Shimon pulled an ugly face at me and stormed off to tell Ima what I had said.

When she came to chastise me, I hadn't yet calmed down, and I was not in the mood to hear it.

'Can't you send Shimon to the fields?' I asked her angrily. 'He is older than Chayyim was when he came out with me, and it will stop him being so perpetually annoying!'

'You were an adult when I sent Chayyim out with you. I cannot ask Chayyim to take responsibility for his brother right now. He is too young and has enough to do covering all of your work.'

'Well, perhaps if Shimon had been put to work before now, he would be more useful and less unruly. That boy runs wild!' I said it in frustration and immediately regretted it.

'Well, perhaps if *you* had looked after Chayyim properly and not taken him into the woods at night, none of this would have happened!' my mother shouted back, then turned and fled towards the river, weeping loudly. Avigayil shot me an accusing look, dropped the basket she was working on and followed my mother.

Shimon and Channah, sensing my mood, went quietly back into the hut. I was left alone, unable to move, having ostracised half of my family with one outburst. I let out a frustrated roar, throwing the contents of my soup bowl towards the plain.

When Chayyim and Abba returned that evening, you could have cut the tension with a stone. Chayyim tried to cheer me up with anecdotes, but it just made me more annoyed that I couldn't be in the fields with him.

By contrast, my father did not even try. His concern for his missing children was consuming him. He scolded me for upsetting my mother, then he told us how edgy the sheep were without their true master nearby.

Apparently, wolves were howling again and could be seen skulking at the edge of the wood. After having something quick to eat, Abba grabbed his staff and went back to the sheep, not willing to leave them for any longer than necessary.

Fortunately, Shimon insisted on going with Abba, grabbing his sling and claiming that he would fight off any that dared come near, just as his brave brother Havel had done. Channah rolled her eyes at him, but no one objected. We would be glad of the respite from his irksome presence.

On the fifth day, the agony of my foot and shoulders grew even more intense, and as the pain increased, so did my vexation. I struggled to get out of my bed. My eyes felt like they had fingers around them, pulling them further back into their sockets. Once the sun had lowered in the sky so that it wasn't unbearably bright, I pulled myself up and practically crawled outside, desperate for something to take my mind off the pain. I lay by the entranceway and watched the family interact.

My father was home and talking with Ima a short distance away. He looked irritated and shortly afterwards retreated into the hut to snatch a brief rest. Everyone seemed tired, and all were on edge. No one said much. Even the twins had grown quiet and were playing a small game near the fire. They too could think of nothing other than the two people missing from our family and when they would come home.

By this time, my nightmares were not confined to times of sleep. Certain sounds and images would trigger their emergence throughout the day. Whenever I was alone – which was increasingly often – they became all-consuming. As the heat built up in my body, I began to hear my heart beating inside my head. I saw my brother and sister die in my mind so many times that I became convinced that they were not going to return from their journey. I sometimes found myself weeping.

'Kayin, what is wrong? Is it so painful?' Ima asked me at one point.

'Not the pain. I can manage the pain. I cannot bear the noise. Or the sight of seeing them die one more time,' I sobbed.

'What do you mean? What noise? Seeing who die?'

'How have you not seen it? They are dead. I see their faces everywhere! His stares at me from the water; hers accuses me from the ground.'

My mother looked at me in astonishment. She put her hands on my head and gasped as she felt the heat of it. Bringing me towels dipped in cold water, she bathed me, praying words over me as she did so. The words passed over me in a blur. I have no recollection of what she said. All was a cacophony of pounding heartbeats, vulgar clicks and the treacherous hiss.

On the sixth day, I could finally think of nothing beyond the pain. As I lay on my pallet, unable to move, Ima came in and uncovered me to wash the wounds, as she had been doing daily. She had tied a cloth over her nose because of the stench. Tiny worms had appeared and begun to eat my flesh.

My clothing was drenched through with sweat, as were the coverings on my pallet. My mother tried to cool me by washing my forehead with water, but it had little effect. She brought me some broth, but it went untouched.

My skin burned as if licked by fire. What I did see when I forced my eyes open bore little relation to reality. Avigayil sat with me and tried to get me to drink water. When I looked at her, I saw Awan's bloodied face. Screaming at Avigayil, I threw the water back over her.

By the time Abba and Chayyim came home that evening, I was seriously ill. I heard voices discussing me on the other side of the room, then my father came and sat on my midriff. I was sure he was trying to kill me for murdering his children – that he had decided he could bear my presence no longer. I struggled to free myself, hitting out with what little strength I had, but Chayyim came and restrained me, holding down my arms and forcing me to be still.

I shouted at them all, my clamped throat making hoarse noises, begging them to kill me quickly and not to keep putting me through this torture. But nobody listened. Instead, Ima leaned over me and poured water down my throat. I felt like I was drowning, I spluttered and spat the water back up, but she carried on, pouring it over and over again. I wanted to be sick. I began to retch, trying to lean forward and empty my stomach, but my father and Chayyim held fast and didn't let me move. Eventually, I gave in. Exhausted and unable to move anymore, I drifted off into another fitful and restless sleep, where noises and faces continued to haunt me.

I must have stayed in this state for several days, drifting in and out of consciousness – reality always evading me. My nightmares grew even stranger as more creatures from the eastern mountains began joining in the chase and helping themselves to the flesh of my siblings.

Every time I was constrained, I would put up the same fight, but stuck beneath the two men, I was helpless to resist the water that my mother poured down my throat.

CHAPTER 10

At some point, my head began to clear slightly. The suspicion that my family wanted me dead lingered, but I accepted their ministrations with less resistance. Or, perhaps, I was succumbing to the idea of death, preferring anything to this life of repeated nightmares. Nonetheless, something felt physically different. My foot felt heavy. I couldn't lift my leg had I wanted to, yet the rest of my body had started to cool down. I was even shivering at points as I lay alone in my soaked linens.

One morning I woke, feeling conscious again for just a few moments. I was alone and noises were coming from outside the hut. I tried to sit up, but the pain that shot through my head was so intense I gave up.

I saw a skin of water on the floor next to my pallet. I managed to reach over to it and drink, desiring water for the first time in days. I tried to curl my body inwards so that I could see my foot without lifting my head. It was heavily wrapped in linen, and there was a green mixture in a bowl near the foot of the bed.

The simple exertion of looking at my foot was enough to exhaust, and I fell back into a sleep that was slightly less fretful.

I must have slept through that entire day, for when I

next woke it was morning again. Sunlight streamed underneath the skin at the entrance to my hut. On the other side of the room, I could still see Chayyim sleeping on his pallet. He hadn't moved back to the other hut since the wolf attack.

The wolves! That seemed like an age ago. How many days had I been asleep? It must be past the time when Havel and Awan should have returned, yet they had not. Were they dead, as I had feared? Once again, I tried to sit up. I felt relieved when I did not get such a sharp pain in my head that I couldn't continue.

The movement from my pallet woke Chayyim. He immediately rose and came over to me.

'Kayin! Are you finally with us?' he asked.

'I think so,' I replied. 'What day is it?'

'It is the day before Shabbat.'

'Again? So how long…?'

'Seven days you have been unconscious. We thought we lost you on the fourth, then Havel and Awan returned with the ointment late that morning. Havel spent the whole day and night in the hut praying for you and caring for you. The next morning you started showing improvement.'

'They are home? Are you sure? I thought they were dead!' I exclaimed in disbelief.

'They are here; I will fetch them.' Chayyim smiled and left the hut. He returned a few moments later with my brother and sister.

I could not believe it. I had seen their lifeless faces so many times that my mind could not reconcile what was in front of me with what was inside my head. They approached, smiling sleepily, and rubbing their eyes. I realised they had been woken from sleep.

I stammered at them, unable to bring words to my lips. Awan beamed and fell beside my pallet, throwing her arms around me and kissing my cheek. I stiffened in anticipation of pain, but it was only slight.

'Havel said you would be fine, but I am ashamed to say I doubted him. I feared for your life,' she said as she looked into my eyes, and I saw hers brimming with tears.

I managed a few words. 'You thought *I* would die? I was convinced it was you who had left us forever.'

A puzzled look crossed her face, then she gently smiled and whispered, 'I would never leave you.'

I found it hard to tear my eyes away from my sister's loving gaze to look at my brothers. They were standing next to each other; arms crossed over their chests and grins plastered on their faces.

'You're back, and I am alive.' I managed to say to Havel, 'You saved me, again.'

'Oh, I'd say we're even now. After all, you once saved me *and* my sheep.' He laughed, then moved to sit on the end of my pallet, gingerly putting a hand near my injured ankle. Awan extricated herself from my arms and sat on the floor beside me, lifting my wet tunic sightly to inspect my shoulders.

'They are good,' she smiled. 'Merely scratches now.'

I looked at my foot properly then. There was something solid underneath the linens that were wrapping it, yet it looked straight on the end of my leg.

'What did you do for my foot?'

Havel told me how they had quickly found the tree they were seeking and had set about collecting the pieces they would need for my wound straight away. They had been delayed on the way home.

'I'm sorry we were later than planned. But Yahweh assured me that you were in His hands, and I could trust Him.'

Following my line of sight, he unwrapped the linen on my foot slightly so I could see underneath. As he did so, my mind tried to focus on what he had just said. They had been delayed but Havel had spoken to Yahweh? Had been told to trust Him? Was he suggesting that the delay was part of Yahweh's plan? My head began to hurt with thinking.

Havel was still talking over my wandering mind. He was explaining how he had poured the ointment from the mountains over my foot, rubbed it with a poultice made from the same and packed the wound with herbs. Then he had fixed my foot back into the correct position, using sticks to hold it in place, then wrapping linens tightly to keep it all together. That explained why my foot felt so heavy, although it certainly wasn't as painful now.

I had no idea how he had known what to do – what my wound had needed. Yet, no one else seemed to find that strange, so I kept quiet. Perhaps I had missed his explanation.

Just then my mother and father entered the hut. Ima came to me, took my face in her hands and tentatively placed a kiss on my cheek. There was something strange in her eyes still, but she looked pleased to see I was well. Abba stood by my bed and put his hand on my shoulder, 'I am relieved you are awake, my son,' he managed, before backing away.

'I will bring you something to eat,' Ima said. 'Awan, come and help me prepare the morning meal.' Awan obediently rose, smiled at me, then left with my mother. The others followed, except for Havel, who remained at the end of my bed, looking at me pensively.

'I have so many questions...' I began.

'I know, Kayin, but you need to build up your strength first. I saw you when you were close to death.' He shook his head, and a tear ran from his eye. 'I tried

91

to protect Awan from it so she would not be scared. We should talk through what happened. However, for now, you must continue to rest. You still have a season of recovery before you.'

Looking at my brother then, and hearing his words, I could scarcely believe he was just a fraction older than I had been when he and Awan were born. I thought back to when I was his age. I had already exceeded my father in the knowledge and skill of the land, and I was a helpful son to my parents, but I had been nothing like the person I saw before me. Now, at thirty-seven summers, I certainly looked more mature than him, with greater height and physical strength. Yet Havel had what I lacked: complete confidence in who he was, along with quiet authority and influence.

Yes, there was something about Havel that was different from everyone else in the family. It drew people to him. And whatever it was, I wanted it.

CHAPTER 11

The next day, with Chayyim's help, I managed to make it outside to Avigayil's seat. It felt good to be in the fresh air again. The sunlight on my face filled my heart with warmth rather than causing my head to throb. I propped my foot upon the stool, and this time the young twins were careful not to run too close to me. Perhaps they had received a stern warning not to knock my foot, or maybe they were just terrified of me after my tantrums and the week of wild fever.

'Today, we celebrate!' Ima announced, coming out of her hut with arms full. She had collected the best of the food we had left from last year's harvest into one of Avigayil's baskets and put it down on the ground, near to where we usually lit the fire. Awan followed her out with yesterday's bread and broth. Then Abba appeared from behind the huts carrying a weighty skin.

'I have been experimenting with making a drink from the fruit of the vine,' Abba said. 'I can't guarantee its good taste, but let us try it today.'

Seeing the procession of food, the rest of the family stopped what they were doing and gathered. Ima passed bowls around, and Abba poured his drink into each of them.

'With thanks to Yahweh Elohim for bringing us all together again,' Abba said, as he raised his bowl. We all copied him, lifting our bowls toward the sky and then to our lips. All together, we took a sip from the bowls and then reacted. Shimon and Channah were the first to spit it out, making a distasteful noise as they did so. Havel and Chayyim had more grace, but their faces told all. They both rushed for the nearest water skin, wrestling each other for it. I swallowed mine quickly and tried hard not to grimace, as did Awan, who even forced a smile. Our circle went silent for a moment as we looked at each other and our father, then all his children burst into hysterics together.

'How can a fruit so sweet make a drink so bitter?' Havel chortled.

'I actually quite like it,' Ima confessed, locking faithful eyes with Abba.

'Perhaps it needs a bit of… adjustment,' he admitted, with a grimace, then laughed aloud. We all joined in laughing then began to tuck into the food.

It was not long before Shimon and Channah were sitting at Havel's feet, imploring him to tell them the whole story of his adventures. And so, as Havel began to recount the tale, I heard for the first time all that had happened since the night they left.

'That first afternoon, we travelled about halfway to the Tigris before seeking a glade in which to rest for the night. I still didn't know how we would cross the river, so I asked Yahweh about it while Awan slept. He was silent, but I could feel his presence with us. I knew he would provide a way, so I ceased to worry.

'The following day, we rose at dawn and continued on our way. As we neared the river, we felt a gentle breeze start up, and on the wind, there was a whisper. I knew this was Ruach Elohim guiding us, so we followed the direction of the wind. As we approached the river, it was clear it was too large to wade across, and the current was strong. Despite our lessons from Kayin, neither of us fancied our chances swimming across. It was then that a stronger wind blew and gained our attention. It lifted the tops of the trees towards heaven and whipped a pile of leaves up into the air. Whilst watching the movement of the leaves, I noticed what Elohim was showing us.

'Just up ahead, two giant oak trees sat opposite each other on the banks of the river. Their branches spread so far across the water that they were almost touching. Then, before our very eyes, the branches began to extend towards each other! I had often imagined what it must have been like when Elohim planted the Garden of Eden and made trees and plants spring up from the ground. I think this was like that! As the voice on the wind spoke, the branches grew – Ruach Elohim was quickening their life!

'In short time, the branches from both trees had entwined to hold hands across the river and thickened so substantially that they were strong enough to hold our weight. We climbed the first tree and carefully made our way out above the water. I cannot deny we were both scared with the rushing river beneath us, but I knew if He could make the trees grow for our sakes, Elohim would certainly preserve us if we fell. So, we climbed across, and soon we were on the other side of the river.

'From there, it was easy to find a path towards the mountains. The sky was clear, and the ground tremendous for walking on. It was uphill, though, and by the late afternoon, we were tired. We stopped again for the night. The following two days, we walked constantly towards the mountain forests. The air grew thinner and colder as the ground rose.

'The views up there were staggering. We saw so many different creatures. Many more flowers and small animals live near the mountains, which we rarely see on the plains. Every colour you can imagine grew over those hills. We collected sweet-smelling herbs and tasted some of the wildflowers. All around us, animals grazed, hopped and skittered. Some even dug into the ground when they saw us approach. Great birds flew in the sky and would sometimes swoop down as if they were hunting tiny creatures far below. How they could see them from their place in the sky, I cannot comprehend! As they neared the earth, we marvelled at the breadth of their wings, which were surely as long as Kayin is tall! It was incredible.

'At night, there were countless noises in the distance, yet no creatures seemed to come near us as long as we stayed near a fire. We were careful to collect kindling wherever we stopped as we could hear wolves howling nearby and did not wish to attract them. It was icily cold at night, so we slept huddled together beside the fire.

'By the high point of the sun on the fifth day, Yahweh had led us to the forest we needed. The air smelt different there; each tree had a unique aroma, and there were unfathomable quantities and varieties of them. They completely covered the mountains as far as the eye could see. The one we were seeking grew another half a day's walk from the forest edge.

'There was no way we could know where we were going, yet the gentle wind still guided us, leading us onto the right paths, paths made by creatures walking before us. At times we would come across significant sections of forest that looked trampled on by enormous beasts: whole trees were felled and stripped of their leaves, and ferns were trodden into the dirt. We realised these clearings were created by giant tanninim of various kinds.

'The smell as we drew close to the area we were seeking gave it away. The air smelt like the poultice on

Kayin's foot, so much so it made our heads dizzy. By this time it was getting dark and we had to stop for another night's rest. As the sun set, innumerable creatures seemed to come alive in this part of the forest. All around us, eyes glinted in the moonlight that filtered through the treetops. We huddled close to the fire, as silently as possible. The howls of wolves were closer now, but we could hear noises far worse than that – screeches in the darkness, distressed screams. The giants were hunting.'

Havel paused for dramatic effect and the little ones wriggled on their bottoms.

'Nothing happened to us *that* night,' Havel laughed as he continued. 'In the morning, we set about collecting ointment from the sap of the trees around us, picking leaves and tearing off loose pieces of bark. I didn't yet know which part of the plant would be most beneficial. When we had gathered as much as we could carry, we set off back down the mountain.

'It should have been quicker coming home as we were walking downhill, but we did not anticipate what happened next. We had just reached a clearing in the forest – one that sat near the edge of some cliffs – when a whole herd of behemoth came near. I knew what they were for I saw them once, watering at the Tigris, when I was collecting herbs with Abba. The path we were crossing must have been one they had created. The ground rumbled as they approached, so we found a thicket to hide in, set just back from the path.

'You would not believe the size of these creatures! They had gigantic necks that reached as tall as the trees and colossal, sweeping tails that floored the plants they swept through. Yet they stripped leaves as they walked and paid no attention to the other creatures around. There was a magnificence and gentleness about these giants. The young ones trotted along in groups, behind their parents, looking about them as if seeking games to play.

'Just as they had passed and we thought we were safe, we heard a sudden screech like the ones heard during the night. Charging through the trees from a different direction was another creature, about the size of three men and much smaller than the gentle giants. It came rushing toward the herd, looking to make a meal of a young one. This tannin had a head too large for its body, with giant, sharp teeth all along its jaws and huge claws on the end of tiny arms that jutted out in front of it. It ran on two legs like a man.

'Several adult behemoth tried to turn back to protect their young, but there was not enough space! They were far too large and merely caused a commotion. The predator seemed to know how to take advantage of this situation. Its smaller size was superior as it pursued its prey into the dense forest, weaving through the trees.

'We did not get to see the end of the story. One of the adult behemoth swept around, aiming for the hunter, but missed. Its giant tail swung towards our thicket! We got up to run but were not quick enough. The edge of its tail clipped our fleeing backs with such a force that sent us flying – right over the edge of the cliff!'

My young siblings gasped. They watched Havel with their mouths wide open, perched on curled up fingers. He allowed a moment of suspense before continuing.

'We did not land on rocks but careered straight into water. Elohim protected us from an impact that should have meant our deaths. You see, the Tigris appears to be fed from streams that begin in the mountains. As we had been nearing the base of one such mountain, this stream had widened into a river that was deep enough to cushion our fall.

'The water was cold enough to take your breath away, but the current was not strong. Even with our limited swimming skills, we both managed to reach the surface within moments, gasping for air and looking around desperately for each other. I spotted Awan just a few arm spans away. We swam for each other, clinging on as our arms locked together.

'The shock prevented us from doing much but treading water as the current carried us downstream. Then I spotted some tree roots jutting out into the water and directed Awan to swim for them. We managed to grab hold and haul our bodies up onto them. This way, we climbed out of the river, for the bank was steep and we wouldn't have been able to get a grip on it without that tree.

'Deeply cold and unsure where we were, we decided to stop and light a fire. We stripped our outer clothing off, gathered some giant ferns to blanket us, and huddled together for warmth as the flames took hold. With great relief, we realised we had managed to retain the contents of our carrying packs, otherwise our journey would have been in vain. We laid the healing leaves and barks out to dry alongside us.

'We stayed the night in that place, managing to gather some berries and mushrooms to eat from near the river. The following morning, we tried to figure out where we were. Clearly, we were now on the wrong side of the mountain, and there was no way of climbing the cliff face. We spent some time praying to Elohim, asking Him for guidance, but the wind did not join us this time.

'We realised that the river we had fallen into probably ran into the Tigris and that, hopefully, we would not go too far out of our way if we followed it. So, we began walking downstream, staying as close to the river's edge as possible.'

'Wait!' interjected Shimon, 'What do mean the wind did not join you? Did Elohim not answer your prayers?'

I was glad my youngest brother had asked the very question that was on my mind.

'It is true, that time I did not hear His voice or feel His touch. He does not always answer me immediately. I think sometimes He withholds Himself for a greater purpose. In this case, we used our reason to work out that we needed to follow the river. It was the right course but, unfortunately, a longer and more challenging route. We could not simply walk downhill as we would have done on the mountain path. Instead, we had to traverse the rolling terrain along the riverbank.

'We followed the river for three more days and nights until it brought us to the Tigris at the midpoint of our ninth day away from home. We knew by this time that you would all be worried. Added to this, we were not at the same spot where we had previously crossed the river by climbing the overhanging trees. Once again, there was no obvious way of crossing. We considered walking all the way back to the bridging oaks but realised that would add another day to our journey, perhaps more. Awan was worried about Kayin; she was sure that he could not afford any further delay.

'So we consulted Yahweh again. This time the wind returned and beckoned us downstream. We did not want to walk further from home and hesitated to follow it. As if in protest at our delay, the wind formed into a swirl above the ground and began to lift the dust from the earth. In front of our eyes, grass, sticks and flowers were churned into its funnel. The sky darkened, and the atmosphere grew cold. The whirlwind forcefully drew us towards it. There could be no mistaking this was Ruach Elohim, so we gripped each other's arms and submitted to Him.

'We were foolish to hesitate. Just around the bend was a point where the river was narrower and the current weaker. We would not have seen it had we gone the other way! We fell on our knees before the whirlwind and praised Yahweh Elohim. We implored Him to forgive our doubt and to help us cross the river.

'He did not fail us. As we stepped into the water, the current ceased and we were both able to cross the expanse at a gentle swim. Soaked again, we made another fire and camped as we had done at the previous river.

'From there, it took us nearly two days to walk to the point where Awan washes linens in the Khabur – where it is easy to cross over to our home. And so we arrived, and not a moment too soon for our brother.'

I had listened to the tale with great interest. Not just because it was the story of how my life was saved but also because it revealed so much about Havel's relationship with Elohim. This was peculiar to me. I could not fathom the expectation he had of communion with Yahweh. I thought that Yahweh had stopped walking with humanity after the banishment. Of course, my parents prayed, but they talked of Yahweh Elohim as if He was distant, as if relationship with Him was something they had lost, not something they currently had. I prayed too, but I had never expected Him to speak or to appear before me. And yet, here He was, not just appearing once, but accompanying Havel in the form of a wind. He had answered my siblings directly every time they had prayed – except for the time they were thrown into the river.

It had not escaped my notice that their prayers went unheeded on the sixth night. The night I had been taken with fever and fallen into the deep sleep that nearly ended my life. Why had He delayed answering then? What greater purpose could justify my suffering? Speaking of which, why would Elohim even choose to take them on this journey? Surely if He could make trees grow unnaturally, control the wind and the river currents for their sakes, He could have healed my foot the very night it was injured. Why bring me to the point of death before healing? Why torment my mind with visions and dreams?

As the others continued to chatter and ask Havel questions, I sunk my head into my hands. I wanted to ask Elohim about these things, but I did not know Him as Havel did. What if He rejected my questions? What if He thought me ungrateful for the healing I had been given? I sensed that He was already angry with me, just as I suspected my parents were. For, despite the celebrations, neither of them could look me in the eye.

Would I ever know their favour again? It was true I had allowed Chayyim to stay in the woods towards dusk, but had I not told him it was time to leave? Had I not grasped him as we ran from the wolves, carried his unconscious body out of the forest, thrown myself over him to protect him? Yet nobody seemed to remember or acknowledge this. I could have run and saved myself, but instead I sacrificed my body for my brother's, and was living with the injuries. They all praised Havel for shooting the wolves with his sling. I only received condemnation.

Perhaps Elohim had forced me to endure weeks of pain as punishment for my mistake. Perhaps He had chosen to spare me in the end only for Havel's sake – because He was willing to do as my brother asked. Yet, why did He speak to my brother only? What was this special relationship? Why did He favour Havel more than me?

These questions flooded my mind as I sat there. I was in the midst of my family, but I felt like a stranger to them all. They all trusted in Elohim, and suddenly I wasn't sure I did.

CHAPTER 12

My confinement continued to frustrate me for the next week. Although I tried to bear it with more patience, I remained too sick to move around. With my siblings returned, I had to watch as everyone else resumed activities and left me alone for most of the day. Though assured of Havel and Awan's safety, my parents and youngest siblings still seemed nervous around me.

Had Awan stayed with me it might have been more tolerable, but now my wounds did not need tending, even she appeared to withdraw. Seeming to have overcome her fears on her journey with Havel, she now happily went out to help the men instead of staying around the hut all day. Almost every time I saw her, she was at Havel's side. In this way, he took from me the one good thing about my confinement.

The following Shabbat, Abba asked Havel if he would lead our prayers. My father seemed keen to delegate the task now that Havel had proven himself. My gut protested that I, the eldest, should have been chosen,but there seemed to be a tacit acknowledgement that I was not qualified for this task. I had never been asked to lead prayers, even when fully involved in the worship.

So, Havel began praying during our times of worship. Prayers soon progressed into something more active as the others responded to his lead. Before long, we were being gathered for worship not just on Shabbat but often during the evenings. Havel would share with us stories and thoughts of Elohim, speaking of His love and goodness. He encouraged my parents to reveal more about their conversations with Yahweh in Eden so that we could all learn from them.

My younger siblings continued to hang on Havel's every word. They asked questions, wanting to know more about Elohim. Chayyim and Avigayil devised ways of acting out the stories Havel told, and everyone would laugh at their antics – especially when they did impressions of my parents. I tried to join in and found some parts genuinely amusing, but my laughter often felt hollow in my ears.

Awan also grew in confidence as Havel encouraged her. She began to sing aloud on her own, rather than just quietly with everyone else. She started singing songs that she had composed – songs of praise to a God that I was struggling to understand. I enjoyed watching Awan sing, but I struggled to follow her sentiment. Whilst the others joined in with her choruses, I held back.

One day, after a family time of worship, Awan came and sat beside me, asking me how I was. I began to say that my foot was improving, but she stopped me – uncharacteristically – and instead asked how I was in my soul. Seeing me speechless, she explained, 'You used to smile when you heard me sing, but lately you always look sad.'

I smiled at her then, trying to reassure her, but hesitant. I was unsure what I should reveal. Finally, I decided if there was one person I could trust, it was her. 'I have been struggling since the wolf attack. I do not feel close to Elohim as you and Havel seem to be.'

She drew her brows together as she pondered what I had said. 'What do you think has changed?' she asked.

I wasn't sure. In some ways nothing had changed: I had never had the kind of bond with Elohim that Havel had. And many of the questions flooding my mind were not just a result of suffering. Some had grown gradually, as I had struggled in my relationship with Abba, or become older and lost my childlike view of the world. Yet only since the wolves had everything come to the forefront.

'I'm not sure,' I responded. 'I don't understand all that has happened recently. I don't know what I have done wrong, yet I seem to have been punished; to have earned everyone's condemnation.'

'I don't condemn you,' said Awan. 'Neither does Havel.'

'Can you read his mind now?'

'Sometimes,' she smirked.

'Why did you go with him on the journey?' I asked.

Awan looked into my eyes. 'I was torn about it, but I wished to help you – and I did not like the thought of Havel being alone in the wild.'

I was surprised that she seemed to have been equally motivated by concern for me as for Havel.

'Weren't you scared?' I asked.

'Of course! But Havel is much braver than I am, and his bravery helps me feel strong. Then, when I felt Elohim's presence… I can't describe it; it was incredible,' she reflected. 'I somehow knew we were safe, even when I thought we might get eaten by the giant tannin!'

We sat still for a few moments. I couldn't help the creeping feeling of jealousy for Awan's trust in both Havel and Elohim. I wanted to experience His presence the way she described it. And I had enjoyed being Awan's strong one. Now I was inadequate for both.

When I didn't say anything further, my sister rose to leave.

'I think if you are confused about Elohim, you should speak to Havel,' she said. He is much better than I am with these things. I will ask him to come here.'

My heart contracted. I instinctively grabbed hold of her arm to stop her from leaving. 'I would much rather speak with you. Please don't go,' I implored. She tried to laugh, yet her laughter cut short as she looked into my eyes. They were searching hers; pleading with her to stay.

'Kayin, it would be better,' she tried to reason, but my expression remained steadfast. She tried to release her arm, but I was unable to let her go.

'Kayin, please.' A flicker of fear crossed her features. I came to my senses and hastily let go of her.

'Sorry,' I mumbled. 'Of course, you are right.'

Awan moved out of arm's length. Fixing her eyes on me again she tried to smile, but could not hide her concern. She turned and went in search of my brother.

Havel joined me a few moments later. He grinned, clapped me on the back, then sat down in the dust. He was facing me at a slight angle, crossing his legs and leaning back on his arms.

'Awan said you wish to speak to me,' he said. Although I had wanted to ask him questions the day I woke up, at this moment I did not wish to speak to him. I just wanted Awan. But I nodded anyway.

'I am glad,' he continued. 'I have been worried about you ever since we returned from our journey, but I was waiting for you to approach me. I didn't want to force you to talk.'

All my questions seemed to flit away as I looked at him. I didn't like the way he was sitting and smiling at me. Being patronised by a brother half my age wasn't a pleasant feeling. However, I decided to swallow my pride for Awan's sake. I searched my mind for those things that had been bothering me most.

'Tell me, Havel, if Elohim cares for me, why would He allow my foot to be bitten? And why did He not heal it straight away? Why did I have to almost die before He decided to help me?' I asked, failing to hide the bitterness in my voice.

Havel didn't look surprised. I'd expected a more significant reaction to my expression of doubt in his God.

After pausing for a few moments, he spoke. 'I too have pondered these things. It wasn't pleasant for any of us seeing you suffer.' Havel ran a hand through his hair. 'I certainly don't have all the answers. However, I think that sometimes Elohim allows bad things to happen to teach us something. Perhaps He wants to teach you how to wait on Him?'

'What do you mean?'

'Kayin, you are very skilful; you have always been strong and capable. Everything you put your hand to flourishes. But now that you have an injury, you might rely less on yourself and more on Elohim to meet your needs.'

'So He caused my injury so that I might be less productive; so that I won't be able to provide as well for this family? That is ridiculous!'

'He allowed the wolves to attack you, yes. However, I don't know if that's the same thing as causing it.'

'It seems like the same thing to me. For if Elohim is all-powerful, then He could have stopped it!'

'Certainly. But then you would always have continued in the same way. Oh, it is a great mystery, Kayin. I feel in my soul that He holds all things in His hand, even the details of our lives, yet we also hold responsibility for our actions! I don't know the answer, but I must trust that He is good and will always do what is right. Perhaps He appointed these things to happen because the way you were heading before was not beneficial for you?'

'How not? Who is the one who feeds this family, Havel? It is not you or Abba. You just play around with sheep all day. You think that Chayyim could do it all by himself now?'

Havel ignored my insulting tone. 'Kayin, we all appreciate what you do, and I have just acknowledged your great skill. But where do you think that skill comes from? It is a gift from Elohim, a gift that has been given to you to use for His glory.'

I did not reply.

'Do you remember the time when I was little, and I bit Chayyim for taking my place on the ground?' Havel asked with a smile. I did remember and, despite my bad mood, I smiled at the memory. 'You asked me then whom the ground belonged to, and I confessed it belonged to Elohim. It is the same with our skills. Everything belongs to Him.'

Was Havel suggesting I wasn't allowed to own my skill – that I shouldn't take pride in the one thing I was good at? If I didn't own that, then I had nothing on which to base my confidence.

'Aren't I using my skill for His glory by providing for His people?' I responded. 'What else can I do?'

'I'm not sure it's all about what we do; more about why and how we are doing it.'

'You're questioning my motivations? Everything I do is for others. Am I not selfless enough for you?'

'That's not what I meant, Kayin. Let me give you an example from sheep – I'm better with sheep,' he grinned. 'When a lamb is born, it is totally dependent on its mother. It needs her for everything: milk, care, warmth. Yet as the lamb grows, it becomes more independent. At that point, what happens? It begins to wander away. It decides to explore rather than keep its eyes on its mother. Then it starts to get into trouble – because the truth is, it is not yet old enough to leave its mother's side.

'We are a little like those lambs, Kayin. We are born reliant on our parents not just to care for us but to guide us. Although certainly capable of doing wrong, we instinctively trust what they tell us about our Creator. Yet as we grow, we become more independent. We may wander away and trust in ourselves when we are not yet trustworthy. We may do things in our own strength rather than relying on the one who created us to give us wisdom.

'Elohim doesn't want us to wander. Like a good shepherd, He desires to keep us safe. He wants to stop us from hurting ourselves in our bid for independence. He wants to keep us from walking dangerous paths. Sometimes, to do that, He will need to use His staff to bring us back in. Or even to discipline us.'

'But what is the right path? How do I know if I have wandered from it?'

'I'm not exactly sure. Perhaps the right path looks different for each of us, but we will not find it unless we allow Elohim to guide us.'

This was all very vague. I tried to think about what Havel was saying. In terms of my parents, it wasn't I who had left: they had withdrawn from me. Yet, wasn't he talking about Elohim? I didn't think I had wandered away from Elohim either. He had never shown himself to me in the first place.

'I have not tried to wander – if you would put it that way. If I have withdrawn, it is due to certain recent circumstances...' I was thinking of my relationship with Abba. '...Due to the suffering and chastisement that I have endured.'

'A lamb rarely tries to wander,' Havel said quietly. 'It happens when they take their eyes off their mother. Then, once they realise they are lost, they bleat loudly, calling for someone to help them.'

'So I should bleat loudly?'

Havel laughed. 'Yes!'

'To whom?'

'Your Creator, Yahweh! Tell Him your concerns; ask Him for His way to be made known. Trust Him that He cares for you and desires what is good for you.'

'But I have no confidence that He does care!' I felt unbidden tears well in my eyes. 'He has shown me no favour! If He cares, why did He allow me to suffer so much? Why is He preventing me from fulfilling my purpose? How can I provide for everyone while confined to a chair?'

'Chayyim has managed pretty well the last few weeks,' Havel smiled.

'Barely,' I scoffed. 'He needs you all to help him. I'm sure the crops will suffer from my neglect. How can you think my injury is good for us? Or for me?'

'Because life is not just about food, Kayin! It is not just about providing for your family – much as we appreciate you doing so. I have a suspicion that life is not even about us, but that He made us for something bigger than ourselves. We were created for the Creator. He has purposes for us that go beyond the skills He has given us, and He desires to know each one of us. We just need to trust Him.'

'Well, I am beginning to think the Creator made a mistake,' I interjected, angrily. 'If He wants to know me so badly, if He wants me to trust Him, He should not have made me suffer!'

I'm not sure what made me snap at that point when up until then, I had been willing to listen. If I could have stormed off, I would probably have done so. Yet, once again, I was stuck on my chair and would have looked ridiculous trying to rise and failing. So instead, I scowled at the ground, signalling that the conversation was over.

Havel refused to take the hint. 'What is really bothering you, Kayin? I know there is more to it than this.'

I continued to stare at the ground. But he didn't leave me.

'If you must know, it is not just Elohim,' I sighed. 'I have lost everyone's favour. Abba has hated me ever since I lost you eight years ago. Ima likewise blames me for nearly getting Chayyim killed. They both hover around me and say nothing of value. And the young ones? They adore you, but they either ignore me or purposefully annoy me. I feel... Sometimes, I feel I don't belong here anymore.'

I realised I had revealed far more than I'd intended to. My brother drew alongside me and lowered his voice, 'Is that really what you think?' He sounded genuinely upset. 'No wonder you are sullen.'

Havel paused before continuing. 'I do not know why you think our parents hate you. I have always thought you were the favourite.'

I guffawed in response, looking at him and raising an eyebrow in disbelief.

'Well, they had you around for so long before any of us were born, and I always wondered why. As a child, I looked up to you, big brother. You were so capable and strong; it felt like you could do nothing wrong. And you had such a close relationship with Ima. I was jealous of you! I have had to repent of that attitude before Elohim.'

He had repented of jealousy? That was odd. I decided to correct his misunderstanding.

'I *was* close to them. Until the day I sent you off that cliff. Then it all changed.'

'I don't think they truly blamed you for that – in the heat of the moment perhaps, but not after you found me.'

'Then why did Abba always refuse to come to the fields with me afterwards?'

'Because he preferred the sheep. Nothing more.'

'No, Havel, you are wrong.' He had not heard the conversation between my parents that I had, where Abba had confessed his hatred for me. 'Besides, how do you explain their behaviour now?'

'That is something different, and I am sorry for it. I believe it relates to your fits while I was away. Do you realise what you were like, or have you no recollection of it?'

'I remember a little,' I replied.

He said the following words carefully. 'I have been told that you were frantic, uncontrollable. You kept screaming that Awan and I were dead. You screamed at Avigayil that she should leave you – that you would kill her if she didn't. You refused to take any food. Ima said you had a look in your eyes – like you were not of this world but belonged to another. Chayyim and Abba had to physically restrain you to give you water.'

'I remember that part. I thought they were trying to kill me.'

'They were trying to keep you alive, Kayin.' He paused before continuing. 'I believe you have frightened everyone quite badly. They do not speak to you because they don't know what to say. They cannot comprehend what you went through or why you would treat them like that. They are simply scared.'

I looked up at him then, searching his eyes. They were pools of deep brown, almost the same colour as the hair falling in wavy tresses down to his shoulders.

Once again, I thought about how much he had grown up recently. A beard had begun to fill out over his chin and around his broad lips. His face was square and angular and sat on shoulders that, whilst not as large as mine, were growing in size and strength. I could not reconcile this person with the boy who had clung to me at the cliff face and cried into my arms. Where had my little brother gone, and who was this man who had replaced him?

After several moments I spoke again. 'I cannot fully explain what happened. I experienced many nightmares when you were gone. I kept seeing you and Awan. You kept dying. Before my eyes. In my head.' My hands dug into my hair and my voice broke as the images flooded back into my mind. 'I could not distinguish what was a dream and what was real.'

Havel put his arms around my shoulders and held me. I began to feel my heart softening.

He started praying, speaking softly into the darkening sky around us. 'Yahweh Elohim, Creator of the heavens and the earth. Ruach Elohim, giver of breath and sustainer of life. I praise you for my brother Kayin, and for the skill you have given him in bringing forth food from the land. I pray that he may soon be able to work the ground again and find pleasure in fulfilling your purposes for him, whatever they may be.

'O Eternal One, Creator of the seasons and the one who numbers all of our days, I pray that you would heal the heart of your son in your good time. O Yahweh, would you weave back together what has torn in his soul? Would you impress upon him your love, your goodness, and your holiness? Have mercy on us, for you are an Elohim of justice, yet you are also our salvation. Blessed be your name in all the earth.'

After he finished speaking, we remained there in the stillness for some time. When I began to fidget, Havel rose, keeping his hand on my shoulder for a moment longer. Finally, he walked quietly away, leaving me alone with my thoughts.

CHAPTER 13

As time went on, I slowly grew stronger. Soon, using a staff to support me, I could hobble to the vineyards nearest the hut. I could just about manage to tend them by balancing on the staff, and could better see what Chayyim had been able to accomplish whilst I had been out of action.

He had done well, considering, but there was much to catch up on. The vineyard certainly wasn't up to my standard as the primary growing season had taken place during the last moon cycle. Not all the vines had been tied in so harvesting the fruit would be difficult unless we quickly got them tidied up.

I spent many days in the vineyard, catching up where Chayyim had missed and instructing him where I couldn't reach something myself. Fortunately, Chayyim still seemed to be the exception in my family. Not fazed by my fits during the fever, he didn't mind me telling him what to do.

After sorting the vines, we moved on to the flax, for it was pulling season. Most would be pulled for linen. A proportion would be left to produce the seed we used for oil and planting next year's crop. Mercifully, the last few weeks of neglect had made no difference to these hardy plants. Once they produced their beautiful blue flowers, it was simply a case of waiting a few weeks for them to be ready to pull; no tending had been necessary whilst I had been injured.

Chayyim and I were able to make good progress in that field. Avigayil and Ima came to help sort the pulled plant into bushels and carry those to a dam I had constructed by the river for soaking. Flax needed retting for one to two weeks: softening in water so the outer wood rotted away, loosening the fibre from the core. Abba, Chayyim and Havel helped by throwing stones over the bushels to keep them submerged as there was no way I could manage that. It was then Shimon and Channah's responsibility to run over the stones every day, ensuring that the stalks stayed submerged and didn't dry out, until I decided they were ready.

Being back out in the fields was good for me. With my body occupied, my mind was less busy, and feeling the earth beneath my hands again seemed to help my soul recover. I was not built for sitting still. I knew what I was doing out here. I knew this was where I was meant to be; this was my home.

Although I struggled to accept what he believed about the purpose of suffering, I began to hope that there was something of truth in what Havel had said about my family – that they had just been scared. If I stuck to what I was good at and proved myself again, maybe time would heal what was broken and we could all forget about last season. Perhaps Elohim had even listened to Havel's prayer for me. If I continued to recover and nothing else disastrous happened, all might be well.

My injury improved substantially as the barley ripened to yellow and its heads drooped towards the ground. I no longer had any traces of fever, and my shoulders had healed. I had some scars on my back but no longer any pain there. Out in the fields, I could even put a minimal amount of weight on my bandaged foot as we began the busiest time of year: the grain harvest.

We had to cut the barley stalks as close to the ground as possible. This would typically be done by bending over and putting your back into it, but as I had strong arms, I found I could manage it sitting down when my foot began to ache.

Whilst my health and my mood improved, my heart missed Awan. She had barely spoken to me since the day I had grabbed her arm. I could not bear the thought that I had displeased her. Although she was in the fields every afternoon tying bundles of barley, we were so busy working we did not speak beyond a simple exchange. There was no opportunity for me to see her alone.

One Shabbat morning, Awan and Havel came to my hut to remove my bandage. Havel placed his hand on my foot and prayed to Elohim as Awan began to unwrap it. As the sticks came loose, I started to swivel my ankle around and was relieved to find that full movement had returned. We all smiled together as the remaining linen strips came off. Then Awan bathed my foot, wiping the last of the strange green poultice away. There was a strip of shiny flesh where the gash had been but no sign of further discolouration or damage.

'It is a miracle!' she exclaimed.

'Much of your flesh had been eaten by worms when we got back from our journey. Your skin has grown again and re-joined,' Havel elaborated.

I lifted my leg slightly and pointed my toes toward the other side of the hut, gazing down my leg. Then I lifted the other foot to compare it. The foot that had dangled at a strange angle had reconnected and appeared almost straight.

'You explained previously what you did,' I said to Havel. 'But how did you know what to do?'

'I followed Yahweh's voice as He instructed me. I don't think I could repeat the exercise, so you may wish to stay away from the wolves next time,' he laughed. Then he stood. 'Take it easy for a while; it will be weak at first.'

They left me alone to stare at my feet. He said he had followed Yahweh's voice. What did he even mean by that? Had he heard the voice alone, or had others heard it? Had it been like the wind by the river or a voice inside his head? I longed to know what it felt like to hear the voice of Yahweh. Perhaps if He just spoke to me, I would get the answers I needed.

I sighed and looked again at my legs. The one that had not been injured looked noticeably more robust than the other. By contrast, the foot that had been underneath the bandage was paler and shrivelled. I slowly got up and put weight on the naked foot. It was still tender, and my leg felt weak, but there was no shooting pain. I began to hobble out of the hut, using my crutch for support and made it to my chair without assistance.

That afternoon everyone seemed in high spirits. They praised Elohim for my recovery and the beginnings of a successful harvest. I was pleased that they were joyful and not scared to approach me. I joined in with their praise of Elohim, repeating some of the words and listening to what Havel said. I was truly grateful for the healing. Yet there was still some kind of barrier inside my soul. It felt as if Elohim was on one side of a cliff and I was on the other, with an impassable river between us. Despite Havel's odd ideas about bleating lambs, I was still too scared to cry out to his God. What if I did so, and heard nothing back?

After our evening meal, Awan began to sing an upbeat song that set our toes tapping. Chayyim beat a rhythm on the stool next to him. Shimon and Channah grabbed small bowls of grain, covered them with their hands and shook them to make a gentle *ra-ca-ca* on the off-beat to the drum.

On the next chorus, Ima and Avigayil commenced a dance, moving around the fire in time to the music, holding hands and laughing. Despite the age difference, they looked so alike – their long, dark hair flowing down their backs and hips swaying to the music. I noticed my father looking on with pleasure in his eyes as he beheld his wife display her beauty. Then he rose and joined her, removing her from Avigayil and taking her firmly in his arms. He sank his lips onto her neck and she threw a giggle into the air.

Unable to prevent myself, I locked eyes with Awan and held her gaze, willing her to join in the dance. Her voice faltered for a moment when she noticed me, then she looked away and carried on singing, staying in her place on the ground. Instead, Havel got up and joined the dance, throwing himself around in wild movements that mirrored those of animals, making the young twins laugh aloud. They lost the beat and Channah jumped up to join Havel. She held his hands and he swung her around as she shrieked with pleasure. Avigayil grabbed Shimon and they galloped about.

I laughed at them then caught Awan's eye again. She had been watching me. I smiled at her and continued to look at her, observing the rise and fall of her chest as she sang. My gaze rose to her lips as she formed each word of the song, and I could not tear it away even though I suspected it was unwise to watch her so.

As the song drew to a close, the dancers collapsed in a heap on the ground, filling the plain with laughter. I chuckled with them until Havel's next words shattered my pleasure.

'When Awan and I marry, I shall force our children to dance every night!' he chortled.

My chest constricted, his statement knocking the very breath from my body.

'What do you mean?' I choked. The merriment froze as all turned to look at me. 'You surely cannot mean to marry Awan?'

'Why not?' Havel asked, still with laughter in his voice. 'She is the perfect companion for me. We have been together since before our birth; we understand each other.'

'You have talked about this?' I looked over at Awan. She was staring at the ground with a deep flush forming on her cheeks. 'When? How?' I stammered. Then I looked at Abba. 'Is it even right that we marry our sisters?'

I loved my family. I especially cared for Awan and Chayyim. I had recently felt a desire for Awan that had confused me, but I had not known until this moment that it could ever translate into the physical relationship my mother and father shared.

'There is no one else on earth, Kayin! I hardly think there is an alternative,' Abba chuckled, then looked at Havel as he continued. 'We have consulted Elohim about this. He has confirmed that joining between brother and sister will be permitted in this generation alone. After that, your children should marry those further removed.'

'*We* have? Meaning you and Havel – Elohim's chosen one? And what about me? Did anyone think to ask me what I thought of this? I am the eldest! Shouldn't I be the first to marry?' I said, my voice rising with panic.

'Kayin, nothing is settled yet! I was merely making a joke, an assumption—' Havel began.

'It is a fair assumption,' Ima chipped in, finally looking me square in the eyes. 'To your father, I am bone of his bone, flesh of his flesh. Havel and Awan were also joined in creation, and they are well suited. They should wed.'

'My children, you may all choose a marriage partner from among your siblings,' Abba continued sweeping his arm around as if to placate me. Yet, I would not be so easily brushed off.

'Really?' I asked, 'Does Awan get to choose? Or must she do whatever is decided for her?'

'Of course she has a choice,' Ima continued. 'That is not what we meant.'

'That's what it sounded like! Havel will take what he wants, claiming the blessing of Elohim, and the rest of us will get what's left!' I rose, grasping my crutch, determined to get away. A new kind of pain was rising in my stomach and I couldn't contain my fear-fuelled anger.

I stumbled away from my shocked family, heading towards the river, dragging my lousy foot which prevented me from making quick progress. I heard Havel rise and follow me and grunted in frustration. Couldn't he just leave me alone?

'Kayin! Wait!' he said and ran round in front of me, taking advantage of my lack of speed.

'I have no desire to speak with you. Please leave me be.'

'Kayin, I don't want to see you upset. I didn't mean anything by what I said, and I had no idea it would affect you like this. Please tell me...' he held onto my arms and looked up into my face, insisting on catching my eyes. 'Do you love Awan? Desire her for your wife?'

'I said I do not want to talk to you! Leave me alone!' I shouted at him. I pushed him out of the way and continued walking. This time he did not try to follow me.

I had little idea what I felt. I had barely even thought of it until that night. How could he expect me to speak of this when I only just found out his intentions? All I knew was that the thought of Havel marrying Awan made me feel sick to my stomach. Besides, he had barely reached adulthood. What did he know of men and women? And how was it possible that he had already consulted his God about this?

As I neared the river, I threw my tunic over my head and half-tripped into the water. Unwelcome tears began to fall from my eyes, and I cupped water into my hands to wash them from my face.

I had just begun to believe things could get better. I had been content again working in the fields – bringing in the harvest to share with the family – doing what I was good at. I had started to believe Havel, to think that his prayer might have been for real. I'd even hoped I was mistaken about everyone hating me. But now – now I felt utterly betrayed. And I wasn't even sure why.

Had I just messed everything up again? I should not have confronted Havel in front of everyone. I was just so shocked; the words had left my mouth before I'd realised it. And, once the question had been raised, there had been no going back. But that assumption of his – that he could take whatever he wanted – infuriated me! I thought he'd changed, but he hadn't! He still thought Awan his possession, just as he had when he was a boy.

My teeth started chattering uncontrollably. Yet, at this time of year it was not particularly cold in the river, even at night. I crossed my arms in front of my chest and rubbed my hands against the bare skin of my upper arms, trying to master my shocked body. When that didn't work, I waded out of the water, not bothering to replace my clothing, and trudged back to my hut in my wet loincloth.

When I got back, everyone had retired to bed. Dying embers of fire lay in the centre of our camp. I grabbed some wood from the stack and threw it onto the fire, poking at it with a long stick and turning it over till it caught into flame. As my body warmed and dried, I pulled my tunic back over my head and considered my situation, still poking needlessly at the fire.

I didn't know what to do. I didn't know what to think. I loved Havel, but he already had the favour of the whole family. Why did he have to have Awan as well? All I could decide was that I must talk with my sister and find out her preference. Throwing my stick into the fire I stood and retired to my bed, anticipating another restless night.

CHAPTER 14

T he next day I rose early and, using my crutch, made my way to the nearest wheat field to inspect the crop. The wheat harvest was typically ready less than two full moons after the barley, and it was important. We used barley for broth and animal fodder. If the wheat failed, we'd be forced to use it for bread, leaving none for over-wintering the sheep. Then they would need shepherding during the winter, in pastures further away from home. After the previous year, it was more important than ever that we had a successful harvest, and we were already behind thanks to my injury.

I heard someone behind me and turned to see Chayyim scampering along, trying to catch up with me. His straight, sandy hair flopped over his eyes as he ran.

'Going without me, brother?' he panted, once he was within earshot.

'I thought I would check on the other crops today and go back to harvesting barley tomorrow.'

'Good idea, I'll join you.'

I sighed. I'd been looking forward to some time alone. If Chayyim was staying though, I may as well find out what had happened after I had stormed off the previous night.

'Chayyim, will you be honest with me? I can count on you to be forthright, can't I?'

'Of course. What is it?'

'Tell me, how did everyone react last night? Do they despise me now?'

'I think *despise* is a rather strong word, brother! We were a bit stunned at your sudden outburst, but we are taught to forgive, as Elohim has forgiven us.'

'Has He, though? Last I heard, He placed us under a curse,' I muttered.

'Where did that come from?' asked Chayyim, holding his hands up defensively and stopping in his stride.

'Sorry, I guess I'm just in a bad mood.'

'Look, I'm not Havel. Save the deep questions for him. You and I have an understanding, don't we? We are alike: we enjoy the land, we work hard, and we bring forth fruit. We leave the heavy stuff to the others,' he chuckled.

'Perhaps that's not enough for me anymore. When I was your age, I was content as you are, Chayyim. I trusted Elohim implicitly because I didn't know any better. But all that has happened recently… I must confess it has thrown me.'

'You've certainly been acting strangely, and it is true everyone has picked up on it. Though I'm sure that doesn't mean they dislike you. You just rarely smile as you used to. And you did give us all a scare with the whole wolf, foot, fever, near-death experience thing,' he grinned.

This is why I loved this brother: he never took anything too seriously – unlike Havel, who had grown up into something entirely different. All this thinking wasn't helping my head. Perhaps I should give up on it and leave it to the others as Chayyim suggested.

'You are a good sort, Chayyim,' I said, clapping him on the back. 'I'm glad I have you to keep me sane.'

'Ha! Not sure I'm succeeding in that regard. You went pretty crazy last night. I've known about Awan for ages, but phew...' he whistled in conclusion to his thoughts.

'What you mean, you have known? I didn't even know!' I exclaimed.

Chayyim laughed. 'I see far more than people think. Your eyes, brother. They follow her around incessantly. When she's nearby you seem to forget I exist.'

'I do?'

'Don't worry. I find it amusing, not insulting. Besides, it's a bit hard not to notice her – she is striking. Yours are not the only eyes she's captured in the last few years.'

'You want her too?!'

Chayyim snorted. 'Oh, you don't need to worry about me! I'm just saying you shouldn't be so surprised.'

'I had no idea. I've been trying to push down everything I've felt about her because it seemed so peculiar. So, you are sure everyone doesn't dislike me? And you don't blame me for what happened with the wolves?'

'Why would I? You saved my life!'

'No one else seems to think that.'

'You are just choosing to see what you want to see. Try getting those eyes out of your head and looking at your family with fresh ones. We love you, Kayin. Get over it.' He began to scamper in front of me before throwing back the words, 'And uh... you'd better get over Awan too!'

He laughed and raced ahead as he said that. I growled and would have run after him, but there was no way I would catch him with my foot still fresh out of its linens, so I just threw my arms in the air.

I hoped he was right about my family; I was more inclined to believe straight-talking Chayyim than I was Havel. Nonetheless, his perspective was that of an innocent child who saw the best in everyone. I still held the suspicion I couldn't trust it. At least I knew that *he* wasn't angry with me.

When I finally caught up to him, Chayyim was already in the wheat field, walking through and carefully lifting tares where they had grown up between the crops. The wheat was almost to my waist in height. I pulled a few grains out of a wheat head and tried them between my teeth. They were still too chewy. They needed more time to ripen and dry out. So far, though, the crop was looking good.

We spent some time re-digging out the channels where water wasn't getting through from the river, making sure they were deep enough that it started flowing again. I knelt in the mud and used a sharpened stick to deepen the channels while Chayyim stood over me, putting his back into the tougher areas. This edge of the field was very close to the part of the river which Awan frequented, so I kept glancing in that direction, hoping to see her coming down to it.

Midway through the afternoon, Awan's form appeared near the river, a stack of linens under one arm and a spear under the other. I told Chayyim I was done for the day. He looked confused until he too spotted Awan, then he rolled his eyes and turned to work in the other direction. I made my way out of the field, hobbling as fast as I could towards the water. It seemed I should have stopped work some time ago, for my un-bandaged foot had started to throb and swell.

By the time I reached the flowing water, Awan had already wet, and was scrubbing at, the linens. She looked up as I approached. When she saw it was me, she flushed and looked back into the water. This didn't feel like a good start.

'Awan,' I began, awkwardly trying to get down to the ground with one leg stuck out in front of me. Unable to deny her sweet nature, she instinctively rose and grasped my arm, then helped me to sit. She returned her attention immediately to the linens, unable to hold my gaze for even a moment. I sunk my swollen foot into the cool of the river and felt instant relief.

'Awan, I owe you an apology. I am sorry if I made you feel awkward last night. I never intended to do that. I was… surprised – no, shocked – by the way Havel talked about marriage.'

'He was having a joke, Kayin,' she almost whispered.

'Is that all then? He has not spoken to you about it?' I asked with disbelief in my voice.

'Well, we have talked about it, just a little, and only in jest. On the journey east, we considered what it might be like to have our own family. We chose silly names for the children, that sort of thing. Perhaps he thought there was an understanding between us, I don't know.'

'You are both so young. I never expected this.'

'Neither did I,' she flushed.

'Is it what you want?'

'I don't know! I haven't particularly thought about it. I am happy for things to stay as they are.'

'So you don't want to marry Havel?' I grew hopeful.

'That's not what I mean. I am content for now. I don't even want to be having this conversation, Kayin. I do not want to upset you. I certainly don't want to choose a new family. I love the family I have! Why can't we all just be happy and content and not have to change things?'

I had never seen her grow so emotional. She threw down the cloth she was holding, covered her eyes with her hands and began to sob. I tried to give her a moment, but I couldn't help but touch her. I shuffled closer, wrapped my hands over hers and drew them away from her face. Gazing into her eyes, I forced her to look at me.

'I am sorry for upsetting you. I never want to see you sad. Please forgive me,' I said softly. 'I have no desire to tear you away from the family.'

She looked at me with those deep, dark, desperate eyes, pooling with tears but still the most beautiful sight I had ever seen. In that moment of fragility, she pierced my heart as rays of sunlight pierce the clouds, highlighting an overcast evening. I stroked her hair, smoothing a stray strand so that it gathered with the rest of her black curls. I knew then that I did indeed love her, far more than I had realised. I glanced down at her lips; everything in me desired to touch them with my own.

'Kayin,' she whispered, and my eyes lifted back to hers obediently. 'Please don't.'

'You don't want me?' I scarcely breathed.

'I love you; you know that. Currently, I think of you as the most precious big brother I could wish for. Perhaps, sometimes, I feel a certain attraction... yet I cannot make this decision now! I had never considered it before last night...'

'Neither had I, please believe me,' I interrupted. 'It was just because Havel said it—'

'I know. I saw the shock on your face, and I felt it too. But the fact remains that I cannot contemplate a life without Havel. He is correct: we were made together; we do understand each other. Right now, I cannot imagine ever parting from him and joining with another. Perhaps that will change as I get older, but...'

'...It is too soon,' I continued for her.

'And we are all making this up as we go along,' she finished with a gentle smile.

'Well,' I said, still savouring our closeness as I trailed a finger down her cheek, 'I am here, and I will wait.' The touch sent shivers through us both. I wanted her to be mine and suddenly became determined to win her from my brother; to prove to her that I could make a better husband than he.

Unaware of my thoughts, she drew my hand to her lips and placed a sweet, chaste kiss on it.

That was the end of the conversation. We spent some time in companionable silence as I helped Awan with the laundry. Then I grabbed the spear she had brought with her and waded into the water. For dinner, I caught several fish that I threw at her playfully. She set about scaling and gutting them, the task no longer producing the disgust that she had shown the day I taught her to swim. I helped her finish them then we threw the entrails back into the river, rinsed the fish and headed home.

The whole family was gathered around the fire and looked up as we approached. I could not judge the expressions on their faces – perhaps a mixture of fear, anticipation and relief at seeing Awan and me happily together. Havel stood and walked towards us. I raised an eyebrow at my sister.

'He will be fine,' she said. 'Just tell him you are sorry for the way you reacted.

'Am I?' I teased.

She gently fisted me in the arm and I laughed, keen to show Havel how well I got on with our sister.

'Kayin, may we talk?' he asked as he approached. I did not answer but shrugged my arms open in a gesture of acceptance. He drew me to the side as Awan continued towards the hut.

'I owe you an apology,' Havel began. I was taken aback. I hadn't expected him to apologise. 'I was insensitive last night. I should not have brought marriage up in such a casual way. Naturally, as you are the eldest, I should have consulted you first. I was wrong. Will you forgive me?'

Frustration rather than forgiveness was the first reaction to rise in my chest. Why did this boy have to be so irritatingly virtuous? Although my temper had cooled, I was still unhappy about his claim on Elohim's will. Whilst the way I'd handled his words hadn't been perfect, my anger at them was justified and, perhaps, I wanted to keep it stoked a while longer. Yet what was I supposed to say, with all my family watching for my reaction?

'Of course,' I grunted. 'I suppose I am also sorry for reacting so badly.'

Havel grinned and clapped me on the back. 'Excellent! Then we will consider it forgotten. When the time for marriage comes – which I'm sure won't be for many more years – we can have a big family discussion about it and decide what is best for everyone.'

Great. I couldn't wait.

CHAPTER 15

While we waited for the wheat to ripen, my foot grew steadily stronger. It seemed clear it would never again be perfectly straight and I might always have a slight limp, but I was soon able to move around with less difficulty. I spent what spare time I could trying to rebuild my leg muscles by swimming or lightly running on soft terrain.

In the throes of harvesting the last barley and the spring vegetables, opportunities to seek out Awan were few. Anytime we were gathered as a family, and I had to watch Awan and Havel together, it pained me. I struggled to comprehend this new feeling which caused an irrational knot in my stomach and consumed my thoughts. Jealousy crept into my mind unbidden, clouding my view of everything Havel said or did with my sister.

I wanted her to love me, but I valued her too much to force anything. I had meant it when I said I would wait. I just hadn't realised how hard it would be. I wasn't sure how long I could cope with watching Havel and Awan together. I kept thinking about what it would be like if she chose him: if she decided that she couldn't, after all, ever part from him. Would they display, in front of me, the kind of affection I saw between my parents?

Part of me longed to speak to Elohim about it, to ask Him for help. However, He had proven himself devoted to my brother, and I doubted I could change His loyalties now. So, I resisted the call.

One day, as I inspected it, the wheat finally looked ready. 'We will begin cutting it the day after Shabbat,' I told Chayyim.

Shabbat was the following day and we'd need it to refresh our strength. Harvesting wheat was a tough job, even with our sharpened stones.

As I was trying to get to sleep that night, I could hear Awan and Havel talking outside. I couldn't make out their conversation, but she was giggling at something he said. I tried to block it out, imagining other things. When it grew quiet, I finally drifted to sleep, only for my dreams to return.

In them, I had lost Awan. Laughing, she had run away from me in the forest. I was searching frantically for her, spear in hand, expecting at any moment to find some wild creature attacking her. Eventually, I spotted her. Unusually, she was not hurt but was lying with Havel under a cliff-face on the other side of an impassable river. At first, they seemed to be clinging to each other for safety so I cried out to them. Then I realised they were not clinging for that reason but for a different one. They had chosen each other.

At the look of conquest on Havel's face, my heart shattered and in place of pain, uncontrollable anger grew. I threw my spear into the river and screamed. A cloud of myriad colours blocked my view. Then the sound of the spear shattering turned into a loud humming noise that beat against my eardrums.

I sat up, sweating and confused. I blinked several times, trying to discern if I was awake or asleep. The loud humming still filled the air all around me. I rose from my pallet, but there was nothing to be seen. Where was the noise coming from? I made my way out of the hut and walked in the direction of the cacophony, letting my ears guide me. It grew louder and louder as I did so. Dawn was just breaking through, sending both light and shadows across the land.

Havel was already awake, and I could see him standing over by the wheat field. Beyond him, there was a great mist covering the crops and reaching up into the sky. It looked as if the dust had lifted from the ground and was encasing the whole area. I picked up my pace. As I drew closer, the noise intensified so that I had to shout at my brother's back to be heard over it.

'What is happening? What is that noise?' A gusty wind was also blowing from the direction of the field.

'Look closer!' Havel shouted back at me. As he turned and I saw his face, images from my nightmares flashed back at me. I could barely repress the urge to launch myself at him. But the situation beyond him rearrested my attention. I passed him, keeping my head down, and continued toward the cloud. Suddenly something struck me in the face, then something else. I began to wave my arms as creatures swarmed around me, hitting my skin.

Inside the dust cloud were countless flying insects. Their combined buzzing was making the incredible noise. Dust was tossed into my eyes by the force of their wings, but I tried desperately to keep them open so I could see what the insects were doing. When I saw it, the blood drained from my face. They were devouring the wheat crop!

'No! No!' I screamed, rushing into the swarm, and trying to wave them off. But I was one pitched against millions. 'Help me!' I shouted back to Havel.

'I already tried; there is nothing we can do,' he attempted to raise his voice over the swarm. 'Kayin, we must gather the family together and beg Elohim for mercy.'

I looked at him in shock. He was in complete earnest. Yet, I couldn't leave these creatures to devour our food. Perhaps if we all ran around the field they would take fright and leave?

'Kayin, come on – quickly! Or there shall be nothing left!' Together we sprinted back to the hut, as fast as my foot would enable me.

The others had risen from their beds and were standing together, concern dominating their faces. Havel immediately took control of the situation.

'It is a swarm of insects. They are eating the crops.'

'Locusts!' my father stated.

'We must all try to chase them away!' I shouted, 'Follow me!'

'Kayin, it won't work!' My father said. 'They will not be afraid of us.'

'I cannot just give up!' I retorted.

'No!' Havel said. 'We will not give up. Everyone must get on their knees. All of you, now! Begin repenting of your sins! Everything you can think of. The best course of action is to beg Elohim for mercy.'

'You would sit here in the dust while they are over there, devouring my wheat?' I cried in disbelief.

'Only the Creator has the power to stop these creatures devouring everything in the land. Abba, you and Chayyim gather some stones and build them into a pile. Put wood on top of it, ready to light a fire. Kayin, you're coming with me.'

It took a few moments for everyone to register what Havel was saying, then they all sprang into action. My mother and sisters fell to their knees and began crying

135

out to Yahweh Elohim; Abba and Chayyim ran off towards the rocky places near the river.

'Come,' Havel said to me, grabbing my arm and pulling me with him as he ran towards the flock who had been put into the sheepfold the night before, ready for Shabbat. When we reached the fold, Havel paused and watched them for a moment, then he opened the gate and walked purposefully in, heading towards one particular ewe who was nursing a lamb. He took the young sheep from its mother and slung it onto his shoulders, then paused in front of me.

'You and I have quarrelled recently,' he began. 'There is bad blood between us. We have not honoured Yahweh's name. This lamb is the loveliest one to be born this year. We must spill her blood to pay for our sin.'

I gasped in astonishment at him. 'You said you had forgiven me!'

He looked up at me with complete honesty in his eyes. 'I have forgiven you. But have you forgiven me?'

The question cut deeply, and I could not answer him. He turned and started pacing towards our home. I remained open-mouthed for a few moments, then urged myself forward to catch up with him, pushing through the aching pain. As we neared the hut, we saw the pile of stones was ready. Abba was arranging wood on top of it. The rest of our family were kneeling with their faces to the ground before the makeshift altar. Before we reached them, Havel stopped and looked at me again.

'Did you ever do what I said Kayin? Did you cry out to Yahweh?'

I shook my head. I was confused. What did my quarrel with Havel have to do with my doubts about Yahweh?

'Then will you repent, Kayin? Will you turn back? I know you have doubts, I know you have questions, but will you beg Elohim for mercy for the sake of us all?'

Everything inside me screamed that I was not ready for this – he was forcing my hand with no explanation! I didn't understand what my feelings had to do with repenting. I hadn't asked for them. And what was this about sacrifice? I remembered something about the very first animal killing in Eden being a blood sacrifice, but I could not put this idea together with Havel's words.

What must have been a moment seemed like an age as Havel waited for my answer. The noise surrounding us grew even louder, the buzz of the locusts was insufferable, and the prayers and wails of my family were too extreme to bear. Eventually, I nodded at him. What else could I do?

Havel gave me a small smile, then he walked over to the stones and knelt before them. He let the lamb down onto the ground in front of him, drew some twine from his pouch, and tied its legs together. Then he lifted it and placed it on top of the firewood. I drew nearer.

'Give me your sharpest stone,' he said. I took it from my pouch and handed it to him. He placed his free hand on the lamb's head and whispered, 'I'm sorry Sarai; you were a beauty.' I saw a tear creep down one of his cheeks then, with one swift movement, he lifted the lamb's head towards him and slit its throat. As its lifeblood seeped out and flowed in front of the altar onto the ground, Abba lit the fire. Havel raised his hands away from the lamb and towards the sky as he prayed:

> O Mighty One, Yahweh Elohim,
>> You speak and summon the earth
>> From the rising of the sun to its setting!
> You determine the ways of the beasts,
>> And direct the course of the sun.
> The heavens declare your righteousness,
>> For you alone are our judge!

Forgive us our every inclination to evil!
We have dishonoured your holy name.
In your mercy, save us, we pray,
    For we call out to you in our distress.
Accept this sacrifice of blood,
    Deliver us for the sake of your holy name,
    That we may fill the earth under your
    blessing.

Our Elohim come; do not keep silent.
For you are a devouring fire,
    You are a mighty whirlwind,
    And we cannot stand before you.
But gather your faithful ones;
    Make a covenant with us by sacrifice;
    Bless us, that we may honour you
    Throughout all generations.

Then the fire roared into life. Havel fell to his knees and planted his face in the dirt. Abba and Chayyim followed him. And, because I didn't know what else to do, so did I.

As the smell of the burnt offering reached my nostrils, I contemplated what Havel had done and the words he had prayed. Bewilderment reigned in my mind. I didn't know why he had killed his lamb that way. Neither he nor Abba had ever done something like this before.

Then, as we all lay there in the dirt, things began to change. It was barely discernible at first, but the noise started to move. It began to grow even louder. My heart sank as I thought that Havel's prayers and sacrifice had failed. Elohim did not care for us. He was still angry with us – or rather, with me.

As the noise grew intolerably loud, I began to realise the insects were withdrawing from the wheat field and flying towards us. I became aware of how close they were when several of them flew into me. Then my eyes were opened, and I saw the locusts forming into the shape of a whirlwind above the place where the burning lamb lay on the stones. The noise was so deafening I clapped my hands over my ears to deaden it. Havel lifted his head out of the dirt, turned to me and smiled, elatedly. He was saying something. I could see his lips moving but could hear nothing above the buzzing locusts.

Lastly, as if that wasn't loud enough, a colossal clap hailed from the sky, and a bright light shot down towards the altar. In an instant, the lamb was consumed. The great whirlwind of insects rose higher above the ground – gathered into the shape of an enormous cloud – and flew away. They were gone.

CHAPTER 16

I stood surveying my devastated crop of wheat. It was like nothing I'd ever seen before; you'd have thought a herd of behemoth had trampled through it. All those seeds I'd planted, shoots I'd tended, thorns and weeds I'd removed with my bare hands. It had all been for nothing. Most of the stalks had been stripped bare of leaf and husk. Many were laid out flat on the ground.

'What is the damage?' Abba asked as he approached with Chayyim. They had been out to assess the other crops and trees.

'Most of the wheat is destroyed. We may be able to salvage some, but nothing like enough,' I replied. I could feel anger begin to build inside me. Not only all my toil, but also everything we had done this morning, was meaningless. The locusts had probably devoured half the crop before we'd even risen from our beds. We had been made fools of – kneeling in the dust and begging Yahweh to save us. We had been too late.

Chayyim, ever the optimist, piped up, 'Don't fret, brother! All the fruit trees are untouched; we shall have plenty to see us through the winter. The grapes are almost ready; the figs, dates and olives will soon be ripe as well.'

'It is true,' confirmed my father. 'The locusts could have devoured it all. Elohim has been gracious.'

'We just lost almost our entire wheat crop and our best lamb,' I grunted. 'I'd hardly call that gracious.'

'I would rather lose every one of my lambs than lose Elohim's favour,' Havel chimed in from behind me. I hadn't realised he was standing there. He walked up and put an arm around my shoulder. 'But I am sorry for your wheat,' he said.

I tried a dry smile, aware that it was his lamb that had been taken from us. As each one was known to him by name, he would feel its loss keenly. But inside, all I could wonder was how he could remain so calm? I expected him to be devastated. Instead, he seemed assured that he had done the right thing.

Havel continued, 'Abba, I would like us to spend more time in worship this afternoon. Would that be alright with you?'

'Don't you think we had better clear up all the mess instead?' I interjected.

'No,' said Abba. 'It is Shabbat. There will be plenty of time to clear up tomorrow. Havel, you will lead us in prayers. Find Awan and ask her if she will sing a special song of thanksgiving to Yahweh.'

'Gladly,' Havel answered and headed off towards the hut. I watched his back in disbelief. What was there to be glad about?

'If I am not permitted to clean the land, may I at least bathe myself in the river? I still feel like I have insects all over my skin,' I asked my father, desirous of an escape to the water.

'Of course. Don't be too long. We will eat soon.'

I had never been more grateful for the river. I stripped out of my clothes, desperate to be rid of the itching feeling all over my body. Every time I thought of the locusts, I wanted to scratch my skin raw. My hair was full of dust from the cloud and I could feel it congealing in my scalp and beard. By contrast, the water was soothing and felt like a friend in the wilderness.

At first, I stayed near the bank, but after having a good soak, I couldn't resist the urge to swim upriver. I loved the challenge of swimming against the current, pushing my shoulder muscles to their limit, strengthening and stretching out my back. In the water, I could usually forget about my troubles and just focus on the movement.

I felt reeds swirling around my legs and fish swimming between them. We had such an abundance of carp that were good for food; I couldn't deny my parents had picked a good spot to set up our home. Tiny fish also swam between my fingers as I moved, tickling my senses, and almost making me laugh, despite my foul mood.

I supposed I should be grateful to Elohim that the locusts had eventually gone away and thankful to Havel for his actions, but why had they come in the first place? Was Elohim still punishing me? And if so, what could I ever do to earn His favour? Had my suffering after the wolf attack not been sufficient?

I continued to swim upstream until I reached a point further than I had gone before. I traversed the breadth of the river and pulled myself onto the bank and out of the water, panting to regain my breath. I began to imagine Havel and Awan making their recent journey across this river. My mind created images of them lying together at the riverbank, their clothes strewn around to dry, their bodies entwined to keep warm by the fire's glow.

A burst of jealous anger rippled through me. Havel and Awan had shared a bed through their infancy and most of their lives, yet it suddenly seemed different now I knew of Havel's intentions towards her. And my dream the previous night! I wondered what had gone through their minds – and bodies – all those nights when they were each other's comfort, out here alone.

Wanting to flee the images, I turned back to the safety of the river and jumped in. I must have been swimming for much longer than I had intended to be so far from home. Swimming back should have been quicker, for it was faster than walking when you had the current to assist you. Even so, my body was weary now, and I had an uncomfortable feeling that I was going to face displeasure when I returned.

I pushed my muscles, refusing to give in to fatigue as I sped through the water. When I arrived back at the place where I had started, I found I was not alone. Abba stood on the bank, his arms crossed over his chest and consternation on his face.

I tried not to meet his eyes as I waded, chest heaving, out of the water and waited for the onslaught.

'I thought I told you not to take long.' Here it came. 'We have already eaten. You missed our family meal.'

'I'm sorry, Abba, I lost track of time,' I replied, keeping my head and my voice low. I was a grown man, but I still cowered before my father like a babe.

'Kayin, I know you are upset about the crops, but that is no excuse for clearing off.'

'I know Abba.' I had said sorry, couldn't he just leave it?

'Don't you understand what Havel sacrificed for you today? Have you no respect?'

I didn't comprehend his words. Why was the sacrifice specifically for me? Hadn't it been to stop the locusts? Did he also think it was necessary because I had argued with Havel? That was so recent and, if we were being honest, there had been bad blood between my father and me for far longer.

I managed to choke out, 'I don't understand, Abba—'

'Well, if you don't understand, then you should have joined us so that you could learn, instead of disappearing!' He was angrier than I had anticipated, and I did not appreciate him treating me like a foolish boy. He wasn't even willing to hear my apology; he didn't care that I was trying. If he continued like this, I was going to lose my temper again.

'Honestly, Kayin, why can't you be more like your brother?'

And there they were: the words I had been expecting for years.

'Havel is trying to lead us all on the right path, but you refuse to listen! You sit in the corner with a frown on your face, rarely joining in with our worship. And then you expect to obtain the favour of everyone in the family when all you do is think about yourself!'

That was it.

'All I do is think about myself? Myself! I spend hours every day in those fields, working myself to the bone to provide food for your family, Father! For your children! I have done all the work that you should have been doing. Elohim gave you the task. He told you to work the land. But you refuse to do it, and you leave it all to me! How can you accuse me of selfishness?'

I was shouting at him. My fear had dissipated in the face of this injustice. I stood over him, my superior height putting my father in the shade. I never imagined I could stand up to him like this, but the grievances that had been building up inside me for years were pouring out.

I watched his face change. Where there had been anger and disappointment, I now witnessed fear and confusion. He stood looking up at me with his mouth partially open, unable to respond. Had he finally realised what his hatred for me had done? As far as I was concerned, he was responsible for the chasm between us and the fact that we had barely spoken in years. So I continued to hold his gaze, refusing to be the first to let it go. Eventually, his eyes dropped to the ground, his shoulders slumped, and he began to turn away from me.

'Perhaps you are right,' Abba mumbled. 'This is my fault. Oh Yahweh, what have I done?'

He stumbled off, a shadow of the man he had once been.

Something inside me felt uncomfortable. I had won this argument, but at what cost? What had happened to my beloved Abba, the man whom I had spent my childhood with? The person who had played games with me, told me stories and taught me to farm? The man walking away from me bore little resemblance to him. Yet, I knew the truth of it. He had not been the same since he had chosen to love Havel over me.

When I returned to the hut, it was beginning to get dark. Channah was lying with her eyes closed and her head in her big sister's lap, and Awan was stroking her hair as she sang a song. The rest of the family were reclining in a circle around the fire. My father was nowhere to be seen. I quietly drew near them and found a space to sit, close to my doorway, where I had a good view of the one singing. Her words and sweet melody lifted above the silence around us:

Sing hallelujah, sing hallelujah,
Hallelujah, hallelujah.

I will praise Yahweh forever,
I trust Him when no-one's around;
He delivers me from all fear,
Sets my feet upon firm ground.

Whom do I have but Yahweh?
There's none I desire but you;
You've given us life and delight,
Your mercy always shines through.

Sing hallelujah, sing hallelujah,
Hallelujah, hallelujah.

Yahweh, come into our silence,
Break into our noise;
Bring your peace into each moment,
Bring us your comfort and joy.

Sing hallelujah, sing hallelujah,
Hallelujah, hallelujah.

I will sing of Yahweh, my source.
I will sing of Yahweh, my strength.
I will sing of Yahweh, my shelter;
My hiding place, my hiding place.

As Awan repeated the chorus, Avigayil sang with her, picking up the tune with ease. Then Ima joined her, and Awan moved into a harmony, blending her voice beautifully with the other women. They returned to the song's beginning and sang through it again, with the others echoing Awan on the verses.

For those sweet moments, I closed my eyes and enjoyed the music, revelling in the sound of the harmonising voices. As usual, while the words washed over me, I couldn't help wondering how they could sing of desiring nothing but Yahweh or how they had such confidence in His provision. When the song ended there was silence again until, in almost a whisper, Havel's voice broke into the peaceful night.

'Our sister has reminded us that Yahweh is the source of all that we have; He is the giver of all life.' Havel paused and looked over at me.

'We have suffered loss today, but Yahweh Elohim has saved us from destruction and proven His faithfulness to us. He has proven that when we repent, He will grant us mercy. Let us continue to confess our sin to him daily and walk humbly with Him. Please spend some moments now considering your position before Him and turning back to Him with your whole heart. Let Him be the ointment to your wounds. Then, tomorrow, we will start anew.'

Havel rose from where he sat, picked up some food that had been left in a basket and brought it over to me. He placed it gently in my hands, then squeezed my shoulder and retired into the family's hut. Everyone else stayed in place around the fire, silently sitting with their eyes closed, presumably pondering as instructed. I lifted a round of bread to my lips and tried to join my thoughts to theirs.

What was my position before Elohim? What sin did I have to confess? I knew I was sometimes foolish, but it was the sin of my father that had broken this family up. His misplaced affections and selfishness had started all this – as he had now admitted to me. And I may have shouted at Havel the other day, but it was his lack of consideration that had caused it – and he had admitted that too. I couldn't help the way he made me feel, and I could hardly help what thoughts came to me in my dreams either.

Furthermore, the thought of laying myself bare before Elohim did not hold appeal to me. If He was indeed in control of all creation, then He must have brought the locusts to us in the first place. Indeed, Havel had made us all repent as if their coming was a judgement against us. A judgement for what? Because

Havel and I had one argument about Awan? That was ridiculous. If He was angry about that, He must be fickle in His affections, or at least not as good as everyone else made out. He had proven that, if displeased, He would take away just as readily as He gave.

I knew Elohim was the source of life. I knew He created everything and I did not doubt His power – I had experienced it that day along with everyone else. However, I did not desire Him as my sister did. I did not feel that He was the source of my strength, for I had worked hard to build that up myself. And how could He be the ointment to my wounds when He was the one who had created them by allowing all these bad things to happen?

I had said that morning that I would repent, but I was caught up in the moment then. Now that it came to it, I didn't know where to start. I had made mistakes – I would admit to that – but was that *sin*? I wasn't intentional in any wrongdoing; I hadn't set myself against anyone, including Yahweh. I had tried to earn the favour of my family and always sought the approval of my father. But it seemed that nothing I did would be enough for Elohim.

Unless it wasn't me. Perhaps the judgement had been against someone else and my father had it wrong? Didn't Havel have us all repenting? Yes, I decided. The fault could lie with any one of my family members. Or even with Yahweh Himself.

CHAPTER 17

Over the following week – not wishing to fight with my father again – I stuck to my old evasion tactics. I rose earlier than everyone else and retired later, always swimming before venturing home. Ima did not question my absence but continued her earlier habit of leaving leftover food in a basket for me to eat on my late return.

During the main part of the day, Chayyim and I cleared the damaged field and salvaged what wheat we could, but by the following Shabbat, I could ignore my father no longer. I had to speak with him.

'Abba,' I asked him, over the family meal on the rest day. 'Do you know if any wheat grows wild nearby?'

'Yes, I believe there is some along the banks of the Euphrates, near the intersection with the Khabur.'

'With your permission, I would like to travel there and retrieve some more seed.'

'Good idea.'

There was a scuffle as my mother nudged her husband in the ribs and he cleared his throat.

'I should come with you.'

I blinked, surprised by his offer, and not displeased. Although I felt trepidation at being alone with him, I remembered with warmth the time we had travelled together when I was a boy. But then I recalled the grapes I had seen the previous day, almost bursting through their skins and ripe for harvesting. The vines would need Abba's attention this week: they were the only plants he still tended faithfully.

'Thank you, but you are needed here in the vineyard.'

My father glanced at the ground.

'Very well,' he murmured.

'Do you want me to come?' Chayyim piped up.

'Actually, I need you to thin out the olives this week so the best ones can catch the sun. I shall be alright alone.'

I left early the next day, knowing that I would need to be swift to get back before the main fruit harvest was ready. Several times on that three-day journey, I regretted refusing the offer of company. My foot throbbed at the end of each day, and I dared not venture far from the river, needing to bathe it each night to reduce the risk of further swelling. Fortunately, when I found the wild wheat, it was dry enough to cut and thresh, but I still wished I had help. I collected as much as I could carry in a sack on my back, then turned for home.

Although it was out of the way, I walked back via our old storage cave. Most of our barley harvest had been carried up to the cave by the rest of the family when my foot had not allowed the climb. This year, I noticed that a proportion of it had produced a better yield than usual and coped better with getting dry. I had already separated those grains, at first intending to give some of them to Ima for food and keep some back for next year's seeds.

However, fearing that Elohim would strike a proportion of the crop again, I now decided it would be better to plant more seed this year than ever before. So, when I arrived at the cave, I put aside all the better barley seed – along with a good portion of the wheat.

Then I spent some time walking around the area, looking for another cave I could use for storage so the seed wouldn't accidentally be taken for food. There was nowhere obvious on the side of the stream where our original cave stood, so I crossed it and explored the next hill.

There I found what I was looking for. Hidden behind some vines was an opening. The cave smelt stale and there were remains of animals inside. A predator of some kind had clearly used it in the past, but dust had settled on the bones of its prey, so I knew it was currently uninhabited. I set about clearing the cave: removing all the bones and nesting materials, burying them in a hole, then sweeping it clean with some branches that I bunched together.

I returned to our storage area, gathered the best seed into baskets, and carried it to the new cave. Avigayil had carefully woven these baskets. They had fitted lids that kept the seed safe from scavenging creatures, and a design that allowed airflow to prevent the contents from growing mould.

By now it was dark. I had a drink from the stream then settled down for the night in our old cave, tucking myself under the skins that we kept there. As I began to fall asleep, I heard the familiar hiss of the resident serpent. I wondered what the lifespan of a snake was. Was this the same one that had caressed my leg, or its offspring? I propped myself up on my elbow. It was too dark to see anything, yet the serpent no longer terrified me. I relaxed, laid back down and dropped almost immediately to sleep.

When I returned home the following morning, the early grape harvest was in full swing, as predicted. These fruits were good for eating fresh, but the ones that followed a full moon later were the most delicious and could be dried out and stored. As this second round of grapes ripened, the figs and early olives were also ready. We treated the figs similarly – eating some and drying others – whilst the early olives were pressed for oil.

As high summer hit and the sun scorched the land, the rest of the olive harvest was ready, along with berries that we were able to gather from hills and groves. I dried some of these fruits and carefully kept a proportion of seed, sorting them into little clay pots I'd made for the purpose. These I also stored in my new cave, along with a portion of each harvested crop.

It wasn't that I wanted to hold it back from my family; I just needed to keep enough for next year's planting and for my experiments. I intended to discover how to increase yields in every variety, rather than relying on what already grew in the land. It would mean we had less food this winter, but I was sure we could manage with some careful planning.

I also decided to keep my new cave a secret. I couldn't risk revealing it and having my preparations questioned – or ruined.

I did not speak with my father again for some time, except to briefly discuss the crops. As soon as the grape harvest concluded, he returned to the sheep fields, and we settled into our familiar pattern of avoidance. The long, busy days of summer also meant I missed spending time with my mother, and, more importantly, Awan. That was the flaw in staying away. If I didn't see them, I didn't get to see her either. Unless I could contrive to meet her at the river.

Awan, a creature of habit, tended to go to the river at the same point of the sun every day. So, I began to plan my work around her, ensuring I would be near the washing spot at least a couple of times in the week at the same point when she was. Then I would escape from Chayyim and join her, helping her with jobs wherever possible, catching fish and, if I could convince her to join me, enjoying a bathe or swim.

Lately, she was always pleased to see me – always sweet and bashful – and, when she was not with Havel, I got all her attention. We would often sit together on the bank of the river with our feet in the water, splashing them and talking. Sometimes I managed to initiate a physical moment, such as the touch of a hand; occasionally, she even returned it. There was nothing I enjoyed more than the radiance of her smile when I made her laugh or the blush of her cheeks when I suspected she was thinking of me in the same way I thought of her. Those were my most precious moments, the ones that gave me hope.

Once the summer harvest slowed down and autumn could be felt in the air, I turned my spare time to searching for discoveries, often wandering in the hills. I was keen to find materials that might be useful for working the land or new plants that I could cultivate. I began to study the trees more, taking samples from seeds and barks and boiling, drying or crushing them. Most of my experiments produced nothing of worth, but for each one I conducted, I learnt something new and gained satisfaction from that knowledge. I did find some alternative fruit in the trees. It was hard to harvest but would be helpful if food became scarce.

The previous winter, I had taken cuttings from a fig tree and tried to coax them into producing roots. The thought that I might be able to make trees grow myself – rather than relying on Elohim to produce them from the ground – was exhilarating. As soon as they had started showing signs of root growth, I had carefully planted my fig cuttings in pots filled with fertile soil dug from the riverbank.

It had been several moon cycles now since they'd been potted and it was time to check what was happening under the soil. I was gently lifting the most robust sapling from the soil when my mother came round the corner.

'Look!' I showed her in excitement, smiling freely at the miracle before me.

'What is it?' she asked, coming to kneel next to me. I showed her the tender roots emanating from the base of the tiny branch, looking as healthy as those on a fully grown stalk of barley.

'Are those figs?' she asked, running her fingers over a familiar three-pronged leaf.

'Yes, I took these cuttings from branches of trees. I can scarcely believe they have grown root! Isn't it incredible?'

'It is! How long have they been growing?'

'I cut them last winter, and potted them here in the spring. I think they'll be ready to go in the ground after this winter coming.'

'You think they'll grow into trees?'

'I don't see why not. Look here – they have already grown in height and you can see nodules on the stem.'

'It will take years for them to fruit at this rate.'

'I'm not Elohim, Ima,' I laughed, 'I cannot hasten their growth. But I am so excited they have taken at all; this is such a discovery. If it works with other trees, imagine how we could increase our yield in years to come? Perhaps in these fig trees, I can create something for the next generation.'

'That would be wonderful, Kayin. I'm so pleased to see you enjoying this success.' She gave me a warm embrace, and I eagerly received it.

'When they are ready to plant, would you like to come with me to the riverbed to choose a spot?' I asked. 'I have five saplings here. We adults could have one each.'

'I'd love that, thank you.' And she gently kissed me.

Just then, Shimon and Channah came running around the corner, fighting over what looked like a stick.

'I need that for the sheep!' shouted Channah, who had begun to fancy herself a shepherdess.

'It's mine. I had it first!' retorted Shimon, who promptly wrestled the stick away from his sister and hit her on the leg with it. Ima rolled her eyes with a smirk and rose to sort out the altercation.

Chuckling at them, I turned and continued my work inspecting the other saplings, pleased I had reconnected with my mother.

As soon as we'd finished harvesting the fruit and olives, it was time to prepare the fields for next year's grain. Harvesting completed, the rest of the family returned to their usual duties, leaving Chayyim and me to do the hard work of digging and ploughing alone. Leaving last year's fields to rest, I prepared the ground in the fields I had used three years previously. Anticipating more planting in the spring, I also crossed the river at the laundry point and began to work on the other side, digging new trenches to water the ground.

One day my father walked out to find us on the far side of the river, with Shimon in tow. 'We thought it was time this one learnt to farm,' he said to me. 'I will stay with him at first, so he is not a burden to you.' I was glad for that, as my youngest brother and I still didn't see eye to eye. True to form, Shimon glared at me in response to Abba's words.

Ignoring him, I extended a peace offering to Abba. 'I have left the area further downstream to grass. One of Havel's wayward sheep grazed there years ago and it looked like good land. You will probably need it this winter as we have less animal fodder.'

My father nodded in acknowledgement. Over the next few weeks, he stayed with us in the fields. He hadn't forgotten what to do and had always been a hard worker when he put his mind to it, so we made good progress on the hard, untamed ground.

Shimon, however, wasn't cut out for hard work and spent most of the day moaning whilst my father tried to keep him occupied. The camaraderie between myself and Chayyim was dampened with Abba there. Once again, I found myself wishing we could get back to the days before things became awkward. I just didn't know how to get there.

One afternoon, when the ground was ready, I announced my intention of heading to the cave to fetch some grain to sow.

'I'll come with you,' my father said.

I faltered, unsure what to say. I appreciated the offer, but if I let him come with me, that would mean revealing the location of my new cave and the fact I had hidden food from the family.

'Thank you, Abba, but you don't need to trouble yourself,' I replied.

'It's no trouble. You won't be able to carry it all on your own anyway.' He drew a little closer to me so that he could lower his voice away from Shimon's earshot. 'In truth, I have been seeking a moment alone with you ever since our confrontation at the river.'

I stammered, realising I had no decent excuse to get out of this. I supposed we could fetch a couple of baskets from the family cave today and I could go back on my own later. Also, despite feeling nervous about it, I too wanted to have this conversation – to hear what he had to say. Perhaps his presence in the fields meant he had realised the truth of my words and was trying to amend his ways.

I smiled and thanked him again. We began to walk towards the hills together. My chest felt constricted in anticipation of his unknown words. As if sensing my nervousness and feeling it himself, he started speaking of how the work was going, the progress we were making, and what Shimon had learned so far. I told him about my fig saplings and he expressed admiration at my successful experiment. We even laughed together when I retold the young twins' argument. I wondered when he was going to address the issue between us. I could tell he wanted to from the frequent pauses, but he was finding it hard to start.

As we were nearing the area where the sheep were grazing in the fainter light of the setting sun, he finally began. 'Kayin, as I said, I want to talk to you about what you said at the river the day the locusts came. I think there has been difficulty between us for quite long enough. When repenting before the altar that day, I felt Yahweh prompting me to speak to you regarding our relationship. I intended to that night but it all went wrong when I grew angry with you for being late.'

I breathed deeply through those first few words. This wasn't so bad. He sounded genuine and humble. Hope rose in my heart that our relationship wasn't irreparably broken. I opened my mouth to respond positively just as a loud call sounded from a distance away. The noise was carrying to us on the wind. It was a holler, with a kind of tune to it. We both knew it was Havel's call. It meant there were wolves about. Abba stood for a moment in indecision, not sure whether to break off our conversation or not.

His face turned to terrified as a second call reached us.

'Channah was helping Havel today!' he said. 'She might be in trouble!'

I decided for him. 'Go!' I said, 'She needs you more than I.'

My father patted me on the shoulder, then began to run in the direction of the call. I started, as if to continue towards the cave, then suddenly realised what I was doing. As much as I didn't want to re-encounter any wolves, I couldn't leave Channah to the mercy of them.

'Abba, wait for me!' I shouted as I darted to catch up with him.

As we ran together towards the call, the sheep around us scattered in multiple directions. We paid little attention to them, looking around frantically for Channah and the wolves. Eventually, we spotted Havel up ahead.

A pack of four wolves were circling a short way in front of him, snarling. A bloodied sheep lay on its side nearby, bleating pitifully, but now they were stalking Channah, who was scrambling, petrified onto a boulder behind Havel. In defence of the injured sheep, it looked like Havel had succeeded in injuring one of the wolves, for it was limping as it circled.

Whilst I always carried sharpened stones, I wished I had a spear now. Abba had a sling, and he raised it as soon as we were close enough, getting a good shot at one of the wolves who yelped and retreated. Havel turned his head quickly and, realising it was us, shouted to me, 'Kayin, my spear is by the fire!'

I saw the fire and sprinted towards it. Abba and Havel continued to defend Channah, hurling stones at the wolves. Just as I reached the fire and lifted the spear, I noticed one of the pack veer off and head for a disorientated, lone sheep. I raised the spear, took aim and let it fly. I hadn't lost my aim. The spear sank into the wolf's side, stopping it dead in its tracks. Reaching it, I retrieved the spear, then turned and headed towards the others.

Havel and Abba had succeeded in pushing back the reduced pack. Startled by my approach, the one remaining wolf turned and fled towards the forest. I was closest to Channah, so I ran to her, gathered her into my arms and held her tightly. She grasped me and buried her tear-stained face into my neck. When my father and brother reached us, they threw arms around us both. Havel thanked me and praised Elohim for our deliverance.

It took us the rest of the evening to round up the scattered sheep. After Havel had accounted for them all, we began walking home. Havel took up the rear with the injured ewe on his shoulders and together we herded the sheep into the fold.

'I am sorry we didn't get the seed or get to talk,' Abba said to me as my alarmed mother ran out to us.

'Some things are more important,' I affirmed. I released Channah, who had been tightly gripping my hand, and watched her run into Ima's arms.

The next day I climbed to the cave with Chayyim. Abba was anxious about leaving Havel and Channah with wolves close by and I assured him I didn't mind him staying behind. After I'd given Chayyim a full basket from the old cave to carry home, I made an excuse to tarry a while longer. Once he was safely out of

159

sight, I crossed the stream, retrieved two more baskets from the new cave, and headed home with them.

CHAPTER 18

We spent the next few days sowing, with Abba showing Shimon the correct way to spread seed across the soil. We had a lot of ground to cover with both the newly prepared and the old fields to sow. I was insistent that we were careful not to waste any seed, particularly wheat.

Shortly after we started seeding the final field, I returned to gather more seed into my pouch, only to find the storage basket empty. I was sure that I had worked out the quantities precisely – I had also now stripped my new cave of all grain – and there was nothing left. I questioned Chayyim and Abba, but they hadn't taken any more from the basket, and all our pouches were empty. It was then that I noticed Shimon was sitting a way off, with a guilty look on his face.

'What have you done with it?' I stalked over and confronted him.

'Nothing. I don't know what you mean,' Shimon replied, sticking his tongue out. Fury rose in my chest at his rudeness. Although he was now eleven, his scrawny body was no weight for my strong arms. I grabbed him by the tunic and lifted him into the air, bringing his face level with mine.

'Tell me what you have done with the seed!' I growled at him. 'You know that we have none to spare!'

'I haven't done anything. Leave me alone!' Shimon squealed flailing his arms about, trying to hit me. 'Abba, help!' he cried when he couldn't get free.

My father walked toward us.

'What is going on?' he asked.

Shimon began to cry, big fake sobs that made me angrier.

'Stop pretending and tell me!' I repeated. 'If you have done anything with it, I shall not be responsible for my actions.'

'Kayin!' My father pleaded, 'Put him down!'

'I will not put him down until he confesses what he has done!' I shouted back at my father.

Shimon's tears continued to flow, and he continued to thrash, but I held him steadfast. Even though he seemed genuinely upset now, it was worth it to get the truth out of him. I knew I was in the right: he must have done something with the grain. It was carved all over his face. My father stood frozen to the spot, unsure whether to intervene and risk trying to remove his son from my arms. It was ultimately Chayyim that did so.

'Come now,' he said gently to Shimon, putting his hands under his little brother's arms and lifting him out of mine. Shimon turned and clung to Chayyim, wrapping his legs around his brother's waist and sobbing into his shoulder.

'No one is going to hurt you,' Chayyim soothed. 'How about you just whisper into my ear what happened to the seed?' After a few more moments of sobbing, Shimon lifted his head slightly and did just that.

Chayyim stroked his hair, 'Thank you.' Then he looked at us. 'He said he was tired of spreading the seed, so he buried the rest under a stone by the river.'

'Tell him to show us where it is, immediately!' I commanded, bristling from the child's shamelessness. If that seed was gone, we had potentially lost half a field's worth of harvest. Chayyim whispered something back to Shimon then put him down. Taking his brother's hand, the younger one led Chayyim over to where he had buried the seed. I grabbed the basket and followed them.

Fortunately, the seed was still there. I knelt and scooped a little into my palm, gently running over it with my fingers. I breathed a sigh of relief when it looked undamaged. After we had safely returned it to the basket, I turned to face my father.

'Are you going to let him get away with that? Shimon is a good-for-nothing lazy boy who gets away with everything! If you refuse to teach him some respect, then I will!' I had spoken quietly, but had allowed myself to tower over my father again, daring him to defy me. Surprisingly, this time he managed to meet my eye.

'I will speak with him. But you are not to lay another finger on that child.'

My father turned away from me and, taking Shimon's hand, crossed the river with him, leaving Chayyim and me behind. After a moment of awkward silence, my brother reached for the basket by my feet.

'I suppose we better get on and finish this field before dark,' he said, filling a pouch with seed and offering it to me. 'Kayin?' he asked, trying to get my attention, which was still fixed on the retreating form of my father.

I grunted in acknowledgement and took the pouch from his proffered hand, then turned and headed back to where we had left off.

❖

As I had suggested, Havel moved his flock to the other side of the river for the first part of the winter. Sometimes he would pack up some food and disappear for a few days as he sought good pasture for them. By the second moon cycle of the coldest season, Havel said it was necessary to head north to where we had initially found the sheep. He went alone, refusing Abba's company, and we did not see him for the rest of the winter.

I expected it to be a relief when Havel left. I was tired of his unrivalled intimacy with those I loved. Yet, everyone else seemed sullen with him gone. Abba was irritable and reluctantly led us through worship on Shabbat days, leaving most of it to Awan's singing voice. Ima carried on as usual, keeping the family together with her joyful service and plentiful preparations. Even so, I would sometimes see her on her own, staring towards the north and moving her lips silently.

Chayyim took on Havel's role of storyteller, keeping the younger ones amused by making up tales of creatures rarely seen and imagining what they might get up to when we weren't looking. Avigayil joined in with these tales, adding sound effects and dramatic movement. Often the accounts would conclude with brave Havel rescuing someone from the clutches of a predator. Avigayil would act the terrified victim, and Chayyim would pretend to swing his sling to defeat the foul beast. I began to slip away during those moments.

I had hoped having Awan to myself would increase her regard for me and that we would get more time alone together, but she too was withdrawn without Havel at home and always stayed close to my mother or father. I soon gave up trying to get her attention and instead spent even more time in the hill-country, making the most of this season when there wasn't a great deal to do in the fields.

As soon as the ground began to warm, the weeds came thick and fast. It was once again a full-time job to keep on top of them. Abba took Shimon to the fig trees by the hills to harvest the off-season figs while Chayyim offered to take the field with the worse thorns – for which I was immensely grateful. They wouldn't show full defiance until later in the year when the sun beat down hard, but they were still a pain now.

Shimon did not return to the fields until the shoots of grain were established. When he did, Abba posted him with Chayyim in a different place to where I was working, intending to keep him well away from me. He did not seriously think I would hurt the child, did he? I had been angry – and rightly so – but I was not a monster. I had merely intended to scare him into submission.

Now that the ground was warm, I decided to try planting the fig trees that I'd grown from cuttings. I was excited to share this experience with the family and hoped it might be something we could celebrate whilst Havel was gone. So, on Shabbat, I asked the family if they would come with me to the river the following morning to choose the planting areas.

At breakfast the next day it seemed my plan to cheer them up might work. All except the younger twins had now taken notice of the little trees growing around the back of the hut and were keen to choose a spot for their own. Avigayil talked of how she had been thinking about it for some time and knew precisely where she wanted hers. She evidently expected that we would not just choose the spot but also plant it together that day. I reminded her that I only had five trees. In response, she said as Havel wasn't here, she and Chayyim should share the fifth one.

'Alright,' I agreed, chuckling at her audacity. After breakfast, I allowed her to drag me to her chosen spot as I carried the sapling she had selected. Surprisingly, everyone else followed, and my father brought a second sapling in his arms.

Each fig tree needed planting close enough to the water that its roots would have plenty of moisture, even when the river was low. Together we dug a good-sized hole for the tree and then partially filled it with the fertile soil from the riverbed before standing the roots in the pit and filling it up completely.

I enjoyed this time with the family as I waded in the water, scooping up the soil with a clay bowl and passing it to Abba, who stood on the bank. He, in turn, handed it to Chayyim who tipped it into the hole and passed the bowl back along the line. We laughed together when once it slipped out of his arms, throwing mud and water all over me. Our troubles were forgotten as we took part in this crucial task of securing food for the next generation.

Once we'd planted Avigayil's tree, Abba called the whole family to gather in a circle around it. We each gently reached one hand towards the slender trunk, and the other hand we put on the shoulder of the person to our right. My father spoke a blessing over the tree, asking Elohim to increase its growth and fruitfulness. Afterwards, there was a moment of contented stillness as we all smiled at each other.

'Awan, would you like to choose your spot next?' my mother asked. Awan nodded enthusiastically. I was thrilled to find that she led us to the part of the river where she did the laundry and where we always swam together. She pointed to a spot of soft soil just near the rocks where we habitually sat. Warmth rushed through me as I realised how important our times in this spot must be to my sister.

After we had dug the pit, I jumped into the water and began scooping up the soil as I had done before. After several bowlfuls had passed between myself and my father, there appeared to be some sort of commotion further from the bank. Awan, who had been watching me intently, suddenly ran off with no explanation.

From my position in the river, I could not see the cause of her flight. Then everyone started talking excitedly and, one by one, they disappeared too, leaving me alone in the water. I pulled myself up on the bank, keen to know what it was that had drawn all their attention away from the task at hand.

Then I saw it—Havel had come home.

He was quite far off but was recognisable by the flock of sheep in front of him. I could now see Awan running towards him, weaving her way through the sheep, pushing several of them out of the way in her desperation to get to her brother. Once close enough, she launched herself into the air and he caught her. She wrapped her legs around his waist and her arms around his neck, burying her face into him.

They stayed that way for some moments, clutching each other as if they'd been separated for far longer than the six weeks or so that Havel had been away. By the time the rest of my family reached them, Havel had placed Awan back down, but she was still holding him. Everyone else then gathered around them, embracing Havel and kissing him.

I glanced at the abandoned, infant fig tree sitting in its hole in the ground – a scattering of soil barely concealing its roots. I looked again at my family. They were all walking with Havel in the direction of the hut. Awan briefly turned and regarded me. She beckoned with her hand for me to come, but I was not willing to leave the sapling half covered.

Feeling the sting of their desertion, I waded back into the water and continued to scoop up the soil by myself.

When I returned to the hut later, everyone was still gathered around Havel. They were eating together and listening to tales of his journeys.

'Kayin!' my father remarked. 'You've finally joined us.'

Havel rose, came to me, and pulled me into an embrace. 'It is good to see you again,' he said. Then he sat back down as I grabbed some food from near the fire.

'Kayin gave me your tree, Havel,' Avigayil piped up. 'He said that, as you weren't here, I could have it. Chayyim and I agreed that the one I chose was the best, so we will share it. We planted it today down by the river.'

Havel didn't look the least upset by her words but chuckled at her and replied, 'I am glad you are so pleased. Perhaps Kayin can grow me one next year?' He winked at me. 'I'm sorry if I interrupted you earlier.'

'We were in the middle of planting mine when you arrived,' Awan said softly, her face so close to Havel's that I only just made out her words. I stared at them both as their eyes connected. Awan was glowing with pleasure at having Havel back, and he was radiant with something else I couldn't put words to. Despite this, Havel turned from her and looked at me firmly.

'May I help you finish planting the trees tomorrow?' he asked. 'I would enjoy it very much.'

I held his gaze, but just as I was about to consent, my father spoke again. 'We should all go back out tomorrow. Today was wonderful, and we should plant them together. I, too, am sorry we were interrupted.'

'Finish telling us what it was like when you were away, Havel,' piped up Channah, who had gotten bored of the conversation about trees. Smiling at her, Havel did as he was bid.

'As I was saying before, Channah, I have no complaints about being away for so long. In fact, despite missing you all, I am thankful for the time of solitude, for it certainly deepened my relationship with Yahweh. Of course, I considered coming back and retrieving one of you for company,' he smiled down at Awan, whose head nestled on his shoulder, 'but decided it was better not to. It is easier to feel closer to Yahweh when alone with His creation, even if that means leaving half my heart behind.'

Everyone smiled at him, but I knew they wished he hadn't left us for so long. I was just grateful he hadn't claimed my sister.

'But Havel, what did Yahweh say to you when you were with Him?' persisted Channah. She was always curious about such things.

'I did not often hear His voice this time Channah, but all creation spoke His praise. Every sunrise, every sunset, every tree, stream and mountaintop spoke of His glory.'

I could understand Havel's appreciation of solitude and nature. I had once felt as he did. And when I had seen the expanse of the stars the night Father and I herded back the original flock of sheep it had been a marvellous sight after all my nights sleeping in a cave up to that point. It had made me appreciate the greatness of the Creator. Had that been what Havel described as seeing Elohim's glory?

As I had grown into a man, I still enjoyed the sights of creation – but the Creator? He had withdrawn from me. Having seen and felt the evil in the banished world, I could not feel the same way Havel did about His gloriousness anymore. Maturing into an adult meant becoming wise to good and evil, as my mother had become when she took the fruit the serpent offered. For this was wisdom, was it not: discerning not just the good in the world but also the brutal reality of life?

Perhaps Elohim had denied my parents that fruit not only because it brought misery, but because that misery would make us question His claim to be good. I suspected that living without that knowledge, as He had intended for us, was living under a deception.

CHAPTER 19

The next day I rose early. Having decided it was warm enough to try growing my fruit seeds, I intended to start work on them before any tree planting recommenced. I didn't know which ones would take when grown from seed or which might benefit from a different kind of propagation, but I was looking forward to the experiment. I made my way straight towards the river to gather some more of the soft, fertile soil which lined the bank.

As I approached, I heard a familiar melody. Awan was singing to herself as she washed in the water. She had submerged fully under it and was rinsing her hair between swimming strokes. It lifted my heart to see her enjoying the water, free of her old fear. It also stoked my curiosity, for I could see her discarded clothing lying on the bank. Desire for her coursed through my body as I imagined what I could not quite see beneath the waterline.

As Awan saw me approach, she broke into a wide grin and waved.

'Swimming without me?' I chided, trying to put aside my thoughts.

'I love coming here first thing in the morning; it is so peaceful and still,' she smiled. 'But you are very welcome to come in!' Then her hand shot up to her mouth in embarrassment as she remembered she was naked.

'It's alright; I can't see anything!' I laughed. 'Shall I throw you a cloth?' She nodded, so I picked up the linen that she used as an undergarment and threw it towards her, then turned away so she could tie it around herself.

'Finished,' she announced. I turned back to the water and threw my own tunic off before wading in. The water was very fresh and took my breath away as I sank my body into it.

When she noticed the chill evident on my face, Awan kicked her legs up and splashed water at me furiously, thoroughly soaking my head. The sound of her laughter rang out across the plain.

'Why you little…' I chortled, and within two strokes, I was at her side, grabbing her around the waist and lifting her over my shoulder. She squealed and wriggled as I spun her in circles. My instinct was to dunk her into the water, but knowing her previous fears, I held back and instead swung her into my arms and began tickling her until she started gasping for air.

'You win! I surrender!' she squealed. I loosened my hold, gently dropping her back down into the river. Then I held her for a moment until she drew back and looked up into my eyes. Hers were shining brightly, whether from tears of laughter – or something else – I couldn't tell.

'You're very joyful this morning,' I said softly, as I considered what it might be like to wet her lips with my own.

'I am. My heart is lightened to have Havel home again,' she replied. I tried to keep the smile on my face, but she must have seen it drop because she quickly added, 'I'm sorry.'

'No, don't be,' I insisted. I brushed aside some wet hair that clung to her brow. 'You must always be honest with me. I couldn't bear it if you hid anything.'

She shivered as I ran my hand over her bare shoulders.

'Shall we leave the water?' I asked. She nodded, so I dropped the arm that was still around her waist and instead grasped her hand as we waded up the bank.

Once out of the water, I turned away, reluctantly giving her privacy whilst she wrapped herself in the dry cloth she'd left lying on the bank. She lowered herself onto the rocks where we always sat, and I joined her. Instinctively dipping our feet into the water, we began swishing our legs up and down as we gazed across the river at the lands beyond.

'Thank you for planting my tree,' Awan said softly, leaning over and stroking the slender trunk next to her. 'Sorry that I ran off in the middle of it.' She touched my arm. 'Though when I realised, I hoped you would leave it and join us sooner.'

'I couldn't leave it uncovered in the midday sun,' I said. 'The roots would have shrivelled. It needed to be properly planted and watered before I left.'

Awan hummed in response, then asked, 'How are things going elsewhere?'

'Good so far. I came here to collect soil to sow more seeds.'

'I thought all the sowing was done?'

'I'm trying something new,' I smiled at her.

'You love to experiment, don't you?'

'I do,' I grinned. 'It amazes me how much variety there is. Most of it we haven't even begun to discover.'

'It's true, Elohim created a magnificent earth.' She hesitated. 'Do you think you will always stay here with Ima and Abba?'

173

I paused to consider. 'I haven't thought much about it. Why do you ask?'

'You're never content. I don't mean that in a bad way; I just wonder if we stifle your creativity. Perhaps you would like to go exploring all over the earth, discovering new things wherever you go?'

'Maybe one day I would. Although, there is someone here that I don't want to leave. I wouldn't want to go anywhere without her by my side.'

She smiled bashfully, fully aware of my meaning.

'Yes, of course, it is you,' I chuckled. 'Perhaps I should not say it, but there it is. Besides, didn't Elohim say it is not good for man to be alone? How could I leave my family when there is no one else on the earth with whom to make a home?'

'You don't seem to mind your own company most of the time.'

'That is merely because several of my family members vex me so much.' I tried to keep my voice sounding jovial but her eyes revealed that she knew I meant it.

'Yes, I am conscious of that,' she began slowly. 'How is Shimon getting on in the fields?' She sounded casual, but I wondered if she knew about the incident a short while ago.

'Alright, I suppose. He has no love for the ground and no natural aptitude for it. Most of the time he stays near Chayyim and ignores me, which suits me fine. Chayyim is trying to teach him which shoots are crops and which are weeds. He keeps pulling out the wrong thing, and Chayyim has to follow along behind him, replanting them!'

She burst into a giggle, flashing another one of her brilliant smiles at me. My breath briefly caught in my chest. Then she suddenly grew serious.

'He will learn, Kayin. Try to be patient with him.' She placed one of her hands over mine as she spoke. I wanted nothing more than to gather it to my lips and pull her closer towards me. Instead, I gently entwined my fingers with hers. I was determined not to mess this up. We sat in the stillness for a few moments more, hand in hand, watching some birds flitter about on a nearby tree.

'Kayin, may I ask you something?' she said after a while.

'Anything,' I replied.

'The day that Havel sacrificed the lamb; did you understand what it meant?'

I stiffened. 'Why would you ask that?'

'I don't wish to upset you, I just... I want to help you. Please allow me this.'

I took a deep breath, wanting to show her I was willing to rise above my feelings. I tried to think back to what Havel had said that day.

'He said something about the blood of the lamb being spilt to pay for our sin,' I replied. 'I must confess, I'm not sure exactly what he meant.'

'Yes, he wanted us all to repent. Later that day, he said that when we sin, it puts a barrier between Elohim and us. One that only blood can remove. In truth, I was also rather surprised – Abba had never mentioned anything like that before. Did Havel say anything else, just to you, when you were alone?'

I wished she hadn't asked that question, for I wanted to be honest with her. I answered with as little detail as I could.

'Yes. He asked me if I had forgiven him and if I would repent.'

'Have you forgiven him, Kayin?'

'Of course; why would you think otherwise?'

She furrowed her brow as she spoke softly, 'You do not look at him with love in your eyes anymore. I fear that you see him only as a rival.'

For once, I wished Awan wasn't so perceptive. I swallowed the lump in my throat and forced a smile onto my face.

'I do love him, Awan; of course I do. We rarely see each other anymore, that is all. We don't have much in common.'

'You look at him like you look at Abba,' she persisted, focusing on the river again. 'As if something is broken between you that only the healing power of Elohim may fix.'

I bristled. 'So you think I am broken too?' My voice gave me away.

'Not you, Kayin; your relationship.'

I didn't distinguish between the two and rushed on impulsively. 'I thought you were different! I thought you and Chayyim were the only ones who didn't hold all my – I don't even know what to call it – my history, against me!' I choked on my words, feeling utterly betrayed.

'Dearest Kayin, please…' She took my face in her hands. 'Please, believe me, I hold nothing against you, for you have never done me wrong. Except—' she stopped herself and looked away. One of her hands fell to her side.

'What? Except what?'

'Nothing. I didn't mean to say anything.'

'Awan? I want you to be honest.'

She clearly did not want to continue, but her eyes flitted back to mine, and then she seemed to relent, still holding my face in one of her hands and gently stroking my cheek. 'There was one time when you grabbed my arm and refused to let me go. You scared me, just a tiny bit, and I can't explain why. I saw a glimmer of something and it frightened me.' She dropped her gaze into her lap and removed her hand. I recalled the time she mentioned; I had seen the fear in her eyes.

'Surely, Awan, you saw someone who adores you, who didn't want you to leave,' I said to her gently, tipping her chin up to look at me. 'Someone who wants to spend every waking moment with you. Someone who... who loves you.'

She did not respond, but as I leaned towards her she turned her head away. I felt my heart begin to splinter. Unable to bear further rejection, I rose, not trusting myself to control my emotions. I began to walk away.

'Kayin, don't go,' she pleaded to my back. I stopped walking but did not turn around. She approached me, and, throwing her arms around me, began to sob into my back. 'Please don't be angry with me. Please, I cannot bear it.'

I did not hold her, nor did I push her away. I just stood there feeling crushed. And utterly perplexed about her feelings for me.

'Why would you be scared of me?' I asked after a time, speaking into the field beyond. When she didn't answer, I turned and looked down at her. 'What have I ever done to make you think I would hurt you?'

She drew away and looked down again, pondering her answer. 'Nothing really; you are always wonderful to me. It's just that I saw that flash of anger, and Havel had said...'

I cupped her chin and forced her to look at me, trying desperately to soften my face even though everything inside me was raging.

'What did he say?' I asked, gritting my teeth.

'He said that you had nightmares while we were away last year; visions where you saw my death, and his. It frightened me.'

They still returned to me often, though not every night. I breathed deeply.

'I did have nightmares, but why would that make you scared?'

'He said that you had grown violent during the fever, and I wondered if—'

'Why would he say that to you? To turn you against me?'

'No, Kayin!' she pleaded, 'He was worried about you! And we prayed for you together. We often pray for you.'

As if I was something broken that needed to be fixed. Yes, I knew. I also knew the real reason why Havel had told her of my weakness. He knew her sensitive nature; he knew it would scare her away from me, then he would have her to himself. Havel had told me he'd sought to protect her from the truth about my fevers. He had lied. Everyone thought he was some great man of God! He was just flesh and blood like the rest of us.

I took another deep breath to collect myself and quieten the pounding inside my chest. 'Awan, there is nothing to worry about. I was sick then; it was the fever affecting me. Now I am better, and that is all there is to it. I would never, ever hurt you.'

'So you are at peace with Yahweh?'

I was momentarily speechless. What did that have to do with my sickness? I gathered myself, smiled and lied, 'Of course.' Then I planted a gentle kiss on her forehead.

She exhaled in relief, a joy-filled smile sparkling in her eyes. 'Praise be to Elohim! All I desire is for you to love Him as Havel and I do; for you to know the joy we find in His presence.'

I felt uncomfortable with it, but there was no option now except to keep up the pretence. 'I do,' I affirmed, smiling.

But jealousy coiled around my heart. Why should she spend time alone with Havel praying? I did not want them to have another bond that I could not compete with. So, I made a decision to go one step further.

'May we pray together?' I asked. She beamed and nodded fervently.

I'm not sure how I got through that prayer; it had been such a long time since I had tried to speak to Yahweh. I drew on words I had memorised by hearing them for many years. I held her hands and spoke of the love of Elohim and the beauty of His creation. I thanked Him for the land and its abundance. I thanked Him for our family and prayed for protection from wolves and other dangers.

As I spoke, I felt Awan's body soften into mine.

CHAPTER 20

While I was still praying, Awan suddenly stiffened. I opened my eyes to see hers fixed on a point in the distance. Following her gaze, I observed Havel walking towards us, digging sticks in hand. He stopped when he noticed us. I held onto Awan's hands, not caring that she was clearly uncomfortable being found alone with me, wrapped in merely a cloth.

'You have done nothing wrong,' I whispered to her.

She tried to smile but still drew away back towards the bank, where her discarded clothing lay. By the time Havel reached me, she was struggling to pull her tunic over her head without dropping the hastily-tied under cloth.

'Let me help you,' Havel said, passing me by and holding her cloth with his eyes averted. I felt myself growl at his proximity to her. Just as Awan righted herself and tightened the sash around her waist, my father arrived.

'Ready for some more digging?' he asked cheerfully, sensing none of the tension between us. He was holding another sapling. 'I chose this tree and that spot, up there,' he continued, pointing to a ledge on higher ground, towards the area where Havel had fallen from the cliff years earlier.

Surprise must have crossed my face, but Abba didn't comment on it. 'Your mother will be along later; she's just preparing some dough. I sent Chayyim and Avigayil to water the crops. I trust that is alright?'

I shrugged, and we made our way up towards the higher ground, Havel and Awan following behind us. The ledge my father had chosen was at the very beginning of the cliff tops. From the river to the place we had to dig was a rise almost equal to my height. It was not the best spot for a tree – too dry and hard – yet, surprisingly, there was a soft patch of ground there.

We were close to completing the planting when Channah burst into view, running as fast as her young legs would carry her.

'It's Naomi!' she shouted in Havel's direction. He looked up from where he was standing, treading down the mud around the tree. 'She is birthing her lambs. They're early and she is in distress!'

Havel immediately dropped his stick and turned to me with an apology on his face.

'Go then,' I said, and the words had barely left my mouth before he was gone, running behind Channah in the direction of the sheepfold.

'Is the planting sufficient?' Abba asked me.

'A couple more should do it,' I replied, passing him another bowl of soil.

Once we'd finished covering the roots, we gathered the tools and began to walk back, meeting my mother on the way.

'How is the ewe?' Abba asked her.

'She is still struggling. Havel thinks he may have to cut the lambs out.'

'Cut them out? She may not survive that!'

'If he doesn't do it, it's likely none of them will survive.'

181

Abba quickened his pace.

On our return, we put down our tools and followed Ima to where Havel was knelt. The ewe had been carefully positioned on the ground in the shade behind my hut. A bowl of water was nearby, and the sheep was bleating weakly as she squirmed in agony. Channah was standing over her, anxiously hopping from one foot to another.

'Thank Elohim that you are back. I must cut her, but I didn't know how I could without someone to hold her down,' Havel said.

My father walked around to the other side of the ewe and began to wrap his arms around her top half. Havel lifted his face. It was tear-stained and streaked in blood where he must have wiped his filthy hand across his face. He looked exhausted already, even though it was only mid-afternoon. I let out a sigh and walked to the rear end of the sheep, peering to try and see the lamb stuck inside.

'She has not dilated fully,' Havel explained. 'Even though the lambs are small, I just can't get them out. I believe there are two blocking the way that may have died. They seem wrapped around each other like a tangled knot. There may be another behind them.'

'Where will you cut?' I asked.

'Here, on her abdomen,' he said, touching a bare patch of skin where he had already ripped away the fleece with a stone and comb.

'Do it; I will help to hold her with Abba.'

The ewe practically screamed as Havel made the incision. Her eyes rolled white, and she tried with all her might to move away from the sharpened stone, kicking furiously. Yet my father and I held firm, keeping her as still as we could. It took a horrible while to cut through the layers of flesh; to make a cut deep and wide enough to get a lamb out of. Before he had successfully grasped anything, the ewe had given up and collapsed unconscious.

After that, it was a more manageable task without her struggling movement. As Havel cut through the birthing sac, blood and water gushed out. The first lamb to be untangled was indeed dead. My father sombrely removed it from Havel's bloodied hands. It then took some time to extricate the next, which was also lifeless. Abba took both the bodies to a place where carrion could dispose of them. With the dead ones gone, the third came free easily. Havel released a deep sigh as it drew in its first breaths and began to bleat. Then, passing the lamb to Channah, he went to the head of his ewe and stroked her face.

'She is still breathing,' he exhaled with relief. Channah cradled the newborn and began to wipe it clean. Havel turned to me. 'Kayin, could you please fetch me something to sew her up?'

'I'm already here,' came Awan's voice from behind us, where she stood with a bone needle, thread and a pot of paste the same as had been used on my foot. She had clearly reserved some of the precious plant they'd gathered. She wrapped her arms around Havel's shoulders and kissed him on the cheek. 'Why don't you go and clean up while I finish here?'

She knelt and began to sew up the ewe as Havel reluctantly rose and walked towards the well.

'You too,' Awan said, looking at me.

'I'm fine.'

'You have blood splattered all over your face and tunic.'

I looked down and was surprised to see that she was right.

'Shout if she wakes up,' I said, gently squeezing her upper arm as I walked past.

When I reached Havel at the well, he was leaning over it and staring into the depths. I put my hand on his shoulder. 'You normally have to lift the bucket to wash yourself,' I jested gently.

He did not reply but continued staring. I leant over and began to tug on the rope attached to the water skin beneath. He took a deep breath and watched as I pulled the water up to our level and hooked it over a wooden post.

'I need to ask you something,' he said quietly. 'I was hoping not to have this conversation again for a long time, but after this morning, I need to know.' He turned to face me. 'Do you love Awan?'

'You really want to discuss this now – after what you've just been through?'

'Not really, but in the emotion of that experience I've somehow found the courage to say something I have been scared to.'

'Why are you scared?'

'Because you may not like it.'

'I rarely like what you have to say,' I quipped, but he did not smile back.

'Just answer the question, Kayin.'

I cupped some water with my hands and splashed it over my face. After rubbing it with a cloth and rinsing again, I spoke. 'I do. I did not know it before our previous quarrel, but I have since – I love her.'

He nodded, then leaned back against the well and looked towards the river beyond.

'What are you so afraid of, Havel?' I asked.

'I don't know how to—' He sighed. 'Seeing you together this morning confirmed my suspicions. I believe Awan is falling in love with you.'

I allowed myself a small smile, safe in the knowledge that he wasn't looking at me.

'You are afraid I will take her from you?' I ventured.

'Actually, that's not it,' Havel replied, turning to me.

'But you do want her? You love her also.'

'It would be useless to deny it.'

'Then what?'

He sighed again and began to wash.

'I am concerned about your walk with Yahweh. We have not spoken in depth since, well... since the day of the locusts. Yet certain things unsettle me. I can't explain it.'

'What does that have to do with Awan?'

'If you do not realise, then my concern is valid. You want her for your wife, yet your wife is meant to be your helpmate, your partner in all things – both physical and spiritual. If you still do not love Yahweh, then how are you meant to aid Awan in her walk with Him?'

I bristled inside. My mind tried to think of a quick retort, but it failed me.

'Oh, she is so naturally affectionate; she has no idea what she does to us!' Havel continued, running his hands through his dampened hair.

'What do you mean?'

'Her touch! I assume it makes you feel the same way as it does me?' If he meant that controlling the urge to take her to my bed became harder with every passing day, then yes, I felt the same way.

'She means nothing by it, though. She is innocent,' I replied.

'Yes. Which is why I am asking you to now do the right thing.'

'You want me to marry her?' I asked, in disbelief.

Havel took a deep breath and turned back to look in the well.

'No. I want you to stop encouraging her. Take a step back for a while.'

'What?'

'I said you wouldn't like it.'

'I can't believe you, Havel. I knew you were flesh and blood just like myself, but I thought you were better than this! Why should I step back? So you can play catch up?'

'You misunderstand me. It is not because I want her for myself. It is because I fear for her. I fear it is not good for Awan to continue along this path. Not right now, at least – while you are yet to find peace with Yahweh. And if you continue to encourage her, it may lead to heartbreak further down the line.'

'How dare you? Who made you the judge of what is good for her? You are her brother, Havel, not her father!'

'Abba agrees with me.'

'He what? You have talked about this behind my back – again? Unbelievable.'

'It was before I went— Oh, I knew you would react this way.'

'Of course I would! I know you think that you are the authority in this family, Havel, but—'

'I do not! I have deliberately tried not to act that way! I am asking of you no more than I would ask of myself.'

'Don't interrupt me! I don't see why I should do as you say! If Abba has an issue, he should speak to me himself.'

'Indeed, I see I have overstepped. Nor should I have spoken in this state of mind. We thought we had time… But Kayin – if you love her, please, please do not pursue her.'

'Why not? Why should I listen to you?'

Havel began to pace back and forth before the well as I glared at him. I had never seen him look so troubled. It was far from the way he had looked yesterday when he returned from his time away. Whether it was his distress at the lambing, at losing Awan, or something else, I could not tell.

'I have prayed for you, Kayin. All the time I was away, I prayed. I have begged Yahweh on your behalf. I long to be wrong about this! But Awan is precious and fragile. What if you pull her away from Elohim? I cannot allow that to happen! I... I will not!'

Fury like none I had ever experienced began to rise in my chest. He still intended to dictate my life for me! His previous apology had been a lie. Oh, he was expert at making his every motivation sound spiritual, but I knew he was bending his words to fit his desires. He could not stand the thought that she favoured me. He would find any excuse to stand between us!

The desire to give him a show of my strength almost overtook me, but – remembering what had happened with Shimon – I somehow managed to control myself. If I was going to win Awan, I needed my father on my side. And, apparently, that meant I needed my brother on my side too.

The words of retort that had failed me earlier now formed in my mind. I knew what to do. I watched Havel's distress for a further moment, then I spoke, in a tone intended to placate him.

'You are wrong about me, brother. I appreciate your concern; indeed, I do. But it is unfounded. Twice now you have interrupted moments when you might have witnessed my devotion to Yahweh. Yesterday, when you returned with the sheep, we had not just been planting those saplings; we had been blessing them together as a family. At my instigation. And this morning, when you came upon Awan and me, we were praying together – I was praying.'

Havel stopped in his tracks and looked at me.

187

'Truly?'

'Truly. Ask Awan if you don't believe me.'

Havel let out a long exhale then took two steadying strides in front of the well.

'Then I owe you an apology. Yahweh is indeed faithful. Forgive me, brother. I am… I am very pleased to be mistaken.'

I almost scoffed openly at him. He was trying to sound sincere, but I could practically hear the disappointment screaming underneath his apology. He had lost his excuse for keeping me away from Awan. I struggled not to smirk. 'Are you sure you are not disappointed?'

He paused. 'I do not want to lose her; I cannot deny it. But we are brothers, are we not? We love one another. Whatever Elohim wills, I submit to Him.'

'Perhaps next time you could speak directly to me before going to our father?'

'Yes. Yes, you're right. That was some time ago – before I went away. But next time I speak to him, I will confess my error. I am sorry.'

I couldn't help enjoying the spectacle of seeing him so put out. The thought that he would have to admit his mistake before our father was pleasant. And yet, it almost seemed too easy – the way he had believed me and backed down. I knew I must ensure I gave him no cause to question me again.

'I suppose you had better check on your ewe, Havel.'

'Yes, I must.'

He moved in that direction, then stopped and looked back at me briefly. For a moment, our eyes locked – his reflected a blend of relief and disappointment, warring for dominance – then he turned away and strode behind the hut. Shortly afterwards, I saw him reappear and pace towards the area of arid land that existed to the east of our home. He was still running his hands through his hair and seemed to be muttering to himself.

That night I allowed myself a rare indulgence as I tried to get to sleep. Pushing aside any guilt about my deception, I imagined Awan was lying in my arms in the forest. We were staring up at the glistening leaves of the treetops and listening to the singing of the dusk chorus. Then I was pulling her in closer than ever before and kissing her gently, exploring every part of her figure.

Yet as I fell into sleep, the images once again began to transform. One of the birds in the treetops morphed into something evil. It swooped down from above and attacked us, trying to slice us with its talons and teeth. We jumped up and began running together. I looked back to check its gain on us. As I did so, Awan let go of my hand. When I turned away from the beast and back to her, she was no longer running with me; she was running from me. I was the one chasing – chasing Awan, who ran ahead with her hand now locked in someone else's: Havel's. Her face was dominated by fear as she tried to escape me. Havel's face was smothered in glee.

CHAPTER 21

When I woke the following morning, it was unusually quiet. Typically, the sound of songbirds assailed me; that morning, I could barely hear them. Their songs were dampened as if a lamentation rather than a dawn chorus. I heard hushed voices outside the hut. Chayyim, who I usually woke, was already missing from his pallet.

I rose, stretched my arms and rubbed the large crusts that had formed in the corners of my eyes. Leaving the hut, I beheld a circle of family members. Havel was kneeling on the ground with Awan beside him, her head leaning against his arm. My father was on his other side, with a hand around his back. Beyond, Shimon sat awkwardly and near to the fire. Next to him, Channah was crossed-legged, feeding a tiny lamb from a makeshift teat: a pouch of animal skin with a hole in one corner. Her tunic was soaked with the milk that dripped from the feeding lamb's mouth.

My mother and Avigayil were the only ones standing, Avigayil was kneading dough, and my mother was pouring herb tea from a cooking pot into bowls. When he saw me, Chayyim rose and came towards me. He spoke in hushed tones.

'The ewe, Naomi, died during the night. Havel and Awan stayed with her all the while, but she succumbed just before the birdsong began.'

My mother walked over to us and handed me a bowl of tea. 'Stay awhile this morning? Show your support?' she requested, nervously.

I looked into her pleading, sad eyes. I didn't particularly want to be in the presence of Havel, especially as he basked in Awan's comfort. Nor did I enjoy witnessing the bond between him and my father. But I could not deny my mother her request so I nodded, 'Of course.'

She let out a quivered breath, then smiled slightly and kissed me on the cheek before making her way back to the cooking pot to distribute more tea. I moved to a gap in the circle and sat down between Chayyim and my father. Abba looked up at me briefly, and I saw in his face the exact look that had been on my mother's.

I silently began to study Havel. He was covered again in blood and gore from the sheep. It mingled with his sweat and the streaks of dirt wiped across his brow. His hair, which usually formed waves around his head, was now tied back with a piece of twine. He looked entirely spent.

Then, from the depths of somewhere in his soul, he began to sing. He sang a long, deep lament that resonated with the distant birds. His words were similar to those my father had sung many years ago when Havel had been a babe. They mourned the fall of humankind, the curse of the earth, the reality of suffering and death. They mourned the lies of the evil one and the destruction of beauty and purity.

Awan started humming a harmony that blended with the melody she had not heard before. Avigayil began to cry. My mother also. Their voices rose together into a wail, accompanied by silent tears that fell down the cheeks of my father, Channah and Chayyim. Only Shimon and I sat awkwardly, trying to hide in plain sight rather than get in the way of their grief.

When the song concluded, Havel spoke. Not with the strong voice that usually characterised his rhetoric, but with a tone designed to preserve serenity. 'Naomi's life was sacrificed for that of her lamb. She bled out to save another. There are many lessons to be learned from this tragedy.'

As the weeks rolled by, the family's grief at losing the ewe was replaced with joy as her hand-reared lamb grew strong, bounding about the place, causing mischief and amusement. After a period of waiting – as a show of respect – I planted the final two fig saplings alone, not bothering to conduct a special event. And so, despite all the promise, Avigayil's tree alone was blessed.

Havel soon regained his joyful demeanour and confidence. He and my father continued to direct worship together, comfortably complementing each other. They would continue in front of the family whatever they had been discussing out in the fields regarding Yahweh. Occasionally they might pause or ask if anyone else had a contribution. I felt disorientated during these times, as if I ought to join in but didn't know what to say.

Images of Havel and Awan continued to harass my dreams. Consequently, I found Havel unfathomably irritating by day and they even left me uneasy around Awan. And so, I found myself evading her at those times when she threw my mind into chaos.

It was soon time for harvesting flax again and I was grateful to find my days busy with this task. Unlike barley, flax had to be pulled from the ground rather than cut, as some of the valuable fibre was underneath the top layer of earth. I watched with amusement as Chayyim tried to show Shimon what to do. The boy still had no interest in hard work, and I was grateful I didn't have to deal with him. Shimon usually quit a short while into the afternoon, moaning that everything hurt. I was always glad when he left us in peace.

It was on one such afternoon that a sheep, followed by a tiny lamb, suddenly burst into our view, apparently running away from something. Her eyes were wide and her ears were pinned back as she jostled this way and that, skittering first around the field and then heading towards us. The lamb followed closely behind her, in danger of being kicked by her jittery legs.

I nervously checked the surrounding area, fearing the sight of a wolf on the chase. Yet it was Havel who came running into view, panting as he caught up with the mother just before she trampled some of our produce.

'I'm sorry,' he gasped once he'd secured her and settled her down. 'Shimon decided it would be fun to play a game involving sticks, stones and screaming at the top of his lungs around my field. This one has just lambed and got spooked.'

'Will that boy never learn?' I muttered, rolling my eyes.

'Don't worry, Havel; no harm done this time,' Chayyim called to him.

He thanked us, then turned and quietly led the ewe back the way she had come. The little lamb wobbled alongside, keeping as close as possible to his mother.

'That's the ewe that produced the best lamb last year; she's his favourite,' Chayyim commented. 'This year, though, her lamb was late and small.'

'I didn't realise you took an interest in the sheep.'

'No, it's just that I actually talk to my brother,' Chayyim chuckled. 'Take an interest in what he does, that sort of thing.'

'You always fought with him when you were little. He was mean to you then.'

'Yes, but he's different now. You know that.'

Yes, Havel was different. Very different. I thought about Havel standing before his sheep pen the day the locusts came, considering which lamb to choose. I remembered how he had chosen the best one.

'So, that ewe is the one whose lamb we sacrificed?' I asked.

'Yes, that's the one. Havel is pleased she won't have to go through the ordeal of losing it again, weakling that it is.'

'Why would she lose another?'

'He intends to make a habit of sacrificing the best lamb every year as a sin offering, and to give thanks to Yahweh for His provision.'

'Will he burn the whole lamb as he did before?'

'Yes.'

My brow furrowed in confusion. We all knew how attached Havel was to his sheep – how reluctant he was to slaughter them, even when we needed the meat. And we were supposed to care for the creation. To willingly slaughter more than was necessary baffled me.

'Isn't that wasteful?' I asked. 'I can understand giving a portion to Elohim, as we have always done, but why burn up a whole lamb when it could provide more food for us alongside His portion? Or why not give Elohim the weakest one that is unlikely to survive, rather than the strongest?'

'I asked him something similar. He says we should not worry about that but should give Elohim our best and trust Him to provide for us. He believes Elohim blesses those who put Him first.'

'When does Havel plan to do it?'

'I think he will wait until they are weaned. After the summer harvest.'

I paused to consider the idea that Elohim might bless those who put Him first; who gave Him their best. If that was the way Elohim worked, then perhaps there was something in this idea of sacrifice. Maybe that was where I had been going wrong.

'Do you think we should put aside some of our crops for an offering also?' I asked Chayyim. 'Does Elohim desire grain too, or just meat?'

'Perhaps you should ask Havel. Though, I think if Elohim desires the best we can give Him, then He would desire the best of our harvest. We can't give Him a lamb but we can give Him grain.'

'Perhaps I will ask Abba if he minds me doing it.' Despite our differences, Abba was supposed to still be the leader of the family. I was nervous about giving up some of my grain, especially after the previous year's wheat shortage. Still, if I could offer barley that might protect the scarce wheat, earn Elohim's favour and increase the respect of my family.

'I have no desire to meet those locusts again, or for any other curse to befall us,' I continued. 'If sacrifice is what it takes to avoid them, then so be it. As long as we still have enough grain to feed the family.'

'If we don't see the locusts again, we should do,' Chayyim replied.

'Yes, despite Shimon's best attempts to sabotage our crop,' I muttered.

CHAPTER 22

I left the fields earlier than usual that day so that I could join the evening meal. Now that I had the idea of sacrifice in my head, I wanted to present it to my father immediately so I could plan ahead with the provisions. After dinner, I took him aside. He looked nervous until I explained why I wanted to speak with him.

'Abba, I have been thinking about offering some of our grain as a sacrifice to Elohim after the barley harvest. What do you think?'

His face shifted from trepidation to joy. 'Really? You desire to sacrifice? I am pleased with you, son! Yet, why do you wish to do this now? We have not offered crops before.'

'No, but we always say thank-you for them and sing praise to Elohim after the harvest. I think it would be good to give something back to Him if He chooses to bless us again. Perhaps we could do this earlier than usual – offer a portion after we have taken in the barley, as it is our main crop.'

I didn't mention my fear that the locusts might destroy the wheat again. If what Havel had said about earning Elohim's blessing was true, I was hopeful that if we gave something to Elohim, He, in turn, would protect us from harm; perhaps even increase our wheat crop.

'I am certain it is a good idea, Kayin,' Abba answered. 'Though you must ensure it is the finest of the crop. We can use the stone altar that we built last year to burn the offerings.'

'You are not worried that we will be short of food?'

'It looks like you planted plenty this year. You saved back far more seed than I thought we had available.'

'I wanted to ensure we did not have a hard winter again, so I was cautious with the rations.'

'I am glad you are showing such maturity and looking after your family. It warms my heart.'

He paused, wanting to say something else, then continued, nervously. 'Kayin, could we take a walk and talk away from the family? We never did finish that conversation we started a while ago.'

I wondered if things had changed again since then, but he appeared to be in a good mood, so I saw no reason to refuse him. 'Of course, Abba.'

As it was growing dark, I took a torch from the fire and we began walking out towards the river. After a few moments, my father spoke.

'Kayin, for several years, I have wanted to have this conversation with you, but I have struggled to know where to start. Now you have come to me with this idea of yours, I feel the time is right to give you a full explanation.'

'An explanation?'

'For why I no longer help you in the fields. As you rightly noted, I do little other than tinkering with the fruit; I have left the management of everything else – and the hard labour – to you.'

I took a deep breath. 'You have.'

'Firstly, you have far superior skills to me. That much is clear to anyone with two eyes. However, I could have laboured under your direction and yet I have not. I

197

have been content to let you toil, especially since Chayyim began to help you. It seems to have caused a problem between us that I should have dealt with a long time ago. That became especially clear when we had our argument by the river.'

He stuttered, struggling to find his words. The pause was hard; I was eager to know what excuse he had for his neglect. Was he truly going to confess how much he hated spending time with me? I knew it was the truth, yet I couldn't believe he would say it. He finished his stutter with a sigh.

'To explain it, I must go right back to the beginning – back to the Garden. It was the moment when I took the fruit from your mother and ate it that everything changed. As I told you when you were a child, I was close to Yahweh before that time. It was He who taught me how to farm the land, and I found much joy in it. Growing provisions there was so different to how it is here and now. In Eden, everything was plentiful; everything was beautiful. It all grew with so little effort as if the very breath of Elohim were sustaining it and making it bloom. When we rebelled, it all changed.'

All of this I knew, yet I did not understand what it had to do with our relationship. I remained silent and he continued.

'I have carried the burden of that sin around with me since that day. When we were cursed, it was as if the very joy of farming was ripped from me. Not just because the land grew harsh and the thorns arose, but because every time I touched the soil, I was reminded of what I had lost. Not only the Garden's perfection but my relationship with Yahweh, which I had broken. It is why we did not settle for so many years after we were banished. I couldn't bear it Kayin. I could cope with wandering from place to place and taking from what was there, but I could not bear the thought of having to work with the soil.

'Yet the burden of sin was even greater than that.' His voice began to break again as he continued. 'You cannot imagine, son, what it was like to have no knowledge of good and evil; to see only Yahweh and His infinite goodness and to know nothing of wickedness or pain. It was glorious! Yet I ruined it all! I ruined it for myself, for your mother and for everyone who will come after me. For all of humanity. It is all my fault!'

He burst into tears then and covered his eyes with his hands, to hide the tears away.

I allowed a moment of silence before asking the first question on my mind. 'Abba, how could you bear the burden of it all? I thought Ima was the first one to take the fruit?'

He took a moment to come back into the present and consider my question. 'Yes, that is true. She did eat it first and then gave it to me. And for a long time, I blamed her for that. A chasm grew between us. We stayed together merely because we knew of no other way to survive. In fact, to my shame, I would bring up her guilt anytime we argued, blaming her for all the wrongs on the earth. But I didn't really mean it. I knew I was guilty and blaming her was just a way of covering my guilt, as I had tried to do before Yahweh Elohim when He questioned us in the Garden.

'The truth is that I am culpable, Kayin. It was my responsibility to protect your mother. I was created first. I spent the most time with Yahweh. I sat at His feet learning from Him, and I walked with Him daily. He set me over the animals, and I named them. He gave me your mother as my helpmate – a beautiful creature to care for, treasure and protect.

'I failed in that duty. When she listened to the temptation of the serpent, I should have warned her; I should have stopped her from eating the fruit – yet I did nothing! I should have refused it when she offered it to me; I should have thrown it to the ground and trampled on it. Instead, I took it, and I ate it.'

'Abba, I don't understand what this has to do with me?'

He wiped his eyes again, then looked up at me with pity.

'Oh, you were such a joy to us, Kayin! After many years of painful detachment, desire was rekindled between your mother and me when we huddled in the northern mountains. In time, you were conceived. As soon as you uttered that first cry, I could at last cope with settling down. I knew it was to provide for you and your mother. Instead of thinking of myself and the burden I bore, you gave me someone else to love, to serve, and something else to think about.

'As you grew, however, things began to change. The older you got, the more capable you became. You loved the land and found excitement in it. By contrast, I began to resent it again. I resented the fact that farming grew harder every year. I longed to return to Eden, where the water covered the ground in the mornings, and there was no competition for the goodness in the soil. I knew that as things grew worse, in time, it would be you that would have to deal with the full result of my sin.

'When we found the sheep, it gave me an excuse to do something different, since they always needed attention. So, I slowly withdrew as you took on more responsibility. Then, eventually, when I saw you struggling with thorns and weeds, instead of helping you, I turned away from you. I couldn't endure witnessing the pain you were going through – of my making – and which I knew would only increase. It was easier to leave you in ignorance than to face up to my fears.'

'I have always known you didn't love farming as much as I did,' I interjected. 'Yet I never detected a hint of dislike for *me* until the terrible day that I lost Havel. That day everything changed, as if you could no longer stand the sight of me. I heard you say to Ima that you couldn't stand to be with me! I heard the conversation where you told her you couldn't forgive me.'

My father looked stunned. 'Kayin, I never said those things!'

'I heard you, Abba!' My voice felt dry and raw. 'You said that being in the fields with me made you angry, and that you could not forgive me because Havel might have died because of my actions. You begged Ima not to force you to work with me!'

My father looked suddenly pale. 'That is what you have thought all these years? Now I begin to understand... Oh, Kayin! It was not you that I didn't love! It was not you that I resented; that I couldn't forgive! Oh, how have I ruined this so badly?' he cried, breaking into another sob. 'You heard that conversation wrong, my son. I remember it well because it was a bitter quarrel after so many years of peace between Ima and myself. I was speaking of the fact that I could not forgive myself! As for the rest – it was the burden of seeing you struggle in the fields that I couldn't endure, it assailed me every time I joined you there. I could avoid it by staying amongst the flock.

'As for Havel, I was indeed angry with you for losing him. But that, too, soon turned to anger at myself. I was the one who had sent him off to find that sheep, assuming you would help him. I should not have assumed. I should have been there with you.'

'And yet you blamed it on me that night, and you never explained or apologised!' I burst out.

'Didn't I?'

'Never!'

'Yahweh forgive me. I didn't even realise, Kayin! When you found Havel again, I was so relieved. But knowing you had endured such danger rescuing his sheep – once again, I could not bear it. It pressed into me even further that it was I who had brought suffering and death into the world. If Havel had died that day – Yahweh forbid – it would have been my fault, not yours!'

He turned to face me, grasped my free hand, looked at it and began stroking my palm. I stared at him, speechless in disbelief.

'Every time I looked at you after that – when I saw your bandaged hands, broken from all the thorns and sharp rocks of the cliff – all I felt was shame and guilt, ten times worse than I had done. I would do anything to avoid those crushing feelings. You must believe me: it wasn't you, Kayin. It was me.'

I took a moment to steady my thoughts. They were spinning – like the twisting wind that Elohim had sent to remove the locusts – as I tried to process what he was saying.

'So all these years you've avoided me because… because I make you feel… guilty?'

'To my shame, yes.'

'Enough about your shame, Father! Have you any idea what this has done to me?' I pulled away from him as the anger began to rise in my chest. 'All this time, I have been convinced you hated me and did not wish to be in my presence! You have spent every moment with Havel. The only time you have spoken to me has been to scold me!'

'I know. I see now that I have deeply failed you! And I have no excuse for leaving it this long. It was simply due to fear that I kept this to myself. I had no idea that you thought I hated you! I am so sorry, Kayin.'

We stood there for a few moments while I absorbed everything he was saying. It was utterly inexcusable, the way he had treated me. Why couldn't he have told me this years ago, when he saw how badly I was hurting? I would have understood more had he been honest with me from the start. A particular question began to simmer and seek a vent.

'Why do you feel this way about me, but not about your other children? You have no issues spending time with them. You do not treat them the way you treat me.'

Abba closed his eyes and tilted his chin towards the ground. 'I do not love them any more than I love you, Kayin. Please trust me in that. Yet, it is true that I often find their presence easier.

'When Havel was young, you may recall he was not the easiest child. But, once he had gotten over seeking your mother's attention all the time, he loved nothing better than to spend his days with me and the sheep.

'We would stand out there in the grasslands, watching over the animals and speaking of Elohim. Havel wanted to know everything about Him. It became apparent that he had a special connection with Yahweh and a unique ability to notice and celebrate the glorious. His growing self-awareness – including that of his own naughtiness – was coupled with a desire to change. This intensified after the incident at the cliff.

'As I spoke of the past with Havel, it rekindled something in my heart. I could almost imagine I was in the Garden again. As I saw him change, it gave me hope that I could too. My burdens lifted when it was just Havel, me and the creation.'

'Until you came home and saw me – then all the guilt came flooding back.'

He did not answer, but his face said it all. I was glad I understood now, yet the understanding did nothing to lessen my pain.

'And Chayyim? What of him? He toils with the land as I do.'

'That is true. But he does not have your disposition. You are so like me, Kayin. You remind me of myself,' he said at last. 'When I see anger in you, it reflects my own. Like me, you take things quickly to heart and do not easily move on. After the wolf attack, you were so intense – it terrified me! Even so, I have mistreated you. I offer an explanation but no excuse, for I have acted wrongly. Please, if I try to spend more time with you to rekindle what we have lost, might you be able to forgive me?'

He looked up at me, his eyes red from weeping, pleading with me to accept his offering. I think I wanted to affirm and reassure him. Yet we had finally been honest, and – despite my desire to impress him with my spiritual alteration and planned sacrifice – I could not fake this. It was clear that in my father's mind, I represented everything that was wrong with the world, whereas Havel represented all that was good. What was I meant to do with that? How was I meant to get over that or do anything to change it?

'I do not know, Abba,' I replied after a time.

We said nothing more but slowly made our way home. At the doorway to my hut, my father placed his large, work-toughened hand on my shoulder, slowly lifted himself onto his tiptoes and tenderly kissed my cheek.

'I love you, son.'

I nodded, turned and went inside. Chayyim was already asleep on his pallet. I collapsed onto mine. I couldn't decide if I felt relieved, bitterly dismayed or outraged. Believing my father hated me for something I had done had almost been easier than knowing he had spent years avoiding me simply because he felt guilty about his own sin.

I could feel my own set of tears building up, but I fought them back. I could not change who I was. I was born to work the land, and I would not betray myself for the sake of others. Was it possible for us to rebuild our relationship if I continued farming? Could he ever view me differently? Whilst I had been stuck at home recovering from the wolf injury, he had not acted any better towards me. Had that truly been because of the fever, or – unlike my foot – was our relationship beyond healing?

I could not deny that I longed to return to those days before my family life became strained. I longed for the childlike innocence that had been mine before. The emptiness in my chest was somewhat relieved by the knowledge that he still loved me, but it was hopeless to dream that his regard for me would ever equal his affection for Havel.

Nonetheless, if there was any chance of it, showing that I could be like Havel was probably a good place to start.

CHAPTER 23

My father was true to his word. He did try to spend more time with me. He came out to the fields in the evening when I would typically be missing our evening meal, and he brought food with him. We would sit and eat for a while, then carry on with the work together. There was no easiness between us – every conversation was awkward – yet he was trying, and I was grateful for that. In return, I made sure to leave early several times a week to join the family at dinner.

'Some of the barley is ready,' Abba said to me one day.

'Yes, I was going to start on this area tomorrow,' I replied.

'Good. I shall tell the others to come and help.'

And they did. In fact, everyone except Havel came the next day so that there wasn't quite enough work for them all. Consequently, Ima and Avigayil left for the river to see to the soaking flax while Abba, Chayyim and I cut the barley. Awan, Shimon and Channah helped by collecting the stalks and tying them into bundles. It took several days to work on the first area and by the time we had finished that field, the next was ready. I always enjoyed this early harvest time: having others with me appreciating the fruits of my labour.

A couple of weeks after the first cut, the women moved on to threshing the first batch of dried barley, beating it against wooden slats laid on the ground. After that, they threw it into the air to separate the grain from the chaff. The grain would fall back down into their baskets while the chaff blew away. This is where my young siblings proved advantageous: they enjoyed chasing the chaff down as it blew and gathering it up for animal fodder.

Six weeks after the first barley had been cut, I carried the last basket of grain up to the family cave. I had set aside some time to sort the barley out before we cut the first stalks of wheat. I intended to choose which grain to store for food or keep for seed, and which to give as my first offering to Elohim. I wanted to ensure I made the offering before we started the wheat harvest to avoid the visit of locusts. I also desired to present my offering before Havel's lamb was ready.

This wasn't just about Awan anymore. My father's confession had produced a new feeling in me. I didn't want to merely go along with the family in spiritual practices; I wanted to prove that I could also be a leader. Havel had taken my rightful place, and I wanted it back. Oh, I knew I could never have the same relationship with Yahweh that Havel had; I wasn't born with that easy connection to Him. Yet if I worked hard enough, kept my feelings in check – even prayed regularly – perhaps something might change.

I longed for the self-assurance that Havel had and the respect that he received. I yearned for my family to look at me as they looked at my brother. I had noted Abba's reaction to my suggestion of sacrifice. He had been so pleased with the change in my attitude that he'd warmed to me again. He had joined me in the fields, even though it was difficult for him. I felt like I was beginning to rise above the curse. If only I could gain the favour of Elohim, I might be able to rise above Havel as well.

Although it wasn't yet dark when I reached the cave, there was insufficient light to see anything inside it. So, rather than grasp around in the dark, I lit a fire outside and waited until it was roaring enough to light a torch. It was so peaceful up here in the hills; I had enjoyed their tranquillity over the last year.

So far, the animal that had previously lived in my secret cave hadn't returned. Therefore, I had continued to store a small proportion of each type of produce there, making sure there was enough for any tragedy that might befall us. I planned to take some of the barley I wasn't using for sacrifice there later. I knew Havel would say that we should trust in Elohim, that He would provide us with enough. However, I wasn't showing distrust; I was just being cautious. Had I not been cautious last year, we might not have had enough food this year.

When my torch was blazing, I turned and headed through the mouth of the cave. There was an immediate commotion of movement on rocks, and I saw several long, scaly tails disappearing into the dark recesses where my light didn't shine. My serpent evidently had offspring now. I wedged my torch into a nearby nook and sat down on a boulder to survey the baskets before me. They had been placed in order of harvest, so I cast my mind back to consider where the best grain was likely to be found amongst the pile before me.

I spent some time sorting the baskets according to the suspected quality of the grain. As it was too early for this year's fruit, I also filled a sack with the best fruit remaining from the previous season. I was planning to add some leaf vegetables to it on the way home.

My burning torch was now almost extinguished, so I went outside and lit two more. Back in the cave, with renewed firelight, I ran grains of barley through my fingers, inspecting and comparing them. I pulled forward the best two baskets. It was the finest quality we had ever had, thanks to my careful planning. The rest of the baskets were fine for food, but I would rather not use them for seed.

Abba and Havel had stressed that we must give Elohim the best, so I knew I should choose one of these baskets to sacrifice and keep the other for next year's seed. The grain to my left was slightly superior to that on the right. It went against every fibre of my being to burn up the best seed as an offering, but I was determined to be seen doing the right thing. And the grain on my right was good enough for next year's crop.

I was standing, ready to carry the left basket home, when one of the serpents that had fled earlier began to slide over the rocks towards me. I was surprised, for they usually avoided the fire. I watched this one approach. Its markings were identical to those of the snake that had wound around my legs before. Leaving the basket safely where it was, I grabbed a torch and waved it, hoping to scare it off.

The snake continued moving forwards until it paused near to the basket for sacrifice and reared up its head. Its forked tongue slid in and out while it assessed me with sharp eyes.

'What do you want, friend?' I whispered. The forked tongue flickered again and the body slithered closer. As it did so, several more serpents slid out of their dark hiding place. They too approached, showing no fear of my torches. One snake did not scare me anymore, but five? That, I was not so sure about. I jumped away, heading towards the mouth of the cave. When I moved, they paused. When I stayed still, they again began to edge forward, ever so slowly.

By now, the sun was beginning to set, yet there was still some light in the sky. I backed further away, transfixed, sure that the snakes would not venture outside the cave. I could run now, but I didn't want to leave the offering behind. Four snakes chose not to follow me out, but the first one boldly began to slither once more. Before I knew it, it had reached my feet. It began to climb my leg, twisting its body around me as if it were scaling a tree.

Fear turned to exhilaration as I stood stock still, my life once again in the clutches of a serpent which seemed much larger than the last time I had encountered it. As it wound around my torso, I noticed a bright red, chequered pattern on its underbelly. I dared not attempt to resist or fight it. I had no choice but to remain calm on the outside while all the blood inside me was racing faster than I could run. The creature reached my ear. Its tongue flickered again, hissing like the whispering Tempter in the Garden.

Its body coiled once around my neck, leaving the tip of its tail reaching down one of my arms and its head next to mine. Its eyes glinted in the moonlight. Its tongue flashed in and out, in and out. The creature didn't appear to mean me any harm. Even so, I stood there for a significant length of time, neither of us stirring as I considered my next move.

Gradually, I began to take tiny steps back toward the cave on slow, cautious feet. I thought that if I could get it back to its home, I might be able to gently remove it without incident. The snake continued to tickle my ear but did not release or tighten its embrace. I passed the other snakes, whose slit eyes followed me.

As I reached the baskets, the four unexpectedly lunged towards me. I was alarmed at the movement and sprang back. The snake around my neck tightened its hold and I felt the breath leave my body. It was choking me! The choke sent me off balance. My legs caved, sending me tumbling. I struck something as I fell, then slipped and came crashing down. Hissing surrounded me as the other serpents attacked. The principal snake tightened its grip on my neck as the others coiled around each of my limbs, squeezing and restricting the flow of my lifeblood. I gasped a final breath.

As I sank into senselessness, images from my nightmares flashed before my eyes: Havel jumping, Awan running, animals attacking. Rocks, blood. Blood everywhere. Lifeless faces. Lifeless faces all around. Suddenly, alive again. Together! They were together, and his gleeful face looked up and saw me. Then, below in the river, the rest of my family appeared, and they were all drowning. Drowning and screaming. Screaming my name. But I was on the bank, held back by serpents, unable to dive in and save them.

I saw Havel's face. He was not drowning. He was safe on the other bank, full of scornful amusement at the sight. His words carried across the river and hissed, like the snake in my ear, 'Why aren't you saving them, Kayin? They will all die! Watch them die, Kayin. Watch them die at your hands – and be content.'

Then I watched in horror as everybody in the river turned lifeless. One by one, the people I loved sank into the water and were carried away by the current. It dashed them against the rocks, breaking their bodies into pieces. Blood in the water, blood on my tunic, blood everywhere.

Suddenly, I was trying to do something; I was trying to sacrifice. Desperately I pawed at the ground, collecting grain. But the grain kept running through my fingers. I gathered it again, but it kept slipping away.

'Why are you sacrificing, Kayin?' hissed Havel's voice across the river. 'You are an undesirable, odious creature. Elohim will never accept you, just as Abba never shall. It is too late! For He loves only me. Do not think that you can ever earn His pleasure. You are everything they hate. You are not good enough for them, Kayin. You will lead them all astray. See, you have killed them!'

Havel dispersed into a cloud of dust, yet his voice lingered – mocking and taunting – even as the dust and grain blew away on the wind. Finally, I was left alone on the bank, kneeling in the dirt. The snakes released me as my vision faded into darkness.

CHAPTER 24

When I woke, I wasn't sure if I was dead or alive. Darkness was everywhere, pitch black, and I could feel rocks beneath me. I tried to move my hands and they brushed over something. It was grain. I tried to move more of my body. Everything hurt, which meant I was alive. I closed my eyes again, waiting for the blood to stop pounding in my ears.

After a few more moments, the pounding settled enough for me to hear wind whistling outside. I must have still been inside the cave. I opened my eyes – still only darkness. Then I turned over slightly and caught a flicker of something a few steps away. It was a dying fire. I began crawling on my arms, dragging my partly numb, partly throbbing legs behind me, pulling myself towards the embers.

I realised they were outside the cave. As soon as I too emerged from it, the wind struck me in the face. It was dark out here too, but a tiny crescent moon in the sky gave just enough light for my eyes to function. It looked as if the wind was simultaneously blowing out the fire and keeping it going. Just as the last ember faded, another would light.

Still pulling myself along, I managed to reach the dying fire and, propping my body up on one elbow, threw a couple of sticks on it. I then pulled up some dried grass from beside me and added that. I dragged my body further round and put it against the wind so that I sheltered the flames. In a short space of time, the fire was going again, warming the front of my body, even as gusts of bitter wind battered my back.

After a while, the wind began to die down and my body stopped shaking. I examined it in the firelight. I had several bruises up my arms and legs consistent with the serpent's constriction, as well as bloodied injuries where I'd fallen. My neck felt achingly tender. Why had the snakes attacked me? And why hadn't they killed me?

Once I had warmed through, I managed to lift myself to my feet and carefully picked my way down to the stream. I knelt before it and washed my face before lapping up a refreshing drink. Then I turned back to the fire, lit a torch and tremulously re-entered the cave. There was no sign of the slithery fiends. A basket lay upturned. The highest quality grain had been spilt all over the ground. I must have tripped over it as I fell.

I propped my torch and began to regather the grain. The vision of it slipping through my fingers flashed across my mind. Though one basket was upturned, the second was just beyond and looked untouched. I turned the first basket over and started to fill it back up again. Dust was inevitably gathered up with the grain. If I used it for seed, this dust would not matter. But what if the grains had been damaged by my fall?

I ran some of it through my fingers next to the light. A good proportion of the sample in my hand was crushed and would be no good for seed. This had been the best grain; now it was mixed with dust and damaged. Did that mean I should offer the other basket to Elohim instead? Or keep the undamaged basket for seed, as originally intended? I could not afford to lose both baskets of my best grain. I halted in indecision.

Just then, I heard someone outside calling my name. The sound was coming from further away and carried on the wind. I instinctively picked up the unspoilt basket and hid it in a recess on the other side of the cave, then rose and staggered out. Havel was climbing up the hill with Chayyim behind him.

'Kayin, are you alright?' he shouted out when he saw me.

'I'm alright,' I shouted back.

When they drew near, Chayyim surveyed me in the firelight. 'You look awful!' he exclaimed.

'What happened?' Havel asked.

'I was sitting in the cave sorting the grain when serpents attacked me – several of them. They coiled around me and tried to choke my breath away.'

'How are you still alive?'

'I don't know, I passed out on the floor. When I woke again, after – well, I don't know how long it was – the night had fully set in.'

'It will be dawn soon, it must have been for some time,' Chayyim replied.

'Praise Yahweh that you are still alive,' said Havel. 'We were so worried when we discovered you were missing.'

'Why were you worried about me?' I asked. 'I often sleep out here.'

'Havel had one of his moments,' replied Chayyim, his eyebrows raised slightly in a knowing way. 'He woke me in the night and said you were in danger, and demanded we trudge out here to find you.' Chayyim rolled his eyes. 'I guess he was wrong. You clearly had everything under control,' he chuckled, sarcastically.

I looked at the older of my siblings. Havel also smiled and shrugged. As he did so, I had a flashback from my last vision: his face morphed into the one surveying from the riverbank and laughing as his family drowned. I blinked and shook my head. The image disappeared, and he became my brother again.

'Can you head home, or would you like us to stay here with you?' Havel asked.

'I've had enough of *here* for one night. Let's go,' I replied. 'I'll just get my basket of grain and the fruit.'

I walked inside and stood before the basket that had previously held my best grain – that which was now crushed and covered in dust. Should I tell Havel about it and ask his advice on what I should sacrifice? I suspected he would tell me to leave this basket and offer the other. Then I would have to plant sub-standard grain for food. All my achievements this year would be wasted. That said, the crushed grain could still be used for food.

As I considered, the hissing voice of the Havel from my vision repeated in my head. *Why are you sacrificing anything, Kayin? You are an undesirable, odious creature. Elohim will never accept you.* If the voice was right, it might all be for nothing. I might never get this quality of grain again, and even my best might not be enough. Yet to stand a chance… This basket would surely be okay if I shook it out, wouldn't it? I had chosen the best originally; my intention was good. That had to count for something.

'Is this your offering?' Havel asked. I hadn't noticed him come up behind me. I briefly paused before replying, and the echo condemned me again. *Do not think that you can ever earn His pleasure… He loves only me.*

My decision was made. 'Yes, this is the basket,' I replied.

'And it is the best grain?' He looked at me, a flicker of disquiet in his eyes. Irritation coursed through me. Did he have to question everything I did? Was it so hard to believe that I would choose to honour Elohim? I put away all the voices competing in my mind and met him square in the face, speaking confidently.

'It is.' *It was the best yesterday.*

Havel began to lift the basket.

'And also that sack of fruit,' I said.

'Excellent,' he smiled. 'I shall carry it all for you. You just concentrate on getting those bruised legs down the hill in one piece.' He swung the woven sack onto his back then took up the basket again. Just before he walked out of the mouth of the cave, he stopped and turned to me.

'Kayin, are we good?' he asked.

I swallowed down hard and forced a smile onto my face. 'Of course. Thank you for *rescuing* me.'

He laughed.

We made our way slowly back home, Chayyim leading at a pace sensitive to my painful joints and muscles. Havel took the rear. By the time we made it back to the huts, the sun had risen and was sending colourful rays across the morning sky. Ima, who still rose early, ran out to greet us.

'Kayin! What happened to you?' she exclaimed.

'He had a fight with some snakes,' laughed Chayyim as he took the basket from Havel and carried it into the hut we shared. My mother's face relaxed when he laughed.

'I thought you'd learnt your lesson as a child, but you seem to be making a habit of fighting with serpents,' Ima gently teased as she motioned for me to sit down on Avigayil's chair. 'I wish you'd find another pastime to keep yourself amused.' She poured some water from a bubbling pot on the fire into a bowl and began dipping a linen cloth into it. Then, when it cooled, she gently wiped at my wounds, removing the traces of dried blood and dirt so they could heal afresh. Shortly afterwards, a concerned Awan emerged from the hut carrying a jar of ointment.

'Havel told me what happened,' she said, sitting the other side of me and touching my cheek. She pulled the lid from the jar, turned it upside down on the end of her forefinger and began to gently rub the ointment onto the scratches Ima had cleaned. The feeling of her finger on my flesh sent shivers down my spine, little to do with the sting of my wounds. Then, she took a little fresh water from the pot and crushed into it some flowers and herbs she had inside a small basket. Whilst Ima fetched me something to eat, Awan rubbed this mixture over my bruises.

'This should help reduce the swelling,' she smiled. I kept my eyes on her face but she stayed focused on tending my body, not meeting my gaze. I looked around, checking no one was watching us.

'I would welcome a snake attack any day to get this sort of attention from you,' I whispered into her ear whilst gently stroking her arm. It was the first time I had touched her in such a way since the day the sheep died.

She didn't reply but I saw that her eyes sparkled, and a flush had crept into her cheeks. The voices in my mind might tell me that everyone hated me, but it appeared that, with Awan at least, I was still winning.

Later that day – after I'd had a rest and recovered my strength – I had a better look at the grain we'd brought back from the cave. I took the basket to an area of arid land that we didn't use for anything, where I could check over it without prying eyes. The wind was still blowing well, so I tossed the grain into the air, allowing the dust to blow away from it. I had to shake the basket for some time before I was satisfied that no dust remained visible.

Next, I placed the basket on the ground and checked through the grain with my fingers. Most of it was still passable. I picked out the worst crushed grains and threw them on the ground for birds to scavenge. The rest I left, satisfied that if anyone checked the basket, they wouldn't notice the damage.

CHAPTER 25

The morning of my sacrifice arrived. I didn't know what to expect. The sacrifice last year had been so dramatic, brought about by necessity – I didn't know if this would be similar or different. I had collected wood and grass the day before and kept it in my hut for the night so that it would be dry and would light well. I had memorised some words to say over the offering; ones that I thought sounded impressive and honoured Yahweh. I wanted Him to change His mind about me; I needed Him to bless me and accept me. As I rose from my pallet, I could feel myself buzzing with excitement – would this finally be the day when my family and their Elohim acknowledged me?

As I walked past our huts to the area where the stones were piled up, I suddenly stopped in my tracks. Next to the stones we had used last year, another altar had been built. I turned around in confusion, in time to see my father and Havel walking towards me with piles of sticks in their arms.

'Good morning Kayin!' said my father. 'Are you ready for your offering?'

'Yes, and I have already collected my sticks,' I replied, an untold question in my voice.

'Havel will sacrifice today as well,' Abba continued. 'We thought it would be wonderful to make a whole day of it – a family celebration of our harvest so far.'

I felt bile begin to rise in my chest and sickness in my stomach. This was meant to be my day; why had Havel set about to ruin it? I tried to think of something to put him off.

'How can you sacrifice today Havel, when the lambs still have a season of growth ahead? You cannot, surely, know which is the best already?'

'I will sacrifice the firstborn of them. I have checked it over thoroughly and the lamb is a perfect specimen to give to Elohim,' he smiled casually.

If only I could dash that annoying smile from your face, I thought. Havel could say what he pleased; I knew the truth: he was going to slaughter it today so that he could spite me and keep his place of superiority in the family.

'But surely the lamb is still a little young?' I said aloud. 'Shouldn't you wait until it's fully grown? Surely Elohim would prefer a more impressive animal?' *See, I can twist things to sound spiritual too.*

'She is not fully grown, I admit. But I slaughtered the firstborn yearling for meat yesterday and have kept its fat portions to sacrifice as well.'

Of course you have. All year you have refused to kill one of your flock. Until you saw my sack of fruit and thought you should do one better. Now, to look as if you are giving more than me, the best of two animals will be wasted in the fire instead of being used to feed your family.

'Don't be concerned, Kayin; it is what's inside our hearts that counts. True, she is young. Nonetheless, if I give her to Elohim today, I am showing that I trust Him to provide. Whereas if I wait until all my lambs are grown and healthy, it shows little trust.'

So, this was about trust? *Trust you to have some strange justification for ruining my day.* Still, I would keep my thoughts to myself, so I didn't give him the satisfaction of knowing he had rattled me.

'I had been hoping this could be my day to sacrifice,' I said through gritted teeth, not willing to roll over just yet, but not sure what else to say.

'Of course, it is a special day for you. But this is Elohim's day, not yours, Kayin, and it will be so much nicer to have a big celebration with everyone involved,' replied my father, while Havel began to stack sticks upon the second stone altar.

I did not agree with him. It would not be nicer to be usurped by my younger brother. Why couldn't we have a big celebration without him being the centre of attention for once?

'I am so happy you have chosen to sacrifice some grain,' Havel chimed in. 'I couldn't be more pleased that you are choosing to follow Yahweh, and I was keen to celebrate it with you.'

I couldn't fathom my brother. Did he really think I was stupid enough to believe his falsehoods? I knew that for all the rhetoric, he wasn't genuinely pleased. Shaking my head, I went back into my hut to retrieve my sticks.

A little while later, all our family had gathered around near the altar. The sacrificial lamb's feet were tied and it was lying next to Channah. She was singing it a song and stroking its soft wool as if it were a babe, even though it was now a decent size. I sat down next to my little sister and stroked the lamb's head. She looked up at me and I saw that her eyes were wet with tears.

'What is the matter, little Channah?' I asked, quietly.

'Havel said we must give this lamb to Elohim. But this is my lamb, Kayin! She is the one whose Ima died. Havel and I have looked after her and fed her milk from a skin. She even slept in my bed when she was tiny. I do not understand why Havel would take her from me instead of choosing another.' She stuck out her bottom lip as it quivered, and tears filled her eyes once more.

So, this was the same lamb that was cut from the ewe that died? The one Havel had been so upset about? No wonder Channah was distraught. I hadn't noticed, for they all looked similar to me and it had been back with the flock since it was weaned.

'Shall I tell you a secret?' I asked. She looked at me and nodded, so I leaned down and whispered in her ear.

'I don't understand it either. I think Havel is being foolish and unkind. It is terrible of him to take your lamb; he should have chosen another. I would not have done such a thing.'

'Why do you think Elohim wants to eat one of the babies? Why can't He eat one of the old, fat sheep?'

'Hmm, I don't know. Perhaps Havel has it wrong. Perhaps Elohim is like us and eats mostly grain.'

Her eyes lit up a little, hope springing to them.

'Will you give Him grain, or are you killing a lamb too?'

'Oh, I will definitely give Him grain. And some fruit and vegetables too. Don't you worry, little sister.' I ruffled Channah's hair. She giggled, a little happier. It was good to know that someone else in the family didn't appreciate Havel's madness.

My father rose, and we all fell silent.

'We are gathered here today to praise Yahweh Elohim for all that He has done, providing us once again with a bountiful harvest and keeping us all safe and together for the last year. He has done many great things. Awan will lead us now in a time of singing to praise Him. Then Kayin, our first-born, will offer his sacrifice, followed by Havel, our second-born.' Abba smiled at us each as he spoke our names. He was evidently thrilled to see all his adult children playing their part.

Awan's voice came next as she sang a song that I barely listened to. I was rehearsing my prayer in my head. She repeated the words and the third time we all joined in. After a few more repetitions, the song gradually drew to a close.

In the silence afterwards, I rose. I looked nervously at Abba, and he nodded at me to continue. I moved over to the altar and placed the basket of grain upon it, removing the lid and arranging the other produce on top. I began to speak, trying to project confidence, lifting my voice to the heavens and pronouncing the words I had memorised:

> O Mighty One, Yahweh Elohim,
>> Creator of the heavens and the earth.
> We praise you, O giver of life,
>> From the rising of the sun to its setting.
> You determine the ways of the beasts
>> And direct the course of the stars.
> Accept this offering of thankfulness
>> For the portion of land you have given us,
>> And the fruit it has produced.
> Continue to bless us with your abundance,
>> For we seek to serve you and multiply on
>> the earth.

Then I walked behind the altar and retrieved the stones I had selected for lighting the fire. I struck them repeatedly towards a section of dried grass in the pile. They sparked and a tiny flame took hold. However, just as it began to grow, a gust of wind blew in and the flame was snuffed out.

I tried again, but the same thing happened. I flushed, embarrassed that my fire had not immediately taken. My family sat looking on, still smiling at me in encouragement. Many times I struck the stones until several areas of grass were lit. Just to make sure, I moved to the other side of the altar and did the same there, then twice more until there was a steady amount of fire taking hold under my offering.

Just as I was beginning to relax, another gust of wind came, and stronger. It blew right over the altar as if it was directed at it. It consumed all of the flames; each one was snuffed out.

'What?!' I exclaimed in exasperation. I would now need more grass.

'Here, brother,' Havel said, removing some from his stack and handing it to me. I grunted at him, then stuffed the grass underneath my sticks and tried to light them once more. I made several more attempts. Sometimes the grass lit then was snuffed out; sometimes it did not light at all. No matter what I did, the offering basket remained untouched by flames.

My family began to grow agitated. I could see them becoming restless as they watched my futile attempts to burn the offering.

'Perhaps Elohim does only like lambs,' little Channah said with sadness after the fifth gust of wind had extinguished my attempt at a fire. There was no sign of wind anywhere else around the hut, and I was beginning to agree with Channah that Elohim had no intention of accepting my offering.

At last, Abba decided to intervene.

'It seems the weather is not allowing Kayin to make his offering. I'm sure it will soon pass. Let us sing another song, then Havel may offer his sacrifice. He squeezed my shoulder and motioned for me to sit down. I took my former place next to my youngest sister, my face burning with humiliation. Channah weaved her fingers around mine and gave them a squeeze.

Everyone else looked around awkwardly until Awan once again began to sing, then they relaxed slightly. I stole a glance at Havel. He looked deep in thought. His eyes were trained on my altar, and his head was resting on his chin. He had not joined in with the singing, but his mouth was moving as if he was uttering silent words.

When the song ended, my father asked Havel to offer his sacrifice.

'Let Kayin try again first,' he offered.

'It's alright,' I returned, 'you go.' I had no desire to be embarrassed again quite yet, and I was curious to see what would happen to Havel's offering. Havel moved to the side of his altar and carefully placed upon it the fat portions he had previously reserved. Then he walked over to Channah and took the lamb's halter from her.

'She needs to come with me now; she has an important job to do,' he said in hushed tones to my sister.

Channah covered her face with her hands and snuggled into my side. Surprised at the affection, I lifted my arm and put it around her, drawing her closer and allowing her to bury her head under my arm so that she did not have to witness the slaughter.

Havel lifted the lamb to the top of the pile of sticks and laid her beside the other portions. Then he spoke, stroking the lamb as he prayed:

Yahweh Elohim, Almighty One,

We do not presume to come to your altar by the strength of our own righteousness, for we are all guilty before you. Compared to your dazzling holiness, we are as black as the darkest cave. We plead with you: accept the blood of this spotless firstborn as payment for the wrongs we have committed against you.

And, in your mercy, accept the best portions of its brother as an offering of praise and thanksgiving for all you have given to us, your children.

Then he took a sharp stone and cut the lamb's throat.

Instantly, before Havel even had time to strike his stones, the sticks underneath the lamb burst into flame. My brother had to jump back to stop himself from being singed by the ferocity of the fire. We were all struck silent and began shivering, unable to believe our eyes as the fat portions were instantly consumed.

Within moments the lamb itself was burning too. Then the atmosphere changed as heat emanated from the fire and a fragrant aroma rose to heaven: the smell of sweet meat and burning wood. I looked around. A peace had settled on all those watching the flames. There could be no doubt that Havel's offering had been accepted by the Master of wind and fire. And mine had not.

Next, a booming voice began to speak from the midst of the flames, so loud that we had to cover our ears and cower to the ground. As it spoke, the flames licked out toward me – arms of wrath seeking to drag me from my place among my family:

Hear, O Kayin, and I will speak.
I will testify against you.
For I am Yahweh Elohim!
Every tree of the forest is mine,
And the sheep on a thousand hills.
I know all the birds of the air,
And all that grows in the field belongs to me.
If I were hungry, I would not tell you,
For the world and all its fullness are mine.

*Do I eat many grains or drink the blood of
sheep?*
*I do not need your sacrifice of grain and I do not
desire it,*
*For I am not a reed that you can bend to your
will:*
I am Yahweh Elohim!

Offer to me a sacrifice of thanksgiving!
Perform your vows to the Most High
And call upon me in your day of trouble;
I will deliver you, and you shall glorify me.
This my servant Havel has done.

But to you, Kayin, I say:
You give your mind free rein for evil,
And your tongue frames deceit.
You sit and speak against your brother;
You slander your own mother's son.
*These things you have done and I have been
silent.*
You thought that I was one like yourself.
*But now I rebuke you and lay the charge before
you.*
Mark this, then, you who forget Elohim:
*The one who offers thanksgiving as his sacrifice
glorifies me.*
To the one who orders his way rightly
I will show the salvation of Elohim!

As I knelt there before the burning lamb, I was
shaken and cut down. I felt every rebuke like a sting to
my soul: every wrong motivation for my sacrifice; every
broken kernel of seed; every word of praise spoken but

unmeant; every prayer filled with false intention; every proud notion about my skill in the fields; every word said and thought against my brother. I felt as if the very flesh covering my heart had been ripped open and scorched in the fire.

I stood and I ran. I ran from the unbearable presence of the Most High. I ran from the family I had wronged. I ran until my breath could no longer sustain me. Then I collapsed and fell into some grass, broken in body and soul. I had desired all my life to hear His voice. I had not known it would be so awful! So terrifying! More so than I could ever imagine. There was nowhere to hide from it for He was everywhere, and He did not see my actions solely but every thought of my mind! How could I ever be good enough for Him? I felt utterly wretched.

Then in my grief, anger began to rise once more. What was the point in trying to sacrifice if Elohim would not accept it? For I had tried; tried to reach Him. I had tried to breach the cavern between us! Why did Elohim have to subject me to such a rebuke? If He had an issue with me, why hadn't He talked to me beforehand, rather than allowing me to get all the way to the altar before humiliating me in front of them all? Why hadn't He answered my prayers before now? Why hadn't He stayed my hand in the cave or stopped the serpents from destroying the grain?

I recalled the hissing voice of the Havel in my vision. The words had been right! I was undesirable; I was odious. Elohim would never love me! Yet why was I singled out for criticism when surely the rest of my family was as sinful as I was? Weren't we all under the same curse? Weren't we all subject to the banishment? Hadn't I seen them all die in my dreams?

As the humiliation sank in and my anger grew more and more ferocious, I began to pound the ground beneath me with my fists.

'Why? Why?!' I cried out.

Then a soft breeze surrounded and enveloped me. The voice was back, yet it was no longer loud and booming. Rather, it whispered as the wind caressed my flesh:

Why are you angry, and why has your face fallen?

He had come. He had finally decided to talk to me alone. Yet, even though I wanted answers, I fought the voice, and I fought the tingle that had begun to descend over my body. How could He come to me now and try to speak to me, as if I had not been humiliated by Him? The indignity of that unburnt offering stung. His voice felt like a spear twisting inside my wounds.

I lifted my head and shouted into the wind. 'You know why! Apparently, you know everything!'

If you do well, will you not be accepted?

'You shall never accept me! Do not play tricks with my heart!' It didn't matter what I did, I would never be accepted. Elohim loved only Havel.

Elohim had favoured Havel from youth. He had never given me a taste of His presence until He was baring flames down upon me. Although I could see the stains upon my soul and feel the rightness of His rebuke, my sinful actions were not entirely my fault! They were the result of an unfair disadvantage and a torturous mind. All I had wanted was to earn the love and favour that my brother had been freely given! Why had Havel been blessed while I had always been condemned?

The voice came again – this time stronger, with warning in its tone.

If you do not do well, sin is crouching at the door. Its desire is to overpower you, but you must rule over it.

To say that I was angry with Elohim now was an understatement. He had betrayed me; He had humiliated me. This was His fault. I no longer desired His ministrations, His warnings or His presence. They were too little, too late.

'Leave me alone!' I shouted again, refusing to listen to the voice of Yahweh. I bowed my head and allowed myself to fall into the dirt as racking sobs of fury and sorrow overtook my body.

The wind withdrew. I was left alone.

CHAPTER 26

I must have fallen asleep where I lay on the ground – another fitful sleep of bad dreams and disturbing images – for the next thing I knew, someone was speaking my name and tugging at my shoulder.

'Kayin. Kayin, wake up.'

Oh no, not him; anyone but him.

I groaned and slowly opened my eyes. Havel was knelt on the ground before me, worry fixed in his features.

'What do you want?' I snarled at him.

'Everyone is worried about you. We didn't know where you were; we have been searching for you all night.'

'Then you have wasted your time,' I sneered, turning away from him and looking into the dirt – anything other than his face. 'I do not wish to see you.'

'Kayin, you were having a fit on the ground; your whole body was convulsing as you slept. Are you well?'

'Of course I am not well! You saw what happened yesterday! Leave me alone!' I growled. He moved backwards as I raised my voice. Perhaps he had gotten the point and would go away. Yet after a few moments, he continued.

'I cannot leave you, brother. No one should endure what you have done and be alone.'

I sat up, exasperation filling my entire body. 'When will you get the point, Havel?' I shouted. 'I do not want to be near you. I hate you and your self-righteousness, and I hate your cruel Elohim!'

The colour drained from his face; he looked as if he would fall dead where he sat.

Good riddance, I thought. I stood and began to walk away from him, trying to get my bearings and figure out where I had run to. I was at the edge of my furthest field. It had not been planted this year, having been given a year to rest. The weeds had grown up tall over most of it, intermingling with long grasses and thorns; providing areas of thistly growth that could hide a man sitting on his knees. Havel remained sitting in the grove I had lain in, where the grass was low. If I'd had my wits about me the previous night, I might have sought longer grass to lay in. Then he would never have found me.

As I walked away, I tried to figure out what I would do. I couldn't bear the sight of my brother. I was also done with pretending: Elohim's rejection had removed that option, and it stung like claws in my spine. The compulsion to run away in order to cope was intense. Yet if I left, I might lose Awan forever. Perhaps I could convince her to come with me. Would she ever defy my father – or leave Havel? I had supplies in the caves; could I make a home up there?

'Kayin. Wait!' Havel shouted behind me.

I ignored him and picked up the pace. I was now thigh-deep in the long grass. Havel ran in front of me, but I pushed him aside and carried on. He ran round again, standing before me with hands held high.

'Kayin! Please talk to me.' *Why wouldn't he get the point?* 'I cannot bear for us to be enemies. You may hate me right now, but I love you, and I know Elohim loves you too. He is trying to reach out to you. He is trying to show you His heart.'

233

'His heart?!' I exclaimed. 'All He showed me was how I can never match up to His expectations! I heard what He thinks of me – I'm some filthy, disobedient child that cannot get anything right! It doesn't matter what I do, Havel! I will never be good enough for Him. I will never be—YOU! Well, I give up now. What is the point in trying?'

'None of us are good enough! I am not good enough! He doesn't desire your actions, Kayin; He desires your heart. That is what He was revealing to you!'

'No, Havel. If He desired my heart, He would not have humiliated me in front of our entire family. And you stood by and let Him do it! You could have petitioned Him on my behalf. But no, you just loved the fact that He chose your offering so clearly. I know that's why you wanted to bring your lamb on the same day as mine: so you could ruin my sacrifice and make yourself look better!'

'No, Kayin, you have it wrong. I wanted to worship *with* you. I thought it would bring us together. I didn't expect what happened yesterday, any more than you did.'

'I don't believe you! I saw you there, whispering to your God while my offering was rejected. I know what you were doing! You were asking Him to reject me.'

'No! That had already happened! I was seeking the truth, trying to understand. I asked Him to explain—'

'So, when He did speak, it was because you had asked Him to? All those words of condemnation, all those words that affirmed you and made me look so terrible in the sight of everyone – that was all your fault too?'

I looked into his eyes, seeking confirmation that I was right. His face fell.

'I knew it!' I snarled. 'You both hate me!' Then I raised my fist and hit him square in the face. It was the first time I had struck anyone, and I felt the exhilarating power of it coursing through me in the reverberations of my muscles. The force of the punch threw Havel to the ground. He fell into a patch of dense thorns snaking out of the tall grass. I walked on but couldn't resist looking over my shoulder.

'Kayin, please,' he was crying out to me, 'I am trapped in the thorns. Brother, help me.'

I stopped walking and shouted in exasperation, 'Why should I help you? I should leave you to rot!'

'Please, if only for the love of your family, help me!'

He was right; my family would be pained by such a thing. They loved him so much more than they loved me. He really had stolen everything from me. I turned around and stalked back to where he lay, barely suppressed rage now threatening to take over my entire body.

A web of thick, thorny branches were trapping his limbs and digging into his flesh. A trickle of blood rolled down his face where sharp spikes had sunk in above his brow. A deep purple bruise was forming around his eye where I had struck him. It gave me a peculiar pleasure to see him in pain and to witness the blood dripping from him. He was getting what he deserved.

I raised my voice in fury against my brother, the usurper.

'You love it, don't you, all the attention you get from them? The way the little ones look up to you. The special bond you have with Ima, Abba – oh, and especially Awan. You desire her above all. You would like to take her from me and gloat in my face every day of my life!'

I towered over Havel, smirking at his discomfort. He said nothing, but struggled in the thorns, trying to free himself with now-bloodied fingers. As I imagined him gloating over Awan, flashbacks transformed his pitiful face. Visions of him triumphing as my family washed down the river. Blood. Faces. Bodies smashing against rocks. Explosions of fear mingled with hissing voices of revenge. I knelt to face him as I continued in a steadier tone.

'You would love it if I left home and you had them all to yourself. But I know that one day you will ruin them all. I have seen it.' He looked so confused I could not resist taunting him further. 'You will blame everything on me, but I know it is all your fault, all of it... Perhaps I should give you a beating then take you back to them, claiming I rescued you from a wild animal? Then I can finally be the hero. Or perhaps I should just end you here. Do away with your irksome presence so I can reclaim my rightful place!'

I grabbed him by his tunic and began to lift him. The thorns that were digging into his brow sliced across his flesh, causing more blood to run down his face. As the barbs refused to yield his body further, he cried out in pain, 'Kayin, please. I'm sorry if I have wronged you in any way. Please forgive me, please let us work this out!'

He was pathetic, begging me like a child. I roared in frustration and released him back down into the savage web. He howled as his back met their blades, then began to whimper. I watched him with scorn, wondering why everyone should look up to someone so weak.

I almost left his wretched form there; almost walked away. Perhaps if I had, my life would have turned out very differently.

However, just as I was turning to leave, an enormous, bright green serpent slithered out of the grass and made through the thorns to where Havel lay. It began coiling itself around one of his arms. He panicked and shook his arm, trying to rid himself of the snake. It hissed back in his face, flaring its neck and opening its mouth wide. This was no cave serpent that killed by suffocation; this was a venomous grass snake!

I scoffed, 'It looks like my friend here might do the work for me.'

'Since when was the serpent your friend?' Havel cried in shock as he fought, once again, to extract himself from the thorns. By now, fear covered his whole face. His body shook from it. 'Kayin, please!' he begged again. I knelt back down, enjoying the spectacle.

Just then, Havel managed to get his second arm free and grabbed the snake behind its head, pulling it away from his face. It uncoiled from his arm as he squeezed its neck. He shook his arm violently, throwing it to the ground. The snake hissed at him, lifting its head high and baring its fangs. I thought it would strike and held my breath in anticipation. Instead, the serpent turned from Havel and slithered into the long grass near where I crouched. Havel's body quaked in relief as mine sank in disappointment.

Then my brother experienced rage of his own. 'How could you?' he shot at me, 'It could have killed me! You can't seriously mean what you said!'

'I meant every word of it, Havel! Ever since you were born, you have set out to destroy me. You have destroyed all my relationships, ripping the favour of the entire family from my grasp and taking it for yourself! You have buried into my mind and destroyed all I care about, tearing all joy from me. Even the good times are marred by your constant presence. And it never gets better; only worse! Now you have committed the ultimate betrayal: turning your Elohim against me. You have convinced Him to reject and humiliate me, leaving me with no hope!'

As I had spewed out all of the twisted accusations that had been building up inside my head, the venomous serpent had slithered up my back, positioning itself around my shoulders. The feel of it there exhilarated me; the squeeze against my muscles made my blood quicken and my heart race. The tongue in my ear encouraged my rage. *Without his Elohim he is pathetic and weak. But you, Kayin, are strong,* it whispered. *You don't need him. You don't need the Creator either. Take back control. He shouldn't get away with what he has done.*

'You are right, my friend. He is weak now; this is my chance. It is high time I did a little destroying of my own.'

I grabbed Havel's neck, squeezing it with my hands. He began to choke as redness surged across his face. Water filled his widened eyes. He tried to speak but could not; he attempted to beg, but I would not hear his cries again. His arms flailed and grabbed hold of mine, uselessly tugging at the hands around his neck. His terrified expression bore into me as he realised I would not relent.

I tightened my hold; I would not give up now. I would right the injustice I had suffered. I could not physically injure Havel's Elohim, but there were other ways to hurt Him. I would start by ridding the earth of the one He deemed most precious.

The life left my brother's eyes, and they glazed over. His whole body went limp. His head tipped backwards. I almost dropped it. He lay there in my hands just as I had seen him in countless nightmares: pale, pitiful, and covered in blood.

CHAPTER 27

I sat there for some time in the tall grass, transfixed by that lifeless face. At some point, the hold of the snake loosened, and it left me. As it slid away, bewilderment replaced clarity. I found myself unable to comprehend what had just happened. Bruises started forming on Havel's neck; bruises like the ones the cave serpents had given me. Had serpents killed him, or had I?

In my earlier dreams, they had wound around me, stopped me from saving him as he drowned in the river, a victim. More recently, Havel had been on the cliff-face – and guilty. Which was it now? Had a serpent been here moments before, or had I imagined it? Had I squeezed the life from my brother, as my nightmares had predicted so many times? Was I now guilty of that which I had feared for so long?

I shook my head and blinked my eyes. Reality and nightmare were too intermingled. Unable to separate the two, I just sat there, holding Havel's body, numb.

Towards noon, I heard someone calling my name in the distance, which snapped me back to the present. From somewhere deep in my mind, I recalled Havel saying that everyone had been looking for me. Fear gathered: whether or not I was guilty, they must not find me here holding my brother's bloodied body.

I gently laid him down in the thorny grass, then tried to cover up the ground we had disturbed in our confrontation. The grass would hide him for a time. Then I ran away from the voice calling my name, hunching as low as possible to minimise the chance of being seen.

Perhaps if I were found somewhere far from the body, everyone would assume it had been the snake that killed him. But a venomous snake would have left a mark. Had his skin been broken? The sight of his body and brow pierced with thorns, and blood trickling down his face, returned to me.

Instinctively, I veered off towards the hills. The cave was a good place to be found; it would make sense that I'd run there after the sacrifice. Although perhaps that would have been the first place they'd checked? I paused in indecision. Not my secret cave! I could lay low there for a while, as no one knew about it.

I managed to make it to my cave without being seen. I knew those paths so well I could tread them with stealth. I crawled inside the cave. Once safe, I found my body was still shaking with nerves from the run. It was hard to calm down. My stomach also felt cavernous. I selected some figs and began to bite into one, hoping the food would settle me a little. Yet, the sweetness rose like bile in my throat and made me feel sick. I spat out the fig and gathered a linen cloth and a sheepskin. Curling into them, I clutched my stomach and tried not to throw up.

As I lay in the stillness that so contrasted with the state of my mind, I tried to make sense of everything that had occurred. I could remember Havel waking me from sleep and an argument, but recalled few of the words spoken. My memories still mingled with my nightmares. One moment we were standing in the grass; the next, we were in the water. Sometimes a snake was wound around me; other times, it was around him. I pictured his face and experienced a myriad of emotions: pain, joy, anger, fear.

For the last few years, my brother had brought me nothing but misery. I tried to block the features of his pale face and the sorrow rising within me and forced myself to think instead of what I knew to be true. He had taken the credit for Chayyim's rescue; he had tried to steal Awan from me – even causing her to fear me; he had turned Abba against me and deliberately sacrificed more than me to ruin my offering; he had cast me out of the family and betrayed me. I told myself that whatever I might be feeling in the wake of his death, he had deserved it.

Where is Havel, your brother?

Had someone spoken? I sat up and looked around. The cave was not completely dark, for the sunlight was bright outside and streamed through its opening. Yet, I could see no one. I shook my head and laid back down.

Where is Havel, your brother?

There was no mistaking it this time. The voice was louder than before, and I knew that voice. It would forever be scratched into my mind as the voice of condemnation. There was no use looking around, for I could not see Yahweh Elohim even though I knew He was here. Anger rose in me as I recalled His rejection. I wondered why He was asking such a question. Was there a chance He did not know what had happened? Sitting up, I took a deep breath, and, into the air, spoke the words of denial:

'I do not know; am I my brother's keeper?'

My words echoed into the cave, followed by silence. Insufferable, unbearable silence.

Just as I could bear the silence no longer, the voice spoke again. It was different now, quiet and piercing: on a statement of inestimable sorrow.

What have you done? The voice of your brother's blood is crying out to me from the ground.

My breath was stolen away. Elohim knew Havel was dead. Of course He knew! How could the one who sees all things not know? Then, as if the words of Yahweh had released the truth in my mind, concrete memories came flooding back in clear succession.

I saw my newborn brother as I carried him through the fields on the first night of his life; felt the indescribable love for him that had entered my heart that day. I saw Havel the toddler laughing at me as I tickled him; young Havel clinging to me in fear at the cliff face, then trying to make peace between Abba and myself in the field. I saw Havel with his sling standing over me and the wolf; saw him praying over my injured foot and passing me food after my fight with Abba.

Scales fell from my eyes as I recognised his insistence on loving me, no matter how I treated him. Tears streamed down my cheeks as I remembered the good things he had done and what we had once been to each other.

Finally, I remembered with clarity our fight and our last words to each other. I remembered what my final thoughts had been as I had held onto the neck of my dying brother: I had desired to rid the earth of the one that Elohim deemed most precious.

Then I knew, with certainty, that I had killed him. I, not the serpent. I had killed him deliberately, and I had done it to spite Elohim.

I gave up the fight against my memories and allowed the full pain of losing Havel to consume me. I bent over in agony with those words still ringing in my ears. *What have you done?* Oh, what had I done? For there was no pretending when I had acted against the one who knew all things!

Yahweh had tried to warn me, and I had refused to listen. Havel had tried to warn me, and I had refused to listen. Sin had indeed overpowered me, and I had become a monster – killing my own brother! Just as Abba had feared I would do to Shimon. Nothing could justify the evil I had committed, and nothing could bring Havel back. I bore my fists into the rocky ground beneath me and wept. I tore my tunic. I sank my face into the earth, willing it to open up and take me.

Then Yahweh spoke again. The sound of it was harrowing. There was no pleasure in the voice that pronounced my fate:

And now you are cursed from the ground, which has opened its mouth to receive your brother's blood from your hand. When you work the ground, it shall no longer yield to you its strength. You shall be a fugitive and a wanderer on the earth.

My judgement concerned the ground – the ground that was the source of my pride, all my achievements, and most of my joy. The ground that had yielded harvest after harvest to my hands. Realisation dawned: that ground had now soaked up my brother's blood and, consequently, it would reject me.

I could not deny the justice of it: I had refused to offer Elohim the best of the harvest. I had refused to trust Him with it. I had been so proud and protective of my skill that I had kept back the best grain for seed and given him broken kernels. So, it was this pride that Elohim was now forcefully removing.

Without the ability to farm, I would be worthless. There would be nothing in which to find joy; nothing in which to find purpose. What did that mean for my future?

I would be a wanderer, just as my parents had been after the banishment – but permanently. I would not be able to settle anywhere and farm. Would I ever go back to my family then? No, I could not go back, for I was destined to be a fugitive, and they would not take me.

My thoughts finally turned from myself to consider everything my loved ones would feel when they found out I had killed Havel. Unbearable anguish would be felt by Abba, Ima and Awan. Also by my other siblings. They would surely hate me and seek my life as payment for Havel's! And they would be right to do so! There was no doubt in my mind: my family were lost to me forever.

What of Elohim? Why didn't He kill me? I deserved it. The way I had treated Him was unforgivable. How could He stand to be here, talking to me? I had to leave. I had to leave His people and leave Him. I thought I despised Yahweh's presence, but now that it was to be taken away, I found I desired it! What would it be like to be a fugitive? Utterly alone forever! I wailed as the force of it hit me. I whimpered into the floor of the cave, knowing that He still heard. I knew I deserved nothing, yet I pleaded with Elohim as tears streamed down my cheeks.

'My punishment is greater than I can bear! Consider, you have driven me today away from the ground, and from your face I shall be hidden forever! I shall be a fugitive and a wanderer on the earth, and whoever finds me will kill me!'

For a moment, there was more excruciating silence. Then in a gentle, almost still voice, Yahweh Elohim answered me in my distress:

Not so. If anyone kills Kayin, vengeance shall be taken on him sevenfold.

Then a fire appeared in front of me, burning with no ignition and no fuel. Tongues of flame surrounded me, and I was caught in its very centre. I closed my eyes as the heat dried them up and prickled my skin. Yet it did not burn me, except in one place: I felt a singe of pain on my cheek as if the finger of Elohim Himself was drawing a mark. Then He spoke again.

Here behold the mark of Kayin: may it be a witness to my promise, lest anyone should find you and attack you.

Then, just as suddenly as it had appeared, the fire was gone. I touched my cheek. It was quite cool and I now felt no pain. I traced the scar from the searing; the flesh was smooth and soft like that on my healed ankle. *The mark of Kayin* – a symbol of Elohim's mercy. Yet His judgement stayed the same: I could not remain between these rivers that had been my home. I was condemned to a life of wandering.

I wiped the tears from my eyes. I gathered as much food as I could carry on my back and made sure I had tools stored in my pouch. I spent the remaining daylight fashioning skins into water carriers and a covering to go over my tunic.

The thought of leaving without saying farewell to my family pained me beyond belief, yet I knew I had no choice. There was no sign of the others outside the cave and no voices. So, as darkness fell, I stepped into the night and set out east, banished once again from the presence of Yahweh Elohim. Fleeing to the place of wandering.

EPILOGUE

Chanoch's father began to falter. He had been standing the entire time he recounted his horrendous descent to depravity, culminating in the killing of his own brother, Havel. Those who hadn't comprehended Tzillah's welcome had soon realised from the tale that this was Kayin: their ancestor of legend who lived in the wilderness, mostly unmet and unknown by the onlookers. Several had turned to scrutinize Chanoch as the tale progressed, awed that he would bring his father to this gathering.

As he had neared the final scenes of his story, the emotional weight had taken a toll on Kayin's body, and he had begun to stoop. Even so, he had refused to take a seat until this moment. Just now, he looked as if he might fall. Chanoch braced himself to dart forwards. But Adah, the first wife of Lamech, had been listening intently throughout the telling. Seeing Kayin weaken, she moved out of the shadows carrying a stool and placed it behind him. He murmured a word of thanks, then lowered himself onto it.

Chanoch, seated at the back of the hall, heard a scuffle as the other listeners grew agitated and impatient. Their wine had worn off as the story was told. Some had fallen asleep on the floor; a few were even snoring loudly. Others had paid more attention but looked unsure what to do with the break in the old man's commanding voice.

Chanoch's eyes were then drawn to Lamech. He knew from experience that Lamech never appreciated silence unless he was the one commanding the room's attention. He was surprised that his host had remained quiet throughout and had been secretly amused every time he'd seen Tzillah giving Lamech a discreet nudge – for Lamech's chin had lowered to his chest in slumber several times. Now faced with lack of sleep, lack of attention and awkward silence, Lamech appeared decidedly grumpy.

Suspecting that his host wanted to discharge his unwelcome guests but was unsure how to do so without being accused of disrespect, Chanoch rose, grasping a cup of wine that lay untouched on the table before him. He thought he might ascend the platform himself and revive his father with it. After all, the interruption was Lamech's doing – it was he who had invoked his ancestor's name when he placed a curse on any who might avenge the death of the persons he had killed. Chanoch had put up with Lamech until that point but such brazen action he could not tolerate.

Daylight, streaming into the hall from the high apertures in the walls, caught Chanoch's eyes. Shielding them, he witnessed Lamech having a stern conversation with Adah, perhaps because she had given Kayin a stool, thereby delaying his departure. Chanoch moved to intervene just as a different woman stood up in the presence of the crowd. It struck him, for the first time, that she looked not dissimilar to Adah, with black hair falling in braids down her back. However, her hair was bejewelled with the white strands of age, rather than flowers, and her umber skin had lost its smoothness.

This woman slowly made her way up the steps, walking with a cane curled under her fingers, until she stood near to where Kayin sat on the stool. Kayin looked up at her in surprise, recognition crossing his eyes. She held his gaze for a moment as if they were exchanging thoughts in a silent conversation, then she turned to the onlookers, who were now captivated in curiosity.

Chanoch realised this woman wanted to speak and wondered how Lamech would react. Again, he prepared to intervene, but again, Adah beat him to it. She moved forward and held a hushed conversation with the elder woman, then crossed to Lamech and spoke in his ear. He grunted an irritated reply before reluctantly standing and addressing his guests.

'Those of you who wish to leave are free to do so. I shall make it up to you next Shabbat,' Lamech sneered. 'For the remainder, there are wash basins in the courtyard and couches in the adjoining rooms. You may use them to make yourselves comfortable. We shall shortly serve a morning meal to those who have energy left to consume it, as it seems we have another riveting tale to listen to.'

The sarcasm lacing Lamech's voice was not lost on Chanoch. Yet, it seemed Lamech had resigned himself to the vexing realisation that many of his guests appeared to be willing listeners – or at least wanted to take advantage of his extended hospitality. To disrupt proceedings now would certainly be worse for his reputation than tolerating its continuation.

The audience were roused into action at the announcement, with only a few choosing to slip out of the compound. Chanoch sipped at the wine that was still in his hands and lowered himself onto the cushions he had previously been sitting on. Just then, he heard a cough at his shoulder. Turning towards it, he saw a man approaching him, one young enough to have energy left after staying awake all night.

'May I sit here, sir?' the young man asked. He had one of those faces which exuded enthusiasm, although in his hazel eyes – rimmed with black – intensity was apparent. A light scar traced the line of his right eyebrow.

'Certainly,' Chanoch replied. 'Do you wish to speak with me?'

His companion confirmed this was the case. Passing Chanoch some of the flatbread that he had brought with him and a bowl of olives, they began a conversation which continued throughout the meal. Indeed, they only ceased conversation when, at Adah's request, the woman with the cane took to the centre of the platform and raised her voice over the crowd.

Lamech – who had ordered a couch to be placed on the stage during breakfast – now propped himself up on its cushions, poured himself a large cup of wine and pulled Tzillah near. Chanoch chuckled at his host's piqued expression. It was indeed going to be a long morning.

TO BE CONTINUED

APPENDIX

KAYIN

Kayin/Cain is a figure who was often demonised in ancient literature; some claiming he was the product of a liaison between Eve and the Devil, others that he grew horns! Why have I chosen to represent him differently? And why tackle this story at all? Besides (I believe) a prompting of the Holy Spirit, there are two main reasons:

1. I think it likely that, despite the horrendous murder, Cain was not especially evil or demonic, but rather his sin reflects the potential present in all human hearts. It is important to note that we are all capable of committing awful acts, given the right set of circumstances. Jesus implied that if we hate our brother, we are guilty of murdering him (Matthew 5:21–22). As such, my intention was to portray Kayin in a human light – as someone we could understand – and the murder not as a random act of rage but as a culmination of allowing sins (such as envy and pride) to take over our lives. That is not to excuse what he did, which is inexcusable. But let us never judge another without first examining our own hearts (Matthew 7:1-5).

2. I wished to redress an imbalance in our understanding of Cain based on the scripture rather than peculiar ideas that have been passed down the generations. To do this, I read Genesis 2–4 countless times in many different versions and considered what the whole line of Cain might look like, from Adam to

Lamech's offspring. I also considered the Bible verses where he is mentioned outside Genesis 4, as follows:

In Hebrews 11:4 it merely says Abel's offering was more acceptable than Cain's. In 1 John 3:11–12, Cain is described as belonging to the evil one, and given as an example of what we *as Christians* should not be: haters of our righteous brothers.

Jude v8–11 is the final reference regarding Cain and is worth quoting:

> *Yet in like manner these people also, relying on their dreams, defile the flesh, reject authority, and blaspheme the glorious ones... these people blaspheme all that they do not understand, and they are destroyed by all that they, like unreasoning animals, understand instinctively. Woe to them! For they walked in the way of Cain and abandoned themselves for the sake of gain to Balaam's error and perished in Korah's rebellion.*

What does this imply about the manner of Cain's sin, given that it was alike to the 'ungodly people' Jude is talking of? Jude is a complicated book, but we can glean some clues from it without getting stuck in the detail.

Firstly, the sin involves a form of blasphemy, blaspheming what is not understood, and being destroyed by carnal instincts.

Secondly, walking the way of Cain has something to do with Balaam's error. Balaam was the prophet hired to curse Israel in Numbers Chapters 22 to 31. Balaam's error was to compromise his convictions for material gain.

Lastly, it resembles Korah's rebellion, which when a group of Levites complained to Moses because they had not been selected for the priesthood (Numbers 16).

THE WANDERER SCORNED

From all of this we can conclude that Cain was a believer (why else would he sacrifice?) albeit one who had rebelled, giving himself to the evil one, and had allowed hatred for Abel to consume him. Additionally, his sin had to do with blasphemy against God, choosing carnal desires over spiritual ones, choosing material gain over spiritual gain, and desiring a holy office that was not given him.

All these ideas are woven into my story. I cannot really take credit for this, for I must confess I had entirely missed the Jude passage until the final editing stage! When I found it, I was staggered at what I had been inspired to write, and I am supremely grateful to the LORD for the reassurance. I hope it also sets your mind at rest that my interpretation is not unbiblical.

NAMES

For most of the story, I used variations of the Hebrew name for God, Yahweh Elohim, where Elohim represents the more formal name for God the Creator, and Yahweh, the personal name that God reveals to His people. The name of the LORD is debated, for written Hebrew did not originally include vowel sounds and the pronunciation of the letters y/j and w/v have caused confusion. Many would use the name Jehovah instead. I chose Yahweh as it is most familiar to me, although I suspect that Yahveh or Yehovah are more likely to be correct. Certainly, as Hebrew does not have a 'j' sound, the first letter should be pronounced 'y'.

The English names God/LORD were used occasionally, for clarity's sake. Havel also uses Ruach Elohim, which is the Spirit of God (Ruach literally means breath).

Why did I choose to use Yahweh when that name is often reserved for times post-Exodus 6 where God tells

Moses that the patriarchs (Abraham, Isaac and Jacob) did not know His name? I believe it is likely that the God who walked with Adam in the Garden also revealed His holy name to the first family. In Genesis 2 (the 'personal' account of creation), The LORD God: Yahweh Elohim, is used. It is also used repeatedly in Gen 4, and is particularly notable in Gen 4:26, where people began to call on the name of Yahweh. Therefore, if the name of Yahweh was forgotten at some point before Abraham and re-revealed to Moses at the time of the Exodus, that doesn't mean it was not used in a personal way by His followers in the most ancient times.

I did choose not to use any later names for God, though, such as Adonai ('Lord', no caps). I stuck to the words used in the first few chapters of Genesis as this was the basis of my book.

The English informal names Dad/Mum were replaced with the Hebrew Abba/Ima. Hebrew forms of the character names were also used, rather than the ones we are familiar with. I did this to give the characters a chance to tell their story without facing immediate judgement. I hope it helped you to get alongside them. Of course, we have no way of knowing if their language (never written down) was similar to ancient Hebrew – it may have been slightly or altogether different – yet it's a reasonable guess.

Hebrew is difficult to transliterate into English because we do not have all the same letters or sounds. For example, the sound written 'ch' is pronounced more like 'ugh' than the 'ch' in cheese. In most cases, I have transliterated the letters as closely as possible. I have used a 'w' in Awan where it should probably be a 'v', just because I preferred it. Where there were several variations of the spellings, I have tried to choose what reads most easily – to my eyes anyway. For the same reason, I have left out some letters, such as the 'y' in

Elohiym. Apologies if you are a Hebrew scholar and you disagree with me on any of the names!

Whilst the meanings of names were significant, some of them were unclear. As I built several name meanings into my character profiles, I picked the meaning that best fitted my narrative anytime there was debate. Here's my list for those of you who might be interested:

Character	Common form	Meaning	Biblical?	Pronounced
Adam	Adam	Red earth (soil)	Yes	Ah-dom
Chavah	Eve	Life (fem.)	Yes	cHa-vah
Kayin	Cain	Acquired	Yes	Kay-in
Havel	Abel	Breath	Yes	Ha-vel
Awan	N/A	Vice/vanity	Apocryphal	Ah-van
Chayyim	N/A	Life (masc.)	No	cHI-yim
Avigayil	Abigail	My father's joy	No	Ah-vi-ga-yil
Shimon	Simon	He hears	No	Shim-on
Channah	Hannah	Favour/grace	No	cHa-nah
Chanoch	Enoch	Dedicated	Yes	cHa-no-ch
Lamech	Lamech	Robust	Yes	La-me-ch
Tzillah	Zillah	Shade	Yes	Tz-il-lah
Adah	Adah	Adornment	Yes	Ah-dah

SONGS & SCRIPTURES

You may have noticed that Awan's songs and Havel's prayers are drawn from the Old Testament scriptures and paraphrased to fit my story. Am I suggesting that

Psalms from thousands of years afterwards were actually written by my made-up first worship leader, Awan? No, of course not.

And yet there is a sense in which, just as our modern-day songs and hymns draw on biblical verse, so biblical verse would have drawn on an ancient pattern of Yahweh worship, featuring phrases, picture language and theology that had been handed down through generations of worshippers since the beginning of time. So we see similar language in the ancient songs of Moses and Miriam as we do in the much later Psalms of David and Asaph, for example.

Nothing happens in a vacuum, and our LORD is wonderful, eternal and consistent in His dealings with His people throughout all generations. I like to think that the first family praised Him for that just as David and others did millennia afterwards.

For your reference, the most significant passage used for this purpose in this book was Psalm 50. Havel's prayer at the first sacrifice and Elohim's words to Kayin are paraphrases of Psalm 50. By using scripture, I hoped to keep the voice of the LORD authentic.

IS IT HISTORICAL?

For me, writing Kayin's story was an opportunity to explore theology through storytelling, not a historical investigation. Nevertheless, I have tried to make it realistic. Some may criticise me for allowing modern concepts or theologies to creep into the mouths of ancient people. Yet, my purpose was to explore the tale within the parameters outlined above rather than worrying about whether it happened this way, which we can never know the truth of. For this reason, I allowed myself artistic license on that front.

Many will have different opinions on the age of the earth and the historical accuracy of what we find in Genesis. I have no intention of causing arguments among Christians, who are called to love one another despite our differences. Therefore, I do not offer an opinion on the age of the earth, which is an incredibly complex debate, but leave it open to the reader's interpretation.

That said, I personally believe there are theological consequences in adopting a narrative of human evolution. Therefore, I wished to demonstrate how it might be possible for a literal reading of Gen 2–4 to fit in with what we know about history and archaeology. Where the Bible is silent (like, for example, on how many siblings Kayin and Havel had and when exactly they were born), I fill in some of the gaps to fit with my story. Where it gives us information, I have tried to stick strictly to that.

I base my farming and geographical descriptions roughly on ancient Mesopotamia, assuming that, before the flood, this would have been a quite different world. Although most scholars no longer hold objections to rain occurring before the flood, I barely mention rain due to the climate I adopted and my interpretation of the curse on the ground.

Rodinia is modern science's name for the first super-continent (pre-tectonic plate shifts.) There is much debate about what it looked like and what parcels of land it featured. Assuming Rodinia to have been the pre-flood world, I based my map of the east on one scientific projection of Rodinia and married it with the four rivers model from Genesis 2.

As regards animal varieties and early hominoid activity, I cannot consider every issue in this story of the very first human family, but – mainly for fun – I begin to explore them.

Tanninim (plural) and tannin (sing.) is a general term used in the Hebrew bible to describe monster-like creatures that inhabited both the sea and land (e.g. Gen 1:21, Job 7:12, Jer 51:34). It is also used of serpents (e.g. Exod 7:9) and refers to the crocodile in later times. However, it is distinct from tannim (pl.), which is Hebrew for jackals. The famous creatures described specifically in Job – leviathan and behemoth – represent a giant sea creature and land creature, respectively. I interpret them to be types of tannin.

Even if some creatures are to be regarded as mythological (which is up for debate), it is possible that during the most ancient times, man inhabited earth with some giant tanninim. They may well have been what we know of as dinosaurs and their contemporaries. All myths start somewhere and, without some kind of cohabitation, it's unlikely that dragons and the like would have made it into so many myths – though granted, the accounts were highly embellished.

MEAT

Again, my intention is not to propose one view over another. Even so, I spent some time considering the question of meat-eating before Noah's ark. Many believe that meat-eating did not happen before the flood, according to Gen 9:3, where God says, 'As I gave the green plants, so now I give you everything.' However, Gen 3:21, 4:4 and 6:11 seem to suggest meat-eating did take place, so I wanted to give this question a fair presence.

Also, in Gen 7:2, before He apparently allows meat-eating, God distinguishes between unclean and clean animals, telling Noah to take seven pairs of clean animals onto the ark. This is the first time this distinction is recorded in scripture, but that does not mean it was the first time God had made it. Noah then offers clean animals on the altar in Gen 8:20. The language for 'every creature' in Gen 9:3 may then refer to God removing the distinction between clean and unclean rather than between plant and animal. Interestingly the language is similar to that in Leviticus 14, which re-establishes the forbidden unclean animals. So, the Mosaic law may have reflected the intended state of things in Gen ch 4–9. Then we make sense of Gen 6:11, where God says the flood was necessary because **all** flesh had been corrupted, particularly concerning the lifeblood mentioned in that chapter and the need to destroy all animals, not just humans.

In conclusion, I do not believe it is theologically necessary to claim that nobody ate meat before the flood. However, neither do I want to abandon the straightforward meaning of the text by suggesting that it was right to do so. Therefore, I have my original family in this story eating some 'clean' animals, but I leave whether this was right or wrong open to the reader's interpretation (consider particularly the incident while hunting in the woods, Havel's reluctance to kill his sheep, and Lamech's family – who have entirely strayed – roasting a hog!).

WASN'T ABEL'S MURDER PREMEDITATED?

In the NIV version of the Bible, we read, 'Now Cain said to his brother Abel, "Let's go out to the field." While they were in the field, Cain attacked his brother Abel and killed him.' (Gen 4:8).

This suggests that Abel's murder was premeditated. However, this may be a case of a paraphrase going beyond the original text. Many translations insert the contents of Cain's speech after the first phrase, following the Septuagint and Vulgate. However, the Masoretic text literally reads, 'Cain spoke to his brother Abel, and while they were in the field...', so we cannot infer from that exactly what Cain said to Abel or when he said it. That Cain requested Abel to come out to the field so that he could kill him is, of course, possible, but I followed the ESV translation when I was writing, which does not insert Cain's speech. It reads simply, 'Cain spoke to Abel, his brother. And when they were in the field, Cain rose up against his brother Abel and killed him.'

IMPASSIBILITY

There is a theological doctrine, which is much debated, regarding the impassibility of God. To be impassible is to be 'not subject to passions'. In other words, because God is immutable (He cannot change), He cannot be affected by the actions of humans or relate to them in an emotional, reactive way. Does this mean that Kayin was wrong to think he could hurt God by murdering Havel in my account? Well, Kayin was wrong about many things! However, I do portray God as reacting emotionally to Havel's death, for the following reasons:

Throughout scripture, we see God portraying Himself emotionally to His people (consider much of the prophets and Psalms and, of course, Jesus himself.) Now it could be, as some theologians have surmised, that God is merely accommodating himself to our limited human understanding – to communicate with us in a way we can understand. However, the sheer depth of emotion in these texts leans me away from this interpretation.

Rather, whilst affirming that humans cannot affect God's nature in order to change who He is, I would affirm that being relational and feeling emotion towards His people is part of who God is. After all, He exists in a relational trinitarian form. I would not go so far as to say God has emotions in the same way we humans do. For example, although he can grieve (e.g. Ps 78:40–41), He cannot be overcome by this grief. And this grief is consistent with His holiness and love. He is always in control; His nature and character remain the same even while He interacts with His creation in time and space. He is not subject to human suffering, but He meets us in it.

Therefore, I am comfortable with the idea that God would speak in a tone of grief at Abel's death, a tone which I hear frequently when I read scripture. He loved Abel and would have mourned Cain's actions. However, I believe my Kayin was wrong in thinking he could actively 'hurt' God by killing Havel. God knew what was going to happen and would not have been taken by surprise. Besides, when he died, Havel went home!

OTHER MATTERS

Finally, the questions these chapters of scripture raise are not new. Indeed, the myriad forms of the story in Jewish, Catholic and Coptic tradition shows that it was often considered by our forefathers.

Several traditions claim that Cain and Abel were both twins and married their own twin sisters. I decided not to go down this route because if Abel had a wife, he would likely have had offspring, which he presumably didn't, as Seth bore out his line (Gen 4:25). Therefore, I left Kayin on his own for a while and made only Havel a twin, which fitted my narrative and characterisations. As the birth of women was rarely recorded in the Old Testament, a female twin being born with Havel is not unscriptural.

Some people suggest that, because they had perfect bodies in the Garden, it would have taken Adam and

Eve little time to conceive, and therefore it is likely Cain was born in the Garden. I rejected this hypothesis for two reasons. Firstly, theologically, if a child was born pre-fall, then it would have been necessary for that child to directly sin and be banished from God's presence, yet the Bible gives us no indication of this. Romans 5:12 is quite clear that sin entered the world through one man, and death through sin, "and so death spread to all men because all sinned." Therefore, it was necessary for Cain to be born into sin after the judgement took place. This is also why I believe that there was only one 'first family' (see also Gen 3:20), although some maintain there could have been many.

Secondly, Seth was born when Adam was 130 years old (Gen 5:3). Clearly, I agree with the traditional stories that other children were born between Abel and Seth (otherwise, who was Cain's wife?) Yet, with perfect bodies, it is not likely that a great amount of time would have passed between the conceptions of these children. It is also probable, in my mind, that Adam did not lie with Eve in the Garden. Jesus tells us that in the resurrection, people will not marry (Matt 22:30, Mark 12:25, Luke 20:34–35.) In the presence of God, we do not need marriage, though we require fellowship. In Gen 2, Eve is given as a helper to Adam, but the pronouncement in Gen 2:24 is abstract from Adam's situation (he had no father and mother to leave) so it does not necessitate that they were cleaved together in sexual union at that point in time.

Therefore, Cain is not conceived in my story until Adam is eighty years old (you need to read the next book in the series to figure this out.) The reason I give for this delay is envisaging a longer period spent in the Garden, rather than just a few days, and a great deal of wandering time after the banishment when the difficult relationship between Adam and Eve inhibits conception.

When you consider what they say about each other before the LORD in Gen 3, such difficulty is not inconceivable!

As I mentioned in the Author's Note, all these things are merely my opinion, and the story is not intended to add to the Bible. It is, if you like, a theological reflection on Genesis 4, in the form of fiction. Even if you disagree on anything above, I hope you were able to enjoy it.

QUESTIONS TO CONSIDER

1. *How do you view the progression of sin in Kayin's life? Can you relate any of his journey to your own? What jealousies or proud thoughts do you struggle with?*

2. *Kayin begins his tale by naming the expulsion from the Garden as 'The banishment'. Is this how you view it from your reading of scripture? What were they being banished from? (see Gen 3:21–24, Eph 2:13, Rev 2:7, Rev 22:1–3.)*

3. *How did this narrative challenge your preconceptions of Cain or other notorious people? What parallels in the narrative can you see with ungodly behaviour as laid out in Jude v8–11? Perhaps you could take some time to pray for those you know who are wandering.*

4. *Kayin is an unreliable narrator: seeing things that are not there and taking words and actions to extremes. (It was a challenge to present the other characters fairly whilst maintaining Kayin's point of view!) Are there areas of your life or relationships that need re-examining? Perhaps you could bring this before the LORD, asking his Holy Spirit to clear your vision.*

5. *Are there times of suffering in your life that have drawn you closer to the LORD or pushed you further away? In the narrative, calling out to God and laying our questions and pain before him is demonstrated as a way of allowing Him to minister to us in those times. Does that match your own experience?*

6. *How did you relate to Havel in the story? Could you see any reflections of Jesus in him? Are there any 'prophets' in your own life who have helped you to hear God's words? Now might be a good time to thank God for them.*

7. *Adam continues to hold onto shame long after he has been forgiven. It has a massive impact on his family. Are you holding on to any shame regarding past sins? Perhaps it is time you claimed the promise of Isaiah 61:7: 'Instead of your shame you will receive a double portion, and instead of disgrace you will rejoice in your inheritance.' Jesus Christ endured the shame of the cross to remove yours – try not to take it up again.*

Enjoyed it?

If you enjoyed this book, please consider leaving an online review. You can do this at Amazon (even if you didn't purchase from there) at Goodreads and at other online bookshops. It will help others find me and help me to publish more books.

Further Artwork, Reviews and Teasers available at
www.natashawoodcraft.com

Keep up to date by following me on
Facebook: Natasha Woodcraft, Writes, Wrongs & Songs
Instagram: @natasha.woodcraft
TikTok: @natasha.woodcraft

Songs from the series are published on my YouTube channel. Find me by searching *Natasha Woodcraft* on YouTube.

THE WANDERER

Reborn

Book 2 in The Wanderer Series

By **NATASHA WOODCRAFT**

Reeling from the shock of Havel's murder, Awan doesn't know how she will ever recover. Kayin's action torments her existence. As the years pass and her younger siblings move on with their lives, she is left behind, feeling bitter and lonely. Will she ever learn to forgive her brother and herself?

Then Awan makes a terrible error which threatens to break up what remains of her fractured family. That same day, Yahweh calls her to undertake a radical journey. A journey that will test her faith and force her to face all her darkest fears.

COMING DECEMBER 2022

Made in the USA
Columbia, SC
19 December 2022

74588576R00164